The Perfect Winter Plan

VANNI SHAW

CANDENT GATE
STORY SHINES THROUGH

This one's for you, El.

Chapter 1

ALLIE

When the wall-length radiator kicks on, everyone in the room groans. Audibly. There's nothing quite like a little extra heat to crank up the stink factor in our ancient elementary school's library.

I came on staff at Sterling Grove Elementary School eight years ago. Since then, our library has suffered countless roof leaks, as well as numerous plumbing failures from the adjacent boys' bathroom. Our entire school is an outdated mess, but if any spot in the building could shout the need for a new elementary school through scent alone, it would be this one.

"We should've gotten after this project years ago," a farmer grumbles as he slips on his coat. "This place smells like a moldy hayloft after a hard rain."

Funny. That member of our Elementary Facilities Committee was one of the most vocal opponents to the idea of building a new elementary school when it was first presented.

I shoot a glance toward my good friend and fellow kindergarten teacher, Raquel. The irony dancing in her eyes probably mirrors the laughter in mine.

Assigning these committee meetings to the library was an ingenious move by our principal, and the architect designing the school ran with it. He's a great presenter, pointing out the health benefits of new construction as well as the educational ones. Every initial naysayer was converted by the end of our second meeting.

Considering our committee is primarily made up of women, it probably doesn't hurt that, as architects go, Grant Covington is rather easy on the eyes.

Wait. Is his first name Grant? Or is it Graham? Or Greg? It starts with G, for sure, but . . . dang it. We've had four of these committee meetings already, and I'm usually very good with names. You'd think I'd know it by now.

Then again, the majority of my life has been spent in one school setting or another. My brain is programmed to address adults by Miss, Ms., Mrs., or Mr.—with the occasional "Professor" or "Dr." thrown in—and their last name. It's called conditioning, and that's science.

In any case, there are plenty of reasons why our sweet little corner of the world needs a new elementary school. And as convincing as Mr. Covington's data is, a few of our more stubborn committee members might not have been so quickly swayed if not for this inspiringly pungent meeting place.

Raquel scoots her chair back. "You ready to head out, Allie?"

"Sure thing." I reach under the table for my bag. When I look up, however, I notice that Sterling Grove's sweetest busybody has cornered the architect.

"I know we haven't known each other long," Mrs. Kellogg says, "but I have a very good feeling about you, young man."

Norma Kellogg is a retired teacher and the real MVP when it comes to community service in Sterling Grove. From her tone of voice to her compact stature and silver-gray hair, everything about Norma is as comfy, rounded, and soft as the snickerdoodles she bakes for every local bake sale. And just like the temptation to scarf down a whole plate of those cookies, it's much too easy to get drawn into one of her well-intentioned schemes.

"I happen to know of a certain young lady, right here in Sterling Grove, who'd be a perfect match for a handsome go-getter like you," Norma continues. "Now, sure, she's a little rough around the edges, but she has the most wonderful heart once you get to know her. I taught her in my second-grade class twenty-odd years ago. Such a unique personality."

Momentary panic squeezes my windpipe until I remember that I didn't grow up here and, therefore, I am already contextually disqualified.

"Allie?"

I force my eavesdropping ears from the conversation at the front of the library just long enough to whisper, "One sec," to Raquel.

It's common knowledge that Norma has a habit of trying to play matchmaker. By all reports, she's terrible at it. But that hasn't stopped her yet. You have to respect her tenacity. It took three years, and at least seven failed set-ups before Norma finally gave up on me.

I count myself blessed.

"She's a business owner now," Norma continues. "Quite successful too. She does travel a lot, but don't believe the rumors about that. She's a good girl."

And with that statement, the identity of the mystery woman clicks in my brain.

I glance at Raquel, whose attention is also now on the conversation between Norma and the architect. When she meets my gaze, I whisper, "Rainey?"

She nods. "Has to be. Should we warn her?"

"On it." Trying not to laugh, I pull my phone from my back pocket and shoot a quick text to my friend Rainey O'Daire, who owns the local pub. I know she'll appreciate the heads-up.

"The tattoos would have been a bit much in my day," Norma says, "but your generation doesn't seem to mind that sort of thing. I would be thrilled, absolutely thrilled, to make an introduction. So? What do you think?"

Mr. Covington's jaw works for a second. "She sounds like . . ." He pauses, as if searching for an appropriate word. "An accomplished young woman."

Evasive, but nicely neutral. I shouldn't be surprised. He's a good-looking guy in his early-to-mid thirties. This probably isn't his first face-off with a matchmaking grandma-type, but the poor guy doesn't stand a chance if he lets Norma keep talking. She will take that carefully noncommittal response of his as an encouragement to hound him until he finally relents.

I bite my lip, once again thanking my lucky stars Norma gave up on trying to matchmake for me. Mr. Covington probably thinks he is doing okay, but he doesn't know our Norma. Should I intervene?

"Yo, Allie. Earth to Miss Hayes. Come in, Miss Hayes."

"Sorry." I give my head a little shake and focus on Raquel. "What's up?"

"The others already left for Cocoa & Froth. I assumed you'd want to go, but . . .?"

I wrinkle my nose. "Of course I want to go."

Behind me, Norma says the name 'Rainey' and something about 'dinner sometime?'

Oh, dear. I absolutely *must* intervene.

"Go ahead without me." I wave Raquel toward the door. "I'll be right over."

"We carpooled," she reminds me. "You drove."

"Oof. You're right. Umm . . ." What should I do? That poor guy is at Norma's mercy. "Give me a sec? There's something I, uh, wanted to ask the architect."

"Sure." Raquel pulls out the same chair she sat in for the meeting and plops down. "Well?" Leaning back like a bored spectator, she gestures to the man up front. "You have a question. Ask it."

A question. A question. *Hmm.*

I move to the front, hoping a question pops into my head. "Hey, Mr. Covington, I wanted to ask you about the— Oh, sorry." I try to look surprised and innocent. "I didn't mean to interrupt."

"No, no. It's fine." The architect's eyes widen a fraction. Is that relief? "Mrs. Kellogg and I were just . . . chatting."

"Cool. If you've got a sec, I have a question about the, uh"—*Come on, brain!*—"the in-room toilets for kindergarten. You know how it is in the lower grades. We spend a lot of time sounding out words." I shoot Norma a wink. "Lots of vowel movements."

Behind me, Raquel snorts. And was that a little twitch in the architect's lips?

"No one but Allie Hayes could make bathroom humor seem cute." Norma chuckles, shaking her head. "Ah, well. It's getting late. I should be heading home to my Stan." She offers me a snickerdoodle-sweet smile and then turns back to the architect, adding an extra dusting of sugar on top for him. "You just let me know if you want any more information about what we were talking about, okay?"

He offers the smaller half of a nod. "See you next week."

This guy has "noncommittal" down to an art. Maybe he didn't need a rescue after all.

He turns a tired but not insincere smile toward me. "You had a question about the toilets?"

"Yes. The, uh, toilets. I was wondering if, uh . . . since they come in little sizes for little students, do they come in different colors?"

"Hmm. It's a possibil—"

"I just thought it might be kind of cool if the toilets could be, I don't know, a fun color?"

Hey, I'd blurted it out. I might as well own it.

"The little ones get distracted sometimes and forget they need to use the toilet until it's too late," I continue. "And then we're losing instructional time cleaning up accidents, and finding spare pants, and all that. If the toilet was a fun place to visit, maybe they wouldn't forget. What do you think?"

I take a breath and glance over my shoulder. Only Raquel, Mr. Covington, and myself remain. "Phew." Wiping imaginary sweat from my forehead, I grin at him, lowering my voice. "Okay, so I just totally made that up. I don't care what color the toilets are."

Mr. Covington tilts his head the slightest bit to the right. "You . . . don't?"

"Nah." Without permission, my brain conjures a picture of what I hope my classroom will look like when the new school is built. It's a bright fairyland of learning that smells like strawberry sno-cones and sunshine—a far cry from my current reality of institutional mint-painted walls and beige linoleum that may have once been white, all overlaid with the sort of scents that might have inspired the funk mentioned in Michael Jackson's *Thriller*. "Huh. Maybe colored toilets would be cool?" I glance over my shoulder at Raquel. "What do you think?"

"I guess." She shrugs. "Depends on the color."

"True. We definitely do *not* want brown." I let out a near-snort laugh. "I've had to deal with too much brown in my classroom's bathroom as it is."

"For real," Raquel echoes, nodding. "But a primary color might be cool."

"True." I nod. "Red? Nah. Too Las Vegas. And yellow is almost as big a problem as brown on the eww-o-meter. What about blue? Blue could be—"

"Wait." Mr. Covington tilts his head the opposite direction. "I'm confused. So, you *do* want colored toilets?"

"Nah. Not really." I laugh but pause, picturing a tiny, bright blue toilet in a bathroom with clouds painted on the ceiling and a meadow scene on the walls and maybe some animals. "A blue toilet might be kinda fun, don't you think? I mean, is that a thing?" I give my distracted head a shake. "No, never mind."

"Okay . . ." He blinks a couple of times. "Did you have another question about the in-room toilets?"

"Nah, I didn't have a question at all."

His dark brown eyebrows reach for the high center of his slightly hipster haircut.

"Sorry. Let me explain." I take a breath. "Don't take this the wrong way, but I overheard part of your conversation with Norma—Mrs. Kellogg, that is—and I thought it sounded like you might need a rescue. She can be a little— Well, Norma's great. But she tends to overstep sometimes." I wince. "Speaking of which, I hope *I* didn't overstep."

"Ah." His eyebrows lower, and then a slow smile pushes through his facial scruff. "No worries. For the record, you were not wrong." He gives a slightly exaggerated wince. "Thanks."

"No prob. Glad to be of service." I glance at Raquel. "Ready to go?"

"Yep." Raquel leans sideways, angling her attention toward the architect. "Hey, a bunch of us have been getting together at the cocoa shop up on Maple Boulevard after these meetings. Just to hang out and relax a bit. You're welcome to join us, if you'd like."

"Thanks, but I should probably—"

"Norma doesn't come to our after-meeting get-togethers," I whisper. "In case you were worried about that."

"Ah." He pauses, rubbing a hand over a shadow of stubble along his jawline that might be the beginnings of a beard. "It's a bit of a drive, and I should probably head home, but . . ." He trails off for a second. "I don't think I've had a cup of hot cocoa in years."

"Not even instant?"

"Not that I recall."

"That, sir, is a literal crime. You haven't *lived* until you've had Cocoa & Froth's cocoa."

"They have awesome coffees too," Raquel says, "if you're a nighttime caffeinator. And a wide selection of herbal teas, sandwiches, pastries, you know. Basic coffee shop fare. It's all good, but the cocoa is perfection."

"I wouldn't want to impose on the group and make it weird."

"Here's the thing. With our group, 'weird'"—I make air quotes—"is a sure thing, whether you come or not. It's only a question of how you time your contribution to the weird."

Amusement lights his eyes. "How so?"

"As I see it, you can risk a possibly weird time while drinking delicious cocoa, or you can be guaranteed a super awkward moment at next week's meeting when our friends ask you why you didn't come. Because I will absolutely tell them you declined our invitation. But even if that doesn't faze you, think of your poor, neglected tastebuds and the truly divine experience they'll miss out on if you don't join our little cocoa club tonight."

He laughs. "You make a compelling argument."

"C'mon. You can follow us over."

Out in the parking lot, I start the car and crank the heat. Even for late October, it's fairly chilly tonight. I can't help but hope for early snow, even though I know it would kind of wreck trick-or-treating for my students next week.

As Raquel fastens her seatbelt, she says, "Did you notice our handsome architect isn't wearing a wedding band?"

"No. But it makes sense." I snort. "It would've been beyond tacky for Norma to try to set Rainey up with a married man."

"True." Raquel laughs. "But you can't deny he's attractive."

"Well, duh." I flip on the radio, but there's a slow song on. I immediately hit the seek button.

"He's tall, but not too tall. And he's got kind eyes," she says.

"Yeah, I guess."

"And good shoulders."

"Oh, for sure. He rocks that button-down with the rolled-up sleeves. Very *GQ*."

"Right?" Raquel nods and her dark brown curls bounce at her shoulders. "Do you think he plays tennis? He seems like a tennis player. He's got that kind of build, don't you think?"

"Yeah, that fits." I hit seek again. Where is the good music tonight?

"And he's very polite."

"Seems to be." When I glance over, Raquel's looking at me like I offered to put sprinkles on her ice cream. "Wait. Oh my gosh. Did you think I was flirting? I was not flirting. Seriously, I felt bad for him falling prey to Norma. I was trying to be nice." I groan. "Do you think he thinks I was flirting? Oh, no. Do you think he thinks I was asking him out when I invited him for cocoa?"

"Hold up. Stop the panic train, Allie. I'm the one who invited him for cocoa, remember?"

I blink. "Oh, right. Good."

"And speaking of which, he's probably waiting for you to pull out, so he can follow us there."

"Yikes! Yes. Driving now." I hit the radio's seek button again and then put the car in gear. It's only a few blocks to Maple Boulevard, where the majority of our small town's businesses are located, but I need my tunes.

"He is pretty cute, though," Raquel muses. "In a manly, successful professional sort of way."

"Simmer down, married mother of two," I say, just as one of my all-time favorites comes through the speaker. "Oh my gosh! I haven't heard this song in forever."

I check the rearview mirror to make sure Mr. Covington is following us and then crank up the volume until I can feel the bass in my bones. There's always time for a dance party, baby.

Chapter 2

GRANT

I step onto the sidewalk and tap my key fob to lock my car. Expecting the two teachers to be waiting for me, I'm surprised to see them still sitting in the car outside the little coffee—er, cocoa shop. In the driver's seat, the blonde one sways. She lifts her hands, waving her arms around like—

Wait. Is she . . . dancing? Yeah, it sure looks like it.

Should I wait for them, or just go in?

She sees me. Her eyes round. She laughs. The car shuts off.

I mentally check their names against the committee roster inside my brain. Allie Hayes and Raquel Dominguez. Both teachers. Kindergarten, I believe.

"Sorry to keep you waiting," Raquel says as the two women climb out of the car.

"Yeah, sorry," Allie echoes, though there's not a hint of apology in her wide smile—not that I needed one. "'Electric Love' came on the radio. Haven't heard that song in a while."

It sounds vaguely familiar. "No, it's fine. I just got here."

I hold the door for the women. Once inside, I'm enveloped by a sense of warmth that's as much atmospheric as it is temperature. An aromatic tinge of freshly ground coffee rides a rich chocolate wave topped with a faint, sugary sweetness that reminds me of buttercream frosting. If this scent came in a candle, my mom would burn it around the clock.

To my left, a wall of exposed brick is decorated with some sort of puffy—or should I say frothy?—artificial white flowers, tightly and artfully arranged to spell 'Cocoa & Froth.' Centered under the words, a brown leather couch and two oversized chairs surround a butcher block coffee table. The opposite wall is painted a warm shade of white and sports a large copper cut-out of a mug of whip-topped cocoa at its center. Beneath it, chocolate-brown upholstered booths hug freestanding butcher block tables. A large corner booth joins the white side wall to the storefront-length windows. In front of those wide windows, three bistro-style tables seat two patrons each.

Sprinkled through the center of the space, wide-seated modern chairs, upholstered to match the booths, surround an assortment of square and rectangular tables. As I stand transfixed in the entry, my gaze moves upward. Hammered copper pendant lights hang over the various tables and booths, adding even more warmth to the overall aesthetic. Above them, Edison bulb string lights crisscross the high, white-painted slat ceiling.

I need to find out who designed this space. We might be able to add them to our interior design referral list.

"Cool, huh?" A woman's voice forces my attention away from admiring the unexpectedly stylish little coffee—er, cocoa—shop. It's Allie. She spreads her arms and turns a full circle. "I love this place. It's a whole vibe, y'know?"

"Uh, yes." I nod. "Yes, it is."

"Right?" Her grin has so much wattage I'm afraid she might have drained a little energy from me to pull it off. "This way." She waves me toward a table holding three other people from the facilities committee meeting.

"We brought a new member to our cocoa club tonight," Raquel says.

"I hope I'm not intruding."

"The more the merrier." Paula Francis, a sturdy Special Ed teacher who appears to be in her early-to-mid sixties, gestures to an empty chair. "Take a load off."

"We rescued him," Allie says. "He was about to become the next contestant on Norma's *Bachelor in Sterling Grove* show."

"Of course he was," Paula says. "Did you manage to escape before she gave you a list of possible wedding venues?"

I laugh. "It wasn't *that* bad."

"Oh, it will be." This comes from Dylan Becker, one of the few men on the facilities committee. He teaches fourth grade. "Once Norma decides she's located the woman of your dreams, she's like a spaniel under a tree full of squirrels. Been there, dude. Would not advise."

"Noted."

"I'm glad she hasn't come for me yet." Lexi Hansen looks like she could still be in high school. She rarely speaks up at the meetings, and if she hadn't introduced herself as the elementary music teacher at our first committee meeting, I would have assumed she was someone's daughter, waiting on her ride.

Paula leans back in her chair. "Your time will come, young one."

An elbow jabs my arm. Allie. "Ready to try out some cocoa?"

I nod and follow her and Raquel to the counter.

"Hey, Josie," Allie greets the barista. "We've brought a first-timer with us tonight."

Josie offers me a smile. "Welcome to Cocoa & Froth."

The menu is, as these two claimed, impressive. Finally, after both kindergarten teachers have their orders in hand and I've asked Josie at least five questions, I make my decision. When it's ready, the wide ceramic mug is handed to me on a matching saucer that also holds a bamboo spoon. I carefully transport my dark caramel cocoa—topped with whipped cream and sprinkled with crushed chocolate-covered espresso beans and orange sprinkles—back to the table and settle into the last remaining chair.

"So you see?" Allie says. "I couldn't stand by and let Norma claim our poor architect as her next victim. I had to think fast. Come up with a distraction."

I'm still the topic of conversation? Not weird at all.

"Allie went off on some crazy tangent about toilet colors." Raquel grins. "Oh, and she made a poop joke."

"Classic." Dylan laughs.

"Totally." Allie grins. "And thanks to my sophisticated sense of humor, Norma soon decided she'd had enough of my shenanigans and took off."

"Remind me to ask my grandsons for some new poop jokes," Paula grumbles with a half-smile. "Always good to have a little extra ammunition when Norma's on a mission."

"Allie can hook you up," Dylan says. "She has poop jokes for days."

"It's true." Allie lifts her mug, as if in salute. "I gotchu, girl."

My first sip of cocoa is nothing less than transportive. An unexpected smokiness lifts the caramel flavoring to the fore, and the dark chocolate foundation, topped by a marshmallow-y whip and crushed coffee beans on top, harkens back to childhood summers at the lake with my grandparents, trading tales around the fire. This cocoa absolutely lives up to the hype, and its goodness helps me soak in the relaxed vibe of the group.

I learn that Paula is happily divorced, well-traveled, and a devoted grandmother. Raquel has two boys—one in fourth grade and one in seventh—and her husband is a radiologist at a nearby town's hospital.

"Hey, Paula." Allie leans back in her chair as she uses her bamboo spoon to stir the whip into her cocoa. "How are you liking that new ceiling fan in your living room?" Her tone holds a teasing lilt that matches the quirk of one side of her mouth.

"How did you know I got a new ceiling fan?"

"I ran into Bill Franklin the other night. He mentioned that he'd been over at your place Saturday night, helping you install it." Excitement sparks in Allie's eyes. "After the two of you went out for dinner. To-geth-er."

"What's this?" Raquel leans forward. "Have you been holding out on us, Paula?"

"Ooh." Lexi clasps her hands together. "Are you and Bill dating?"

"Well, I . . . we . . . it's not . . ." Paula splays her hands on the table and then drags them toward her, dropping them in her lap. "We've only gone out three times."

"Three times?" Allie's mug clatters back down onto its saucer. Cocoa sloshes up the sides but somehow does not spill. "Holy love connection, Paula. That's practically a long-term relationship."

"Maybe in Allie World." Raquel chuckles.

"Hey! Not nice." Allie's mock offense melts into a grin. "Can I help it if every man I date turns out to be utterly forgettable?"

"What about Preston?" Paula offers, and when Allie groans, she laughs. "That boy was anything but forgettable."

I can't help but smile in response to the laughter around me, even though I'm not in on the joke.

"You have to admit," Lexi says, "Preston was *hot*."

"Hot, schmot." Allie wrinkles her nose. "The guy launders his shoelaces."

What? I've been known to wash my laces. Especially the ones on my hiking boots. Shoelaces get dirty. "And that's bad because . . .?"

"He doesn't just wash them," Dylan explains. "He irons them."

"Twice a week," Paula adds. "And then there was the thing with the car radio."

Allie shudders, and Raquel answers my unasked question. "He will not listen to music while driving. Says it's too distracting."

Allie shudders again. "It's unnatural."

"Whatever happened to that financial planner guy?" Paula asks. "What was his name? Vincent?"

"Vic." Allie rolls her eyes.

"Oh, right. Vic. He was nice."

"Was he the long chewer?" Lexi asks.

A laugh bubbles through my lips. "What's a long chewer?"

"Someone who takes entirely too long to chew their food before swallowing," Allie supplies. "It is utterly annoying and really drags out a conversation." She turns back to Lexi. "But that wasn't Vic. Thomas was the long chewer."

"That's right," Dylan nods. "Vic was the coaster guy."

"Let me guess," I say, feeling a smile tug my lips. "He was obsessed with amusement parks?" I'm surprised to be enjoying myself this much. Maybe it's because Allie seems to take the discussion of her less-than-stellar dating history in stride, with good humor that carries neither self-deprecation nor discomfort.

"Nope." Dylan shakes his head. "Apparently, he didn't use a coaster on Allie's coffee table and his glass left a watermark."

"The coasters were *right there*." Allie's voice pitches upward. "I set his glass on one when I brought it to him. How hard could it be to put it—"

"The coaster thing was an excuse." Raquel pats her friend's arm. "You were already tired of him."

"True enough." Allie shrugs and leans back in her chair. "But enough about me. I believe we were talking about Paula's love connection with Bill, the magic ceiling fan man." She clasps her hands by her cheek and bats her eyelashes. "Tell us more, won't you?"

"We've gone out to dinner three times. He helped me install a ceiling fan," Paula mumbles. "That's all there is to tell."

"And you're going out again, when?" Allie prompts.

A puff of air leaves Paula's lips. "Tomorrow night."

"Woo-hoo!" Allie's fist pumps the air. "I do love me some romance. Especially going into the holidays. Wintertime is absolutely the *best* dating season." She takes a deep breath and sighs through a smile. "So many romantic date possibilities."

"Like what?" Dylan asks. "Not that I don't have my own ideas, you understand. But a guy can never have too many, am I right, Grant?"

I nod. Can't argue with that.

"You fellas need wintertime date ideas?" Allie's smile widens, and everything from her posture to her eyes brightens. "You have come to the right place, my dudes. I may be hopeless when it comes to sustaining my own romances, but I am full of ideas. The days between Halloween and New Year's Day are absolutely the best. Romantic opportunities simply abound."

"Do tell," Dylan says.

"With pleasure. But first, you have to admit that the season of calendar winter and the better, truer idea of wintertime as a state of being are totally different things."

"What do you mean?" Lexi asks.

"Calendar winter starts on what, December twenty-first? That's ridiculous. As far as I'm concerned, wintertime starts November first, the end."

"Go on," Paula prompts.

"So first you have all the sweater-weather stuff. Like sipping hot cider while chilling around a bonfire. And don't even try to tell me hayrides aren't romantic. In November, hayrides are all about the snuggling."

"You know that's right," Raquel nods but then frowns. "Which is scary, now that my son is a teenager. It seems like someone's organizing a hayride every other weekend around here."

"They totally are." Allie laughs. "Then there's Thanksgiving, which is the least romantic of all holidays because of the whole stuff-yourself-until-you-pop thing, so definitely skip that as a date idea. Eww. But after Thanksgiving? It's on, baby." She grins. "You can shop for holiday gifts together, and bake cookies, and drink cocoa under the stars on a clear, cold night. You can go pick out a tree together, if that's your thing, and put up your favorite holiday decorations. There's caroling, making gingerbread houses, watching holiday movies, and driving around to look at all the lights. Any of that can be a date. And if you're lucky and it snows?" She does four quick claps and then leans back with a sigh. "The simple act of cuddling on the couch and watching the snow fall gives all those top-tier romance vibes."

Allie's enthusiasm is contagious and, as I tear my gaze from her illumined expression, I see I'm not the only one infected by it.

Allie runs her finger around the rim of her mug as she continues, "Snow brings that sparkly winter mood with it. It's practically glitter, y'know? And who would turn down free glitter? Not me. No, sir." She shakes her head. "If you want to get out in it, you can go for romantic walks in the snow, or make snow angels and snowmen."

Allie's palms slap down on the table.

I'm not the only one who startles.

"Oh my gosh, you guys!" She leans forward. "Can you imagine how fun it would be to build a snow fort on a date? It would be so—"

"Geez, Al." Raquel winces but laughs. "Take a breath."

"I'm just saying"—Allie splays her fingers—"when it comes to cute wintertime date ideas, the possibilities are endless."

"For someone whose every relationship comes with an expiration date of approximately three weeks," Paula says dryly, "it sounds like you've given this a lot of thought."

"More like I've watched a lot of Christmas rom-coms." Allie takes a deep breath—which she no doubt needs—and lets it out on a sigh. "But seriously, guys. Wintertime is the most romantic season of them all. That's why they make all those movies. And how awesome is it that Paula is on the cusp of something-that-could-be-something this time of year?"

"It is entirely awesome," Lexi grins, nudging Paula with her shoulder. "And I agree with Allie. The holidays are super romantic."

"You know it." Allie thrusts her hand toward Lexi, who gives her a high five.

"You should find your own wintertime romance. Then you won't need to stick your pert little nose into mine." Paula arches an eyebrow. "Maybe you could try one of those online dating services or something."

"No thanks. That's where I found Preston. Andrew too."

"What about Brody? He's a really nice guy," Raquel protests. "You two dated for like, almost a year, right?"

"Eight months, give or take," Allie corrects. "It only felt like a year." She laughs but then claps a hand over her mouth. "Please don't tell him I said that. Brody's such a sweet guy. But we were doomed from the start. If you recall, we did not meet through a dating site. That was a Norma set-up."

"Oh my gosh, that's right!" Raquel laughs. "I forgot Norma had a hand in that. With her track record, it's kind of a miracle you made it that long."

"If you don't mind me asking," Dylan says, tilting his head. "Why did you break up with him?"

"Brody broke up with me, actually. But it was time. With all his responsibilities at the farm and stuff, trying to keep up with my energy simply exhausted the poor guy. It was an amicable break-up, obviously, and it was long overdue." She shrugs, but I can't find even the slightest trace of sadness in it. "Face it, guys. I'm just not cut out for long-term relationships. Or maybe long-term relationships aren't cut out for me." And when her lips break into a fresh smile, it overtakes her face. "But I could totally go for a limited-time, just-for-the-winter romance. That's exactly my jam."

Dylan snorts. "Maybe you should put *that* in your profile."

"No freaking way." Raquel shakes her head. "Do you know what sorts of guys respond to 'not looking for anything serious' posts? Just, no."

"She's right." Allie shrugs. "I already tried something like that."

Raquel gasps. "You didn't."

Allie shrugs, but her tone is a tad defensive. "I needed a plus-one for a wedding. I thought I'd try to find, y'know, a boyfriend of convenience."

Paula barks a laugh. "Now that's a rom-com plot if I've ever heard one."

"Right?" Allie nods. "I figured if it worked in the movies . . . but alas." Her frown matches the melodrama of the back of her hand pressed against her forehead.

Allie Hayes seems like kind of a mess, but I've never met anyone with such a positive, silver-linings attitude. I join in the table-wide chuckle and then tip my mug, draining it of its deliciousness.

"You'll find the right guy someday, Allie." Raquel pats her hand.

"Maybe, maybe not. And you know what? I'm okay either way. I don't hate being single. Honestly, I love my life."

Her tone and body language proclaim her statement as true, and it's . . . refreshing.

"Sure," she continues, "if I could find a nice, sane guy to be my winter boyfriend—you know, someone who would agree from the start that we would graciously, mutually ditch each other before I discover that one annoying trait I can't help but think about every time I see his face?—I wouldn't turn that down." She grins. "But trust me. Even if that perfect winter boyfriend guy existed, I'd get tired of him before long. I'm sure I'd be relieved when it was time to go back to my contented singleness after the holidays."

"Oh, come on." Dylan crosses his arms. "The books. The movies. The way you devour every detail of your friends' relationships. You're a certifiable romance junkie."

"No argument there. I'm *totally* addicted to romance. But since I suck at sustaining it for myself, I'm utterly in awe of those who can. I'm perfectly happy to get my romance addiction hit through the rest of you. So keep it comin', my friends. Between you guys, my books, and my movies, I'm set. I don't need to go looking for it for myself."

"I, for one, wish you would." Paula's tone is dry. "Then maybe I could keep *my* love life private."

"Oooh." Lexi nudges Paula with her elbow. "So it's love, is it?"

"Don't you start," Paula throws Lexi a scowl. "I'll have enough trouble reining *that* one in." She angles her thumb toward Allie's end of the table and then lifts her mug, taking a big swig before setting it back down. "And before she gets going again, I'm gonna call it a night."

"Aw, don't run off on account of me. I'm just teasing." Allie stands. "Who's up for cocoa, round two?"

"I am." I tilt my empty mug toward her. "This cocoa was superb, but I didn't want to seem like a glutton if no one else was going for seconds."

"A new convert, my friends." Allie laughs. "You can't out-glutton me where this cocoa is concerned. I always get a second cup. Sometimes a third." She pauses to frown down at Raquel. "I keep forgetting we rode together. Did you need to get home?"

Raquel glances at her phone. "Yeah, probably. But if you're not ready, I can—"

"No prob. I'll get mine in a to-go cup."

By the time Allie and I return to the table with our cocoas-to-go, everyone has their coats on.

"Glad you could join us tonight," Paula says, and it seems sincere.

"Yeah, man," Dylan adds. "Thanks for aiding my gender equality in this equation."

Lexi punches his arm. "That is not remotely what 'gender equality' means, doofus."

"I know that." He tosses her a wink. "But still. Glad to have another dude in the cocoa club. You should come again next week."

A chorus of nods, *please do*s, and *yeah you should*s round the table.

It was fun being around new people socially instead of just through work interactions. And the cocoa here is just as amazing as promised. A smile tugs my cheeks. "I just might."

Chapter 3

GRANT

Friday afternoon, Howard Iverson pops into my office. "Oh, good. You're still here."

I glance at the clock in the corner of my screen. "It's only four. Where else would I be?"

"And that is exactly what I want to talk with you about." Howard comes in, closing the door behind him. "Do you have a minute?"

It's not unusual for Howard or Wallace Forsyth, the firm's other senior partner, to pop in on a Friday to sit and chat for a while or offer a dinner invitation. But this feels different somehow.

I lean back in my chair. "What's on your mind?"

"Wallace and I have been talking about my upcoming retirement, and the partnership position that will open up when I take my name off the door," he begins, and my pulse speeds up. "We couldn't be prouder of the architectural team we've built, and you, in particular, show real leadership promise. But we have some concerns."

"Such as?"

"Wallace and I have great faith in your abilities, and great affection for you, as I'm sure you know. That's why, before we consider a bid from you, we need the assurance that partnership is truly the best thing for you as a person."

"I'm not sure what you mean."

"You're aware of our Family First policy, yes?"

"Of course." I nod. "I admire how you both have prioritized your families, and how you've allowed your employees to do the same."

"Thank you. And you're aware of our flexibility with employee scheduling? And how we occasionally work from home and encourage our staff to do so too?"

"Absolutely. All excellent policies."

"Of which you do not benefit, by choice."

"I don't have a family yet." I shrug. "I hope to someday, but I've been focused on my career."

"Exactly." Howard's expression is thoughtful, almost fatherly. It's a familiar look. "We—Wallace and I—have long held the belief that our craft as architectural professionals will only be as creatively excellent as the fuel we provide that creativity. Do you know what fuels creativity, Grant?"

Easy. "Study, planning, and hard work."

"Those are ingredients for success, to be sure," Howard nods. "But the vibrancy, the freshness of a creative spark? That's found beyond these walls, out of the office, where we're fully removed from the study and work of architecture. It's found in the places where we're living—truly living—the best parts our lives. When we prioritize access to that spark, we can bring it back to work with us and infuse its energy into our designs and the staff we lead."

"Well, sure."

"Where would you say you are living the best parts of your life?"

"Right here. I love my work."

"That's what I was afraid you'd say." Howard takes a deep breath. "Your professional drive is admirable. You are passionate about your craft, and it shows. But there's more to life than work, Grant. We don't want the burden of partnership to rob you of the very thing that will allow you to excel as a partner in this firm."

My stomach clenches. "Are you saying I shouldn't make a partnership bid?"

"No, that's not what I'm saying. We want you to make that bid."

My stomach unclenches the tiniest bit.

"What I am saying," he continues, "is that I cannot guarantee your bid will be accepted if things continue as they are."

"Oh."

"This is coming from a place of friendship and respect, Grant. We need to see some evidence of a work/life balance in you. One that leans harder toward life, without sacrificing the excellence of your work. We need to see you actively pursuing those things that will fuel your creative spark." He stands. "I hope you'll give it some thought."

I swallow hard and give one solid nod. "I will."

Howard tells me to have a good weekend and leaves me to my gut-punched thoughts.

I sit, staring at the door, completely shell-shocked that a seventy-two-year-old man just told me to get a life.

But I do have a life. A good life. Don't I?

I play racquetball with some guys every Sunday night. Well, not every Sunday night. But I have a lot of friends. We hang. Not as much as we used to, but occasionally. A lot of them got married in their twenties and are busy with wives and kids now. Even so, it's not like I'm bored on the weekends. My entire family lives within a ninety-minute radius of my condo, and we're pretty tight. And there's always work. Power lunches. Networking events. Planning. Doing.

Always moving forward.

Yet clearly, those in charge of the decision that will set up my future think I've fallen behind. If I don't catch up, and soon, I'll have missed the mark.

It's been seven days since Howard dropped that "get a life, or you'll blow it" bomb on me, and while a corner of my brain is still a little shell-shocked, I'm determined to crush this goal. I'm not the type of guy who can sit around and wait for a solution to fall into my lap. When a clear expectation is given to me, I will absolutely meet or exceed it. Every time.

Planning leads to strategy. Strategy leads to action. Action leads to results.

Howard may not be aware of it, but all that *get-a-life* stuff he talked about? It was always the plan. I just have to move up the timeline a little bit. It'll be tight, sure. But if I'm going to ensure that the end-of-quarter meeting in March begins with announcing the venue for Howard Iverson's retirement party and ends with the acceptance of my partnership bid, it must be done.

I lean back in my chair and crack my knuckles. *Forsyth-Covington Architectural Associates*.

That sounds pretty good.

Once that detail is cemented, I will have completed Phase I of my life plan and will be ready to begin Phase II: Marriage and Family.

Nearly every evening this past week has been spent on some aspect of planning my introduction to Phase II, and its revised timeline.

Well, not every evening. That first night was spent sitting on the sofa, staring at the wall, and craving hot cocoa while having an existential crisis.

That craving, however, led my mind back to the "cocoa club" conversation, which eventually spawned an idea. The more that idea spun around in my brain, the more sense it made. So, I got to work.

I started with a pros and cons list. Strategically speaking, the pros of my idea outweighed the cons. With that settled, I dug into the necessary research. Took notes. Made lists.

Next came the creation of an optimal timeline and the crunching of numbers to develop a project-specific budget—setting a little extra aside for contingencies, of course.

Finally, while polishing the data, a strategy emerged.

I crafted a logical, professional, and highly detailed presentation. On my personal tablet, of course. This is not the sort of thing I want flagged by Iverson-Forsyth's I.T. department—the gossip hub of the firm.

Tonight, following my weekly meeting with the Elementary Facilities Committee in Sterling Grove, I will give my presentation and hope it's well-received.

I am confident that I've crafted a solid plan, but I can't seem to sit still. I'm not an anxious guy. I'm a planner and a do-er who excels at follow-through. I trust in the structural integrity of the plans I design—be they architectural plans or dinner plans. That's how I landed this corner office before my thirtieth birthday and how I paid off my condo with merit bonuses over the following four years. But a lot rides on how my presentation is received, and my nerves are so on edge they're practically popping out of my skin

I can create the work/life balance required to be both professionally and personally successful.

I can, and I will.

I'm aware this next phase could prove to be a lot trickier than its predecessor. Partly because I failed to plan for any overlap between Phases I and II, and partly because my lack of foresight was so poignantly pointed out to me by my boss last Friday.

I could have been dating—at least for fun and practice—long before now, but it wasn't the priority it obviously should have been. Now, I'm thirty-four and starting to notice echoes in corners of my life I hadn't realized were empty before.

But it doesn't matter. Phase II begins soon. I may be a bit behind due to the lack of overlap, but I have a plan to catch up and get back on track.

I glance at the clock. It's 2:37 p.m. A full three minutes since the last time I checked.

I'm accomplishing very little in the way of work today.

I haven't been this excited about going to an elementary school since my P.E. teacher introduced our class to dodgeball.

I haven't been this nervous since . . . I don't know when.

My career is thriving. My Phase I goal—partnership and long-term financial security—will soon be in reach. It's time to lay the groundwork for Phase II. I'm ready.

Today, however, time is standing still.

I shift forward and wake my computer screen, only to have a menu of cocoa concoctions stare back at me. A near-Pavlovian response awakens my tongue, and a tingle of anticipation tickles the bottoms of my feet. I need to figure this out. When I arrive at Cocoa & Froth after the meeting tonight, I don't want to waste time at the counter like I did last week. I want to walk in knowing my order.

Five minutes later, the decision is still unmade when an intern knocks on my office door.

I wave him in with one hand and minimize the Cocoa & Froth tab with the other. "What's up?"

"Package." He hands me a padded envelope. "I think it's the specialty toilet catalog you ordered for the Sterling Grove Elementary project."

"Awesome. Thanks." As soon as he leaves, I rip the envelope open and slide the catalog out. I can't believe I forgot this hadn't arrived yet. Considering what a crucial albeit small role this catalog has been assigned in the timeline of my micro plan for this evening, that memory lapse is a little disconcerting.

I click the Cocoa & Froth menu open again. I peruse, imagine, and finally choose my order. I write it on a scrap of paper and read it aloud a couple of times. I want it memorized so I'm ready when the time comes.

I glance at the clock in the corner of the screen. Finally, it's time to start packing up for my trip to Sterling Grove Elementary School.

I have to set the cruise control to avoid speeding. Even so, I arrive ten minutes earlier than planned, which is still twenty minutes before the meeting's 6 p.m. start time.

A custodian recognizes me but still makes me show my district-issued ID badge before she lets me into the building. Sterling Grove is a small rural community, but full staff vigilance at school buildings is priceless these days. I thank her for her caution and for letting me in early.

The moment I step into the library, the scent of decay and rot assaults my nose. The smell of the library is never pleasant, but whatever died in these walls since our last meeting has to be bigger than a mouse. Luckily, I came prepared. A baggie in my satchel contains a peppermint oil-coated cotton swab. After I dab it under each nostril, I can breathe a little easier. Once the scent situation is as managed as it can be, I set up my equipment.

I understand why the building's principal chose this space for these meetings. It was a strategic move for sure, but it seems a little like torture when, surely, there must be a less-odiferous space somewhere in the building.

Oh well. Not my call.

After rearranging tables and chairs in a staggered v-formation that allows every chair a clear view of the screen, I distribute tonight's printed meeting agenda. After double-checking my presentation to be sure every slide is in the correct order and no typos exist, I glance at my computer bag but manage to resist the temptation to pull out my tablet and rehearse tonight's *other* presentation.

My knee bounces. I press my heel into the floor. Deep breath in . . . and out. In . . . and . . . out.

The library door clicks, and I open the eyes I closed while getting a grip. "Dylan." I lift my chin in greeting. "Hi."

"Hey. What's up?" He shoulders off a bag and sets his own laptop on a table near the middle of the middle row. "You down for cocoa tonight?"

I nod. "Planning on it."

He grins. "Finally. Another dude."

A few more people start to filter in. I leave my chair and mingle, thanking each committee member individually for showing up. I cringe inwardly when Norma Kellogg walks in. Thankfully, she just gives me a little wave and takes her seat.

Raquel arrives alongside a pair of community members, both parents of elementary students, and I greet them all by name.

At six, my smartwatch vibrates, and I move to my place at the front. "Thanks for coming out, everyone." But it's *not* everyone. One chair is empty. "Before we jump into tonight's agenda items, does anyone have questions about what we talked about last week?"

I give it a minute. When my gaze has roved over the assembly, to the door, and back three times, I wake up my laptop and, projector remote in hand, begin the meeting.

An hour later, I open the floor for questions, comments, and concerns.

One chair is still empty. The chair I most wanted to be filled tonight. Not for this presentation, but for the one to follow.

It's okay, I tell myself. *One week's delay won't make or break the plan.*

I field the few questions that come up, taking notes on suggestions and ideas. At 7:32, I thank everyone for coming and express that I'll be looking forward to seeing them again next week.

"We can't have a meeting next week," Paula pipes up. "It's Parent/Teacher Conferences."

On some level, I knew that. I've just been too preoccupied with my non-work plans to realize that the date in my head—and on my calendar—was next week.

"Do you need me to get you a copy of the school calendar?" Norma beams at me. "It's no problem."

"Thanks, but I already have it." I aim those words at her before lifting my gaze. "Sorry. My mistake. Due to Parent/Teacher Conferences, we will not have a meeting next week but will reconvene the following Thursday. Have a good night, everyone."

I close my laptop and start packing my stuff.

"See ya in a few." Dylan doffs a two-fingered salute from the door.

"See you there." With my Phase II starter plan on hold, my enthusiasm for cocoa has dimmed, but since I already told Dylan I'd be there, it would be rude not to show.

No meeting next week. I grit my teeth. That means I'll be two weeks behind on the new plan. Of all the meetings Allie Hayes could have skipped, why did it have to be tonight's?

Chapter 4

ALLIE

I should probably feel guilty about skipping the facilities committee meeting, but I totally don't. This bulletin board is epic. Probably the best one I've ever made. My kiddos are going to walk in tomorrow morning and lose their sweet little minds over the sheer awesomeness of this thing.

By the time I've put away all my bulletin board crafting supplies and turned off the fairy lights in Storytime Corner—which might soon lose its place as the kids' favorite part of the room—I'm starving. I started carefully disassembling the old bulletin board design as soon as the last student left my classroom at 3:15. A quick glance at my phone shows I've been at work on this project almost five hours, during which the only sustenance I ingested was a juice pouch and a handful of Skittles. Thankfully, it's only 8:00. Cocoa & Froth is open until 9:30.

There aren't any parking spots in front, so I have to park around the corner. When I walk in front of the window, I see the gang has gathered around the usual table, and—

Oh, crap. The architect is here. And I skipped out on his meeting.

Busted.

Ah, well. I'm a teacher first and a committee member second. I'm here now, and a girl's gotta eat. Besides, I'm already salivating for a chicken salad croissant—the perfect accompaniment to a hazelnut cocoa with hazelnut whip and chocolate curls on top.

But I should probably apologize first.

I sidle over to the table, plopping my bag in the chair at the head of the table—my usual spot, conveniently unoccupied even in my absence. I shed my coat, draping it over the chair back. "Greg," I say, making eye contact with Mr. Covington, who tilts his head, frowning. "I'm sorry I missed the meeting. I was working on a project in my classroom. I'll make sure these guys get me caught up before the next one."

"No problem," he says. "And, er, it's . . . Grant. Not Greg."

"Grant." I facepalm myself. "Sorry. I knew that. My bad." I rummage through my purse and pull out my debit card. "I'm starving. Be right back. Carry on."

About twelve minutes later, I've demolished the chicken salad croissant. With a satisfied sigh, I lean back in my chair. "What did I miss?"

"*Aaaand* she's back." Dylan laughs.

"I don't think I've ever seen Allie go that long without talking," Paula adds. "That must've been some sandwich."

"The best." I pat my belly and then clasp my hands over it. "So? Dish. What are tonight's hot topics?"

"Nothing, really," Paula says, at the same time Lexi pipes up with, "Paula and Bill are putting together a team for the town library's trivia night fundraiser."

"Paula *and* Bill?" I waggle my eyebrows. "That certainly sounds cozy and officially-a-couple-y."

"Keep that up and you won't be invited to join my team," Paula growls halfheartedly.

"Oh, but I can't be on your trivia team. One of my students' parents already asked me to join hers. Too bad for you and Bill," I tease, "because my team is going to dominate."

"Good luck with that," Raquel says. "They've already recruited Karen Louise and Colin Jacobson."

"You're kidding me."

"Nope."

Karen is a high school social studies teacher and a total sports fanatic. She's famous for the bracket systems she creates—some for sports I've never heard of. Nearly every time I've seen her outside of work hours, she's wearing some team's insignia, and most often that of her favorite team and alma mater, Purdue University. Colin is a middle school science teacher, but his main income comes from his pop culture podcast.

The original Cheshire Cat could not smile more devilishly than Paula is right now. "With those two alone, we've covered sports, science, entertainment, and history. Good luck dominating, Al."

"In the end," I say, closing my eyes and bringing my hands together in a prayer pose, "winning doesn't matter. It's for the *children*." I open my eyes. "Seriously, though? You're going to kick our butts. I'll just have to make sure our table has a good view of yours so I can witness your budding romance with Bill."

"You're such a child." Paula rolls her eyes at me, but she's smiling, even as she shakes her head. "I suppose that's part of why we all love you."

"Probably. So, what else did I miss?"

"That's pretty much it," Lexi says. "Oh, and Dylan ripped out the seat of his pants in the lunch room and had to rush home to change, but you probably already knew that."

I nod. "I was there. That was a rough few minutes, my dude."

"Don't remind me." Dylan groans and stands. "I'm gonna head home. These were my last pair of clean pants, and I dripped a little cocoa on them. I have to do some laundry."

Almost everyone else starts scooting back their chairs.

"Seriously, guys? I just got here," I protest. "I haven't even had my second cup of cocoa yet."

"I could go for another mug," Grant offers. "If you don't mind the company."

"Not a bit. And if you don't mind, maybe you could catch me up on what I missed at the meeting?"

He smiles. "Sure."

Raquel pauses in putting her coat on just long enough to arch an eyebrow at me.

It's good to have friends who look out for your safety. I'm fairly certain Mr. Covington—Grant—is harmless, but you never know. "I'll text you when I leave," I reassure her. "And when I get home."

"Oh. Umm . . ." She gives me a confused look and then zips up her coat. "Okay."

By the time Grant and I have decided on our final cocoas of the evening—he decided much faster than I did—the teachers are all gone, but Cocoa & Froth is far from empty. In one booth, two middle-aged women are deep in conversation. The big corner booth holds three teen girls whose expressions—and one telltale propped-up textbook—proclaim they have an Algebra II test tomorrow. At a table for two by the bank of front windows, my neighbor, a not-quite-elderly man named Dennis Lee Rose, sits alone with a faraway smile, tapping a pen against a scrawl-covered notebook page. I decide to make a quick detour by his table while awaiting my order.

"How's the new book coming, Dennis?"

"Hmm?" He turns the smile toward me, and it widens. "Well, if it isn't my favorite neighbor, catching me daydreaming again." He laughs. "The book has taken an unexpected turn. But a good turn, I think."

"Ooh, that sounds interesting. Is it a Dennis book, or a Rosalie book this time?" He writes true crime novelizations under his real name, and swoony romance using the handy pen name 'Rosalie Dennis.'

"This one is Rosalie. Takes place in the Scottish Lowlands."

"Is there a duke?" I splay my hands on the table and lean in. "Please tell me there's a handsome, rakish duke."

"I'm mixing it up a bit. This time it's a young, widowed duchess and an outlaw. But he's a rakish outlaw, if that helps."

"Why, yes it does." I lean back and fan myself with my hand. "Can't wait to read it." My name is called from the counter. "Back to your daydreaming, sir. I'm gonna need that book soon."

"See you later, Allie-neighbor."

"Back to your prose, Dennis Rose."

We grin. That's been our schtick since the day we met over the waist-high white picket fence between my house and his. It was at least a year later before he admitted he was also Rosalie Dennis.

I head up to the counter just as Grant's name is called. He's disappeared, so I grab his drink and head back to the big table.

The bell above the door jingles. I look over the rim of my mug. It's Grant, with a satchel in hand. He must have gone outside while I was chatting with Dennis.

He pulls a magazine from his satchel. "Toilet catalog." He sets it down in front of me. "You'd mentioned a possible interest in colored toilets for the kindergarten classroom bathrooms last week, so I thought maybe you'd like to see some of the available options."

"Cool." I'd nearly forgotten all about that on-the-spot toilet tangent. I honestly don't care about toilet colors, but since he went to the effort of bringing the catalog, I'll take a look. "That's yours." I point to his mug.

"Thanks."

I open the catalog and flip through pages. "Holy cow. I had no idea toilets were so pricey."

"Specialty toilets tend to be fairly high-dollar fixtures."

"In that case, let me declare my undying love for boring white toilets. There are much better things to spend that kind of money on." I slap the catalog closed and push it back toward him. "But thanks for remembering and going to the effort of bringing the catalog and all."

"No problem." He takes a sip of his cocoa. "You didn't miss much at the committee meeting tonight. There was some discussion about the arrangement of the upper elementary classrooms and how we can combat the reflective glare from the southern windows at different times of day, but other than that you didn't miss anything of import."

"So how many more weekly meetings do you have to suffer through before you can begin the actual architectural work?"

"Oh, it's already begun." He smiles. "And I don't mind the meetings. It's good to get a feeling for what the staff and community consider important. Every community is different, has different priorities." He rubs his thumb back and forth over the top of the mug handle. "But to answer your question, I think we should be able to wrap up the committee meetings before school lets out for winter break in December. We'll see how it goes. I expect to present the committee-approved plan to the school board at their January meeting. I believe it's scheduled for January 17th, but I'd need to check my calendar to be sure."

"They meet on the third Tuesday of every month, so you're probably fairly close. Well, poo. Once the committee approves the design, I'll have to find a new excuse for my Thursday night cocoa run."

He leans over to pull a folio of some sort from the satchel resting against the side of his chair. "Actually, there might be a few extra opportunities for cocoa. At least for you." He shakes his head. "Wow. That was a clumsy segue. Sorry."

"Segue to what?"

"I've been thinking about something you said when we were here last week, and I wanted to follow up on it."

"Uh . . ." I squint, as if that will help my brain recall what I might have talked about last Thursday night. Nope. "I'm drawing a blank."

"Right. Sorry. The group was talking about Paula's new relationship, and then you shared all of your ideas for romantic winter outings."

"Not nearly all of them." I laugh. He chuckles, and I note a dimple in his cheek as he opens up the folio case to reveal a tablet computer.

He taps the screen a couple of times before propping the tablet on the case's built-in stand, and then it hits me. "Oh! You need ideas? Do you want to take notes and plan some romantic stuff to impress your girlfriend?"

"Not . . . exactly? I don't have a girlfriend. To be perfectly honest, I haven't had a serious girlfriend since undergrad. I've been focused on Phase I."

"Phase one?"

He nods. "My career. But now that I'm established in the firm, I'm ready to start moving into Phase II. Marriage and Family."

"Oh. Um, right. Sure." I look over my shoulder toward the door, but everyone from our table is long gone. At least Dennis is here in case things get weird.

Scratch that. Weird-er. We've already passed regular weird.

"You said you're content being single," he continues, a remote in his hand. "Which is perfect. Honestly, a little unusual. But you also said you would enjoy a winter romance, as long as it had an expiration date." He meets my gaze. "I have an idea to present to you that, I believe, will benefit us both."

He turns the tablet to face me.

The screen is black, but out of the corner of my eye I catch a slight movement from his thumb on the remote, and the black screen dissolves via my favorite of all digital transitions: sparkle.

When the gloriously glowing glitter clears, it reveals a still image of Princess Anna from *Frozen*, knocking on soon-to-be Queen Elsa's door. "Uh . . ." I look up at him, confused. "So . . . you want to build a snowman?"

"Yes!" He grins, but it quickly falls. "Wait." He turns the tablet back toward himself. "What the— Why is that slide . . .?"

He trails off, his frown at the tablet growing more severe with each tap to the screen.

Chapter 5

Grant

What happened to my carefully designed presentation?

I tap the remote again. Nothing happens. I set the remote down and lean in, as if closer proximity will make the technology work like it's supposed to. I tap the screen to put it into presenter mode, but . . . there are only two slides. The blank starter slide, and the final slide.

"I'm not sure what happened. I had a whole— There should be twelve slides." I click back and forth between presenter and presentation mode, but the missing ten slides do not return. "I don't know what . . . Oh. I opened the wrong file."

I glance at Allie. She isn't smiling. This is maybe the first time I've seen her *not* smiling.

And her gaze keeps darting over to where an older man sits, writing in a notebook.

Honestly, she looks a little creeped out.

Ohhh. She *is* creeped out. Because of me. I did that.

"Now that I think about it," I say, closing the tablet, "maybe a multimedia presentation was a little overkill." I cringe at my own word choice. Considering she probably thinks I'm some sort of psycho at this point, using any incarnation of the word 'kill' was not a great move. I take a deep breath and then close my eyes and run a hand over my face.

"Should I ask to see the file?" She sings the question to the tune of that song from *Frozen*. "Or will it freak me out?"

She's being a good sport, in any case. "Valid question, all things considered." I meet her eyes. "Wow. This illustrates the point I intended to make, but a lot less subtly—and with a good deal less professionalism—than I planned." I push the tablet out of the way and lean back in my chair. "But maybe that's where I went wrong." I laugh, but it's a dry and self-deprecating sound. "Howard was right. Clearly, my after-hours-interactions style needs help."

"Who's Howard?"

"My boss."

She tilts her head, appearing more curious than creeped out. Good. Maybe I still have a chance.

"He told me I need to get a life. Outside of work." I take a deep breath. "I plan to make a bid for partnership at my firm soon, but for it to be successful, I have to prove to my bosses that I can balance work and a life away from work."

"That makes sense."

"It does now." I nod. "Unfortunately, I never gave it much thought before it was pointed out to me." I've thought of little else since. "Like I said earlier, I haven't dated anyone since college. It just hasn't been the priority. I thought dating anyone seriously would actually distract me from the Phase I priority."

"Your career."

"Right. I plan to start dating—intentionally—after the first of the year. But my dating skills are a tad rusty. I thought maybe . . . ?" I glance at the tablet. "Do you want to hear the pitch?"

"The pitch? Like, a sales pitch?"

"Uh, yeah." Wow. I made a sales pitch for a conversation about dating. With visual aids. "I am a complete idiot. Never mind."

"Are you kidding me? You're not getting off that easy, buddy." She shakes her head, and her lips part into a smile that practically sparks with energy and challenge. "I'm gonna need to hear that"—she does air quotes—"pitch."

"You're serious?"

"Soooo serious."

Honestly, I deserve to be humiliated. "With or without visual aids?" I nod to the tablet.

"Absolutely with visual aids."

I take a deep breath and scoot my chair back. "Here goes."

Chapter 6

ALLIE

I cannot believe what I'm seeing. And hearing? Was that a sleigh bell sound accompanying the transition to the next slide?

It was. It totally was.

This guy created a multimedia presentation to . . . I'm not sure what the goal is here. He's delivering talking points in an ordered and concise way, but with such an easy, conversational tone that even though I know they're memorized—he more or less admitted to memorizing the presentation—they sure don't come off that way.

I'm a little disappointed the sparkle transition hasn't yet made an appearance, but maybe he decided a cleaner transition was better for the jingle bell sound?

In any case, it's pretty smooth. If I hadn't been mildly freaked out a few minutes ago, I would be tempted to pull out my credit card and order at least two of whatever it is he's selling.

Which seems like . . . his life plan and organizational skills?

To be honest, I haven't quite figured out where he's going yet. So far, he's only told me about his background, his hobbies, and such. He outlined his Phase I: Career, and it's impressive. If you're into that sort of laser-focused professional drive. But we're only on slide seven or eight, and he said there were twelve, so . . .

He clicks another slide. This one features a gorgeous gingerbread house.

"You described having a just-for-the-winter boyfriend. Someone with whom you would agree to part ways after the holidays, with no hard feelings." He looks so directly into my eyes that I can't help but notice his green irises have a little brown and a little gold sprinkled through them. "I couldn't stop thinking about the perfection of that idea. And how it might figure into my plans for Phase II."

The next slide features an idyllic two-story modern farmhouse with the heading, *Phase II: Marriage and Family.*

Whoa.

No, for real. *Whoa, fella.*

"Hold on," I say. "A winter boyfriend would have an expiration date. How did you jump from there to *marriage*?"

He startles but recovers quickly. "It's not a jump, just a detour possibility that could prove beneficial prior to me actually starting Phase II." He smiles. "Hang with me just a little longer, Allie. It will all come together and make sense, I promise." He clicks to the next slide, which is a picture of a desert highway with a "road closed" sign blocking the way. "Unfortunately, when I crafted my three-phase life plan—"

"Three? What's phase three?" I interrupt to ask.

"Retirement and leisure."

Wow.

"As I was saying," he continues, "back when I crafted my plan, I was so focused on my career that I didn't think to provide overlap to prepare for Phase II. That's where you come in."

"Me?"

"Yes, Allie. You, and your unconventional dating philosophy."

His smile is disarming, to say the least. I still don't quite know what he's selling, but he baits an attractive hook.

I blink and tear my gaze away, only to see my name appear on the next slide—via a sparkle transition, yay!—above two cups of steaming cocoa.

Grant talks through the bullet points that appear under my name. Presumably, this is his take on the stuff I talked about last week when trying to give my friends some wintertime dating ideas.

"You want to be in a dating relationship during the wintertime season between November first and the end of the year." His name replaces mine, and a new bullet point follows. "I am woefully out of practice dating."

He clicks another bullet point. And then another, detailing how he intends to show his bosses he's a good candidate for partnership within the next couple of months and then achieve his goal of being married and starting a family within the next three years. "But to do that, I need a dating refresher course."

This guy is something else.

Except with a flawlessly sculpted jawline, thick brown hair, kind eyes, and a solid set of shoulders.

I do enjoy a solid set of shoulders. But other than that, he seems way too organized to be able to handle someone like me.

The slide changes. This time, the background is a snowy field where two people appear to be building a snowman.

Ah. We must be near the end of the pitch.

"Our long-term goals differ, but I think our short-term, more imminent goals might align." He leans forward, clasping his hands on the table between us. "To that end, I've devised what I believe is the perfect winter plan for both of us."

Is he saying what I think he's saying?

"Allie." He pauses, and the vaguest hint of insecurity passes through his eyes, but disappears into a warm, earnest smile. "I would like to apply for the position of your winter boyfriend."

Oh. Oh, wow.

"So . . . let me get this right. You're offering to take me on all of my romantic wintertime dream dates without a commitment beyond January first?"

He nods. "I am."

Grant smiles, and his dimple shows through his end-of-day stubble. But only on one side. I imagine what he would do if I poked it when I have frosting on my finger after baking Christmas cookies together.

Hmm . . .

A flash of light turns my attention to his tablet, which is still facing me.

Oh, no. Heaven help me. Sure, I agreed to watch his presentation. I didn't expect—or want—to see a *spreadsheet*.

I lean as far away as I can from the screen. "What happened to all the pretty slides?"

"This is the budget I've set for this plan." He angles the screen slightly toward himself. "Complete with a little extra for contingencies and spontaneity."

"Spontaneity via spreadsheet?" I've found the hole in his plan. "I think you need a refresher course on the definition of spontaneity."

I roll my shoulders back in an attempt to relax what had tensed up as soon as that spreadsheet appeared. "Grant, you seem like a great guy with good intentions, but I'm not sure we're a good match. You're obviously a meticulous planner, and I'm . . .? Well, I'm about the furthest thing from that. Things like spreadsheets, and concrete plans, and schedules outside the bounds of the school day give me literal hives." I'm not even kidding. "I kind of doubt our vibes are going to gel enough to last very long. I hate to disappoint you after you've gone to all this work, but I don't think I'm the girl for you."

"Exactly." His face lights up. "That's why going into a romantic relationship with a predetermined expiration date makes so much sense for us."

"Fair point." I lean back in my chair. Could this actually work? Might it even be a little bit . . . fun?

Chapter 7

GRANT

"I have some questions." Allie crosses her arms. "First off, I need to know this isn't some fake-dating thing where we lie to everyone we love. Because I'm not about that." She tilts her chin down at an angle. "And frankly, I wouldn't want to hang out with someone who is."

The unexpected steel in her gaze makes me feel like I'm five years old and just pushed somebody over on the playground, unprovoked.

I wasn't prepared for that question, but it's reassuring to know Allie is a person of character—especially since we're bound to interact with people I care about over the next couple of months. "We would be dating for real, but casually."

"So I could tell anyone I wanted that we're only planning to date through the end of the year?"

"Of course."

"And you would be honest with your boss about it?" Allie's tone matches that steely gaze. "Because if you're looking for someone to help you pull one over on your boss just to get a promotion, that's a hard pass for me."

"If I were willing to lie to my boss like that, I wouldn't deserve a place of leadership in the firm."

She holds my gaze for a moment, and then her expression relaxes into a smile. "Good answer. Okay. Moving on. I've set a fairly high bar in my mind for what constitutes a romantic wintertime date. Are you up to that challenge?"

Okay, she's open to the idea of a winter boyfriend, but she's not sure I've got what it takes.

That makes two of us. But then again, that's why I want to do this.

"I understand your reticence," I say. "Last week you supplied a lot of ideas. Since then, I've been doing some research and planning on my own. I'd be happy to take more input, of course. Or participate in things *you* plan," I offer. "But I will try to do my best. You don't have to answer tonight. Take the weekend, or—"

"Happily?"

Is she asking me if she should be happy while deciding about this? "I'm sorry, I don't quite—"

"Will you *happily* participate in the fun-slash-romantic winter outings I plan without your input? Or don't plan, per se, but spontaneously suggest? Because that is about a bajillion times more likely."

My smile muscle pulls to one side. "One little spreadsheet and you think I'm a giant fun-killer, huh?"

"There's that word again." Allie gives an exaggerated shiver. "Stop saying that word."

"I can be a fun guy." Can I in this context, though? I haven't been anyone's boyfriend in years.

"Okay. But when you do plan fun-slash-romantic wintertime dates in what appears to be your very, um, thorough style, are you willing to keep those plans to yourself? You won't suck the fun out of them for me by telling me about them too far in advance?"

Wow. She's serious about that spontaneity thing. "Won't you need to know what to wear, when to be ready, things like that?"

"I guess?" She shrugs. "You can tell me the basics. What I need to know. Just don't tell me too much all the time, okay? Eliminating the element of surprise kind of diffuses a moment's magic, don't you think? And a wintertime romance deserves its magic."

I am not a big fan of surprises. But I am a big fan of diplomacy. "I've never thought about it that way."

"If you were my winter boyfriend, you would definitely need to consider that sort of thing." She sputters a laugh. "Hey, maybe being around me will take some of that starch out of your shirt. Your future wife might just thank me one day."

Ouch. "You could be right." My preparedness did not make the best impression, but she hasn't left yet. Maybe I still have a chance. "Like I said, I need a refresher."

"Clearly. Now about that expiration date."

Clearly?

"When we hit that date, when we 'break up'"—she makes air quotes—"or expire, or whatever? We're cool, right? No hard feelings, no typical angsty breakup stuff?"

"None. We go our separate ways in a friendly fashion, each having achieved our short-term goal."

"Cool. Cool." Allie nods several times and then sits up straight, scoots her seat back, and crisscrosses her legs on the chair. She closes her eyes and brings her elbows toward her sides, her arms at forty-five-degree angles from her waist, palms up. Her thumbs gracefully meet her middle fingers. She takes a deep breath in through her nose, holds it, and exhales through her nose.

It's a lotus pose. She's doing yoga? In a chair at a cocoa shop?

Huh. She doesn't strike me as someone who does yoga.

Then again, I probably don't strike her as someone who does yoga either.

Three breath cycles later, I'm intrigued. The way she swerved from animated conversationalist to silent yogi in a fraction of a heartbeat is somehow the perfect coupling of spontaneity and stillness. I haven't known Allie Hayes long, but my limited observations would not have led me to believe she possessed this capacity for serenity and silence. And yet, she does. Interesting.

Then again, the pose could be exactly that: a pose.

I tense, half-expecting her to jump out of her chair and yell, "Boo!"

Allie goes through another three breath cycles before her expression subtly changes. I can't put my finger on what that change is, only that it happened.

A moment later, she gracefully flips her palms over to rest on her still-criss-crossed knees and then opens her eyes. "Okay." Her smile contains both the serenity of the lotus and the enthusiasm that seems to be her signature mood.

I tilt my head, feeling a little bit like a dog hearing a high-pitched sound. "Okay . . . what?"

"Okay to the plan." She shrugs. "I accept your application. Congratulations, Grant Covington. You got the job. You are officially my winter boyfriend."

Chapter 8

ALLIE

Grant blinks at least three times. "You don't want to see the rest of the . . ." He looks down at the table before giving his head a small shake. He lifts his gaze to me. "I'm sorry if you thought I expected an answer on the spot. I didn't. I don't. I can email you the file. Take some time to think about it, and then let me know next week. Or if you need more time . . ."

"Nah, I'm good." This guy. Seriously. "Dude. Lighten up. Being my winter boyfriend is supposed to be *fun*, remember?"

"I— Um, right." He lifts his cocoa to take a sip, but it's a slurp of air. He mumbles an apology for the sound and gazes into the empty cup as if that mug of cocoa held the secrets of the universe, but now that it's empty, he can't remember what those secrets were. Is he that shocked that I said yes?

I swallow my laugh, lest any sudden sound or movement causes Grant to have a cardiac event. This successful, good-looking architect went to the work of creating a full-on multimedia presentation to basically ask me out. Okay, that's odd. But it's even stranger that he is figuratively choking now because I said yes.

Maybe he wasn't exaggerating about not dating anyone since college. Wow. If that's true, my guy *does* need a dating refresher course. And unless he turns out to be a creeper, which I won't rule out but kind of doubt, I am absolutely up for the challenge.

I carefully place my hand on his arm. "It's a great idea, Grant. You be my winter boyfriend, and I'll be your winter girlfriend-slash-dating-tutor. We'll have some harmless wintertime fun together. *Fun*." I squeeze his arm, but he's still staring into his empty cup like he didn't feel it. "Let that soak in, okay? I'm going to get you a refill. Hold tight."

He has a bit of a death grip on his mug, so I leave it with him and take my empty mug and saucer to the dirty dish return before heading to the counter. After I put in an order for a fresh pair of cocoas, I glance over my shoulder to find Grant putting his tablet back into the satchel.

Good. He's recovered basic motor functions.

While I await the cocoas, I bop over to see how Dennis is doing, hoping a couple more minutes will help Grant reestablish some equilibrium.

"Allie." Dennis lifts his face, gracing me with an inquisitive smile. "Who's the new guy?"

"You noticed? Oh, dear. Does this mean the outlaw and the duchess are being stubborn about sharing their story with you tonight?"

"A bit." He lets out a deep sigh and then arches one eyebrow at me. "But it looked like a lot of sharing was going on at your table."

"You have no idea." I laugh. "His name is Grant Covington. He's the architect designing the new elementary."

"Ah." He nods. "Is that all he is? You two were looking rather cozy."

"Says the romance author."

"People-watching is an occupational necessity." Dennis smiles. "And if I'm not mistaken, I believe I detected a hint of intensity, if not outright romantic chemistry."

"Chemistry, huh? Well, that's good, I guess. I'm not sure how compatible we are, to be honest. But we've been talking about hanging out some this winter. Dating. But nothing serious," I clarify and then shrug. "Could be fun."

He smiles. "I hope it is. You deserve to have some fun."

I step back and put my hands on my hips, feigning offense. "Don't you know by now that I *am* the fun?"

"I most certainly do." He laughs. "You're a good kid."

"I know," I say with a grin, just as my name is called from the counter. "That's me. Gotta jet. See ya later, Dennis-neighbor."

"'Til next we meet, Allie-sweet."

We both laugh. It never gets old.

As I set Grant's fresh cocoa down on the table, he reaches for his wallet.

"Not this time," I say. "My treat."

He gives me a look like he's going to argue, which I counter with my *do-not-test-me* teacher face.

His wallet stays where it is. He's a fast learner.

I take my seat. "I couldn't remember what you ordered, so I thought I'd surprise you with something adventurous."

"Adventurous, hmm?" He lifts the mug and takes a sniff. "Spicy."

"Spicy good, or spicy bad?"

He takes a sip. His eyes widen. He takes another sip. "Wow. That's good."

"Right? So good." He likes my favorite cocoa! "It's called *The Golden Hour.* It's ginger- and turmeric-infused white chocolate cocoa with chai-spiced whip and a buttery caramel drizzle."

"It's amazing." He takes a long, slow sip and then sets his mug down. "Just so we're clear, it's okay if you want to take some time to think about this."

"I've swiped right with a whole lot less information than what you've given me here tonight. I'm good, but . . ." I pause, running my finger around the rim of my mug. "Are you having second thoughts?"

"No, not at all."

"Neither am I." I shrug. "Halloween's over. It's November. Wintertime. Temperatures have been in the mid-30s at night, and the weatherman says we could get our first snow of the season this weekend. Why waste time thinking when we could be out building snowmen?"

"Good point. If you're sure, I'm sure."

"Wait." I hold up my hand. "Speaking of snowmen, what happened to the Princess Anna slide?"

"The wha— Oh, that." He cringes. "We didn't get through the whole presentation."

"Oh. I'm sorry." Oops. "How much was left?"

"Just a slide or two. No big deal."

"I should have saved my questions until the end. I'm sorry I interrupted your pitch."

"Don't be." His lip quirks upward. "Besides . . . mission accomplished. Even without the final few slides. We're doing this, right?"

"Yep." I lean back and cross my arms. "But let's say we do get snow this weekend. Will you behave in a way that honors the spirit of that final slide?"

He chuckles. "If it snows, and if it is the right kind of snow to build a snowman," he adds as his smile widens, "I *might* call you up to see if you'd like to join me on a snowman building date. But I won't tell you when I'm going to call. I don't want to ruin it for you."

"In that case . . ." I reach for my phone. "You're going to need my number."

Chapter 9

GRANT

"Hey, Covington."

I look up from my desk to find our IT guy standing in the doorway. "Hey, Brenton. What's up?"

"A bunch of us are watching the game at Peabody's tomorrow. You in?"

"Thanks, but I can't." My lips stretch a little too near my ears. "I have a date."

"A date?" He takes a few steps into my office. "Like, with a girl?"

"No, with an actual adult woman."

"Har-har. You know what I meant. But, seriously?"

"Seriously."

Brenton's posture perks up. "Anyone I would know?"

"Highly doubtful." I lean back in my chair. This might take a minute.

Brenton is a good guy, mostly. He came on staff about a year ago. Ever since, the office gossip stream has become more of a river. If I don't give him at least a few details, some sort of misinformation with my name attached will be making the rounds next week.

"Her name is Allie," I say. "It's our first date."

"Allie, huh? Cute name. Cute girl?"

"Yeah. She's attractive. For the record, though, I don't think a lot of women like to be called cute." My sister would smack me upside the head if I called her 'cute.'

She has, as a matter of fact.

"Are you going by her online dating profile pic, or have you seen her for real? Because those online photos can be misleading. One time, I got catfished by a girl, and lemme tell you—"

"We've met. In person," I interrupt. "When I asked her out, it was face-to-face."

"Bold." Brenton nods in that *bruh* kind of way. "Where are you taking her?"

"Not sure yet. But I have some ideas."

"Yeah? Like what?"

Would Brenton consider '*go someplace cool and do something fun*' an idea? Because that's all I've got at the moment. I wasn't expecting Allie to agree on the spot last night. I thought I'd have at least a week to plan a good first date. Now, I have less than twenty-four hours. "I . . . uh . . ."

His eyebrows rise. He laughs. "Hey, if all else fails, just bring her over to Peabody's. Cute date plus football and beer sounds like a winner."

"Yeah, I'm not doing that. Any other ideas?"

"Uh . . . nope. Good luck, man." And with a quick pivot, he exits like he didn't just crank up the *make-it-good* pressure by ten degrees.

A few hours later, as I leave the office behind, I shoot a text to my brother-in-law, Jamie. I'm sure he'll have a great idea. He takes my sister out on two official date nights per month, and I generally babysit for at least one of those.

I could ask my sister, but while Rae would be more than happy to offer her input, she would also need more details than Jamie will. And then she would probably stalk Allie on social media or call Mom to share the news.

I'm not quite ready for Rae and Mom to know I'm dating someone.

Wow. I'm actually dating someone.

I have a girlfriend. A just-for-winter girlfriend, sure. But . . . progress. Forward motion.

When the text finally dings, I'm already driving, so my phone stays in my pocket.

While the garage door closes behind me, I check Jamie's text. His suggestion? Dinner and a movie.

Are you kidding me?

I promised Allie a series of wintertime-specific dates. Dinner and a movie? C'mon, man.

I guess I can't really blame Jamie. He doesn't know the parameters of my agreement with Allie. Dinner and a movie would probably pass for a decent first date in most cases. But our situation isn't "most cases," and I'm on track to have the lamest first date in history.

After ordering pizza delivery, I sit down and type 'winter date ideas' into my favorite search engine. A few clicks later, I've landed on Pinterest—a site my mom and sister talk about all the time, but I've never visited.

Within a few scrolls, however, I get it. There's so much stuff here. Tutorials. Organizational tips. Recipes. Memes. The app sucks me into some sort of vortex. Before I know it, my doorbell is ringing, announcing thirty minutes have passed and my pizza is here.

I devour the first slice while using my free hand to set up my own account profile and immediately start organizing ideas on boards—setting them to private, just in case.

The ideas for first dates are seemingly endless, and several users have linked to articles tailored toward wintertime and holiday-centric first dates. With upwards of twenty-five ideas per article, I have hit the motherlode.

I sort through ideas, tossing out those that are too isolated or that would work better for established couples. Eventually, not only have I discovered how freely the exclamation point is used on this website, but I've found the winning idea: *Attend a paint & sip class together.*

A search for "paint and sip classes near me" offers three options for tomorrow, but only one features a paint project that feels wintery. Luckily, its location—a local winery—also seems the most date friendly. I fill out the online form, pay the registration fee, and think about how to present the idea to Allie for a little bit before I text her.

> *Hi, Allie!*
> *Are we still on*
> *for tomorrow?*

Three dots appear and then vanish.

Is she having second thoughts? Maybe something came up. Maybe she forgot?

The dots return. The phone vibrates.

> *New phone, who dis?*

My breath stutters. Did she . . .

Did she program the wrong number into my phone? And if she did, was it . . . intentional?

Of course it was. I asked her out via multimedia presentation, like a total weirdo. I freaked her out so badly that she gave me a fake number and pretended to go along with it to get away from me. Honestly, can I blame her?

Not one bit.

With a sigh, I set my phone down on the coffee table and collapse back into my plush leather sofa. Looks like I'll be volunteering myself as babysitter tomorrow night so Rae and Jamie can go paint and sip.

The phone vibrates. With a sigh, I reach for it, intending to apologize for the mix-up. Instead, I find this:

> *Just messing with you.*
> *I'm in.*
> *When and where?*

I stare at the message, close my eyes tightly, and then open them again to reread it.

My heart restarts. Maybe I'm not as hopeless as I thought.
Trying to keep that vibe going, I type:

> *Should I pick you up,*
> *or would you feel*
> *more comfortable*
> *meeting me somewhere?*

> *Pick me up at*
> *Cocoa & Froth.*

> *Great!*
> *Cocoa & Froth at 5.*
> *We'll grab a quick dinner*
> *and then go to …*
> *our destination.*

> *Your "surprise me" skills*
> *are showing promise.*
> *Any wardrobe advice?*

Huh. Maybe I have better skills than I thought. Definitely more than Allie
expected. I consider her question.

> *Casual and comfortable.*
> *Nothing that would*

break your heart
if it was ruined.

Ooh! I'm intrigued.
See you tmrw!

I send her a thumbs-up and set my phone down.
This is happening. The intro to Phase II has begun.

Chapter 10

ALLIE

"This is fun!" Grant says, a paintbrush in one hand. He's perched on a tall metal stool beside mine. On his right cheek, two smears of dark blue paint serve as double exclamation points at the end of his smile.

Should I tell him? *Nah, it's kinda cute.*

I've done paint-and-sip classes before, but not in this cute little winery's event space and never as a date.

The building we're in looks kind of like a machine shed or barn from the outside, but inside it's decorated in what I would call 'barndominium chic.' The cement floor is stained a tawny brown that warms it up. A few snazzy, modern chandeliers hang here and there from the dark beams above us, and a wine bar at the far end of the space has been free-flowing all night. We're sitting in the center of it all at a counter-height table covered with butcher paper and topped with our masterpieces, which are still in progress.

Grant is wearing jeans and a navy button-down with the sleeves rolled, once again displaying his toned forearms. I'm not complaining.

I'm also wearing jeans, but with a loose-fitting, comfy brown pullover sweater with a wide neckline. I'm having a hard time keeping the baggy sleeves from falling down into my paint, but oh well. Over our clothes, Grant and I are both wearing what the host called "one-time-use artist smocks," but I'm pretty sure they're just disposable rain ponchos like you find at the dollar store. It's a smart choice. I buy them in bulk at the start of every school year and pull them out on the days we're doing messier lessons. They do the job, on the cheap.

"This was an awesome date idea." I take a sip of my sparkling white dessert wine—the only kind of wine I like—and peer over at his painting. Tonight, we're recreating the northern lights on canvas, with some tree silhouettes backing a snowy meadow. In the meadow, a lone snowman peers up at the sky in partial profile, with just one side of him illuminated.

Grant is coming in hot with his winter boyfriend game, and I'm happily surprised to be having a relaxed kind of fun.

My date chose to light his night sky in shades of teal and light green. I decided my aurora needed to honor the movie version of Princess Aurora from *Sleeping Beauty* and added in some subtle pink.

"That looks almost real," I say. "You're really good at this."

"Thanks. It's been a long time since I've painted anything. Other than rooms in my sister's house." He chuckles. It's a nice, warm sound. "She's a compulsive redecorator."

"Me too." It's true. I've lived in my little house for seven of the eight years I've taught at Sterling Grove Elementary, and I've repainted at least one room every year—usually more. "Raquel says I'm probably safe if a tornado plows through town because all those layers of paint will hold my house together."

He laughs. "As someone who understands a little bit about structural engineering, I wouldn't count on that. But if Raquel's paint layer theory turns out to be true, my sister's house will withstand any twister the sky might throw at it."

We talk a little about our families. I learn he's very close with his parents, as well as his sister and her family—a husband, identical twin daughters, and a baby boy.

"I'm a twin," I offer. "But my brother and I don't look that alike. Adam is six minutes older, about six stories taller than me, and his eyes are closer to gray than blue." My twin brother also has a different last name, but I don't go into all that. I'm a firm believer in keeping first-date conversations light and easy.

Instead of going into more detail about my twin, I give Grant the quick run-down on my blended family and tell him how much I'm looking forward to our family Christmas, when my mom, dad, brother, stepparents, and stepsiblings all gather together in a huge rental house for the weekend.

His eyes widen in the typical way people react to my unusual family dynamic. "And everyone gets along?"

"Yep." I can't help but smile. "It's awesome. We have our family Christmas the weekend before actual Christmas. That way, we don't have to worry about Santa knowing where to take our gifts on Christmas morning."

"Smart." He chuckles, smiling.

"Right? I do not want to miss out on that." I shoot him a wink. "It's a core family belief that each smaller unit within the whole should be able to claim their own unique Christmas Eve and Christmas morning traditions in their own home, if they want."

Although it does leave the few remaining single adults in the family kind of in the lurch on years like this, when the parental units announce they're going on a cruise right after our early Christmas weekend.

This year, I'll be alone on Christmas Day.

Gross.

"How many people is that?" Grant asks, pulling my attention back to our conversation. "I lost count."

"Twenty-one— No, twenty-two this year and counting. Two babies are on the way within the next few months—that I know of." I grin. Every baby makes our family better. "My family is kind of a *party*. Our Christmas gatherings are a little nuts, but I love it."

Just thinking of getting to see everyone, overloading on sugar, watching Christmas movies, and playing games sends a rush through my system. I bounce a little in my seat.

What does it matter if I'm alone on December 25th? Christmas is as Christmas does. The calendar date is just a date.

"Your family sounds great." Grant gestures to my painting. "I like what you've done with the pink. It's subtle there beneath the green, but it adds an extra touch of magic."

"Thanks. Can you imagine this same picture idea, but huge?" It's something that crossed my mind the second I saw the instructor's example painting, which also has a few rosy tints. "I think I might try to make a bulletin board mural for my classroom like this. Maybe do it over winter break. Ooh! I could find a way to squeeze some Northern Lights science stuff into the curriculum." I wipe off my brush and grab a different one. "Although it might be easier to buy a couple of kindergarten-appropriate picture books about auroras to read to my students during story time."

"Do those exist?"

"Probably?" I shrug. "I've yet to search for a topical children's book I can't find." I start adding some snow to my trees. "It feels weird to use blue paint to make snow."

"It is counterintuitive," Grant agrees, wiping a brush on a paper towel. "But that pale blue works with the lighting."

"Trust the process," I say, more to myself than him. "If all else fails, add glitter."

He chuckles. "I bet you're an awesome kindergarten teacher. I'm sure the kids adore you."

"I love my job. Most days," I add, because it's true. "Working in public education isn't always glitter and fairy lights, though. Some days I dream about owning a taco truck, just so I can give certain people food poisoning. Or at least some embarrassingly bad gas."

Was that a snort that just exited Grant's grin?

"Sadly, I've been told that's a bad business plan. I guess I'll stick with teaching for now."

He's smiling. Good. Not everyone appreciates my sense of humor.

"There's an amazing taco truck about a block from my office," he says. "It's only there on Tuesdays, though."

"Any other day would seem wrong, wouldn't it? What's it called?"

He lifts his face and stares over the top of his canvas for a second, squinting, before turning to look at me. "You know what? I have no idea."

How can he not know the name of his favorite taco truck? "What's it look like?"

"It's a greenish, aqua color. Kind of like this"—he points his paintbrush toward one of the paint blobs on his tray—"with big orange dots. And there's a sombrero affixed to the truck's front grill."

"I know that truck. It's called 'Have Tacos, Will Travel.' Ohmygosh. Have you tried their triple decker tacos? They are the best." I turn so fast that I accidentally smear light blue paint across several of my trees. "Oops. Umm . . ."

He glances at my painting and winces. "I think you can probably go back in with the black after a couple of minutes and put in some more branches to hide that."

And that's what I do. It isn't perfect, but it isn't terrible. "Live and learn, as they say. At least I know what *not* to do when I make my mural."

"Yeah? What's that?"

"Get distracted by tacos, duh." I nudge his shoulder with mine.

It's meant to be a soft nudge, but my stool tips, smashing my face into Grant's shoulder. I'm teetering on only two legs of my stool for a split second before it scoots out from under my bum.

Seeking something to balance myself, my hand slaps down hard on the paper plate holding Grant's globs of paint. I gasp into a sideways fall, barely registering a tug on my sweater before my hip slams into the ground. As the rest of me flops gracelessly across the floor, I exhale an *"Oof."*

Once I've recovered my breath, the sensation of cold concrete against bare skin creeps into my consciousness. But I can't see anything because my sweater is now up over my face.

Chapter 11

GRANT

I slide off my stool and to my feet. "Are you okay?"

Allie is lying on the hard floor. Thanks to my too-slow reaction fail, her sweater and smock are almost inside-out, covering her face and revealing way more than she would probably like anyone to see on a first date, let alone show off to a whole room of strangers. I face away from her and drop into a crouch, using my body to block prying eyes. "Sorry I, uh, messed up your sweater. I was trying to catch you."

"Thanks. Hey, I appreciate the chivalry, but I'm not totally naked back here or anything. This bra could pass for a bikini top at the right beach. Would you mind scooting out a couple of inches?"

My brain conjures Allie in a bikini, which is probably why I'm a second or two late responding to her question.

"Grant?"

"Right. Sorry." I scoot. "Are you hurt?"

"Nah. Well . . . my left cheek might end up with a bruise," she says, "but other than that, I think you slowed my descent enough with that quick reaction to prevent any real injury. So, thanks for that. Okay, I'm good. You can turn around."

I stand and offer her my hand. She takes it, and I pull her to her feet, having to tighten my grip when hers starts slipping.

The class breaks out in applause. When our hands separate, they're both covered in green paint. Allie raises hers high in the air, does some sort of queenly wave thing that encompasses the room, and then grins and takes a dramatic bow.

"I, uh, think your sweater is ruined." I tear several paper towels off the roll at our station and hand her a few and then get my own and wipe my paint-smeared hand.

"You may be right." Allie examines the paint smears produced by righting her clothing after the fall. "No worries. I followed your wardrobe advice." She shrugs. "It's a $3.00 thrift store sweater. It won't break my heart to lose it. And it will give me an excuse to go shopping, so . . . win."

I chuckle, shaking my head. "You are quite the silver-linings person."

"What can I say? I like shiny things."

"That's good, because the right side of your face has some shiny paint on it."

"Maybe I was just trying to match you." Her smile angles toward sly. "You've had two smears of blue paint on your right cheek for over an hour. And now there are some green splatters too. I'm guessing those are courtesy of my epic paint slap on the way to the floor."

I rub my hand over my cheek, feeling the texture difference where the blue paint has long since dried as well as some moisture. I get a new paper towel for each of us.

"Did you hit your head on the way down?"

"Nah. Why do you ask?"

"You said you thought your cheek might bruise."

"Oh. I meant this cheek." She slaps her backside and then winces. "Um, yeah. Definitely gonna have a bruise there."

"I'm sorry I didn't catch you. If that jolt you got at the bottom ends up causing issues, I can recommend a good chiropractor."

"Thanks. My stepdad is a chiropractor. So I'm good." She glances at our paintings, now dotted with green. "With a little imagination, that could be wintertime lightning bugs." She laughs. "Sorry I ruined your painting."

I step back and cross one arm at my waist with the other at an upward angle, one finger tapping my lips. "The couple at table five took an avant-garde approach to their scene," I say, affecting a British accent. "Adding bioluminescent insects to a winter scene is something of a risk, but it does offer the piece a touch of whimsy."

Allie shoots me a grin and then takes on a serious expression—something I don't think I've seen cross her features quite so strongly before—as she mimics my posture.

"Yes, yes. I see what you're saying. The unique splatter paint technique is very rare to find in a pastoral scene, but after the rave reviews these two pieces are sure to garner, I predict more artists will attempt this rather genius approach quite soon."

"Quite," I agree, nodding. And then we're both laughing.

"Should we try to fix it?" she asks when we settle down.

"Nah." Only a few other painters are still at their stations. Most have left their paintings to dry and have gravitated to the area near the bar. "If you ask me, these works of art perfectly represent the first official date of our winter relationship."

She arches an eyebrow. "How so?"

"Like our uniquely seasonal relationship, they're a little . . . out of the ordinary. A little unexpected and a little whimsical."

"Did you know that whimsy and whimsical are two of my all-time favorite words in the history of words?"

"I did not."

"Well, they are." With hands on her hips, she gives a solid nod. "And I agree with your assessment. They are the perfect representation of an unexpectedly memorable night."

I wince. "I hope at least some of the 'memorable' aspects are good."

"Of course they are. Ask the internet. Watching people fall down but not get seriously hurt is top-tier entertainment."

"I wish you would have been watching instead of the one falling, though."

"That's sweet of you, but I have a vivid imagination, and I bet that was hilarious to see. Hey! Do you think they have cameras in here? I'd love to see my epic flailing fall on instant replay."

I laugh. "I'll ask."

"Awesome. You, sir, are doing an amazing job on the winter boyfriend front."

"Does that mean you'd be willing to go on a second date with me?"

She grins. "Abso-freakin'-lutely."

Chapter 12

ALLIE

It's Thanksgiving evening, and I'm stuffed to the gills. I'm sprawled on my mom's sectional sofa with one hand resting lightly on my happily bloated belly. The other hand holds a glass of cider, taken from one of the three gallons I brought here as my contribution to the feast. All courtesy of Grant's awesome date-planning skills.

My second date with Grant was every bit as fun as the first. And without any injuries this time, which was a bonus. We went to an outdoor artisan fair. I was fascinated by the glassblowing demonstration, so my sweet winter boyfriend bought me a Christmas ornament from the artist's stand.

Last Saturday, we drove about an hour west to an apple orchard and cider mill.

After touring the orchard, we browsed their apple and cider displays and hiked on some nearby trails. When the sun set, we took part in the orchard's end-of-season hayride and cookout, roasting apple-chicken sausages, mini caramel apple pies, and apple slice s'mores over a roaring fire. It was so much fun. But since the date had more of an autumn than winter feel—not that I was complaining—the drive there and back featured a playlist of wintery songs Grant especially curated for the occasion.

Not gonna lie, I think Grant is getting a raw deal. My first impression of what dating him would be like was way off. I thought he was stiff, maybe even boring. But that's not who he is at all.

Grant is a *fantastic* date. Sure, he takes a little time to warm up at the start, but he settles in after five-to-ten minutes. He's an engaging conversationalist, keeping things light and fun. For all he claimed about being out of practice with dating, he's planned three dates loaded with all the things that make this season romantic, but none have pushed the 'let's be *romantic*-romantic' thing, which is also great.

But that leaves me wondering. When we agreed to this limited-time relationship, we never talked about physical stuff. Only fun winter dating activities. I'm not sure what to expect from him in the physical realm of our relationship.

Oh well. Doesn't matter. We'll cross that mistletoe moment when we come to it.

If we come to it.

Which we may not, and I'm cool with that.

I haven't told anyone we're dating yet. Winter dating, that is. But I probably should. Otherwise, a few of my friends and family members are going to be shocked if we run into them on Black Friday.

I almost always run into people I know on Black Friday, even though I have to go to a larger town to participate. This year, it's a sure thing. I've been working on what I call 'A Christmas Cheer Gift to the World' for months. A few friends and I started planning it right after last year's Black Friday madness, and the idea grew and grew. It's gonna be a little retro . . . but a lot of straight-up, awesome fun.

I just hope Grant's into it.

I'm picking him up and handing him a preprinted schedule with times we need to be at certain locations, so that should give him a little comfort. If I had been stupid enough not to pick up his appreciation for structure from his initial winter boyfriend presentation, I would know it for sure now after our two extremely well-structured dates. The man is a fan of a good plan.

Wow. Rhyming again, even in my thoughts. Another weird occupational hazard of reading a lot of picture books aloud and teaching memory skills stuff through song and rhyme, I guess.

"Hey, Al."

I flop my head toward my stepbrother, Jackson. Thanks to the copious amounts of carbohydrates I've consumed, and the glorious tryptophan content of Thanksgiving turkey, the motion feels like I'm the Dread Pirate Roberts about to storm a castle after being mostly dead all day.

Seems about right.

"Pass me the candy corn."

"Can't," I groan. "That would require movement."

"Ugh. You're such a spoiled baby."

"Says the guy who won't get his own candy corn."

He shrugs. We share a grin. We don't see each other very often these days, but old habits have a comfort all their own.

"You two." Mom smiles as she rises gracefully from her plush chair. She doesn't have the same overindulgence weighing her down that Jackson and I are quite contentedly suffering. Mom is a health and fitness nut who watches her portion sizes, even on holidays. Luckily, she is also an amazing cook who loves feeding people as much delicious food as they want.

Jackson and I are the only ones on this side of our blended family tree who came here for turkey day this year, but by the look of the spread she laid out for dinner, you'd think Adam—my twin—and Jackson's sisters Mikayla and Cassie were expected, along with their spouses and kids. As soon as the meal ended, Mom packed up leftover bundles for me and Jackson to take home. I won't have to buy groceries for a week, at least.

My mom is awesome. I tell her so.

"You're the best," Jackson echoes as he takes a handful of candy corn from the bowl she holds in front of him and then shoves it in his mouth.

"Oh, hey," I say, taking a couple pieces for myself when she offers. "I'm taking a guy with me for all the Black Friday-ing fun."

All heads swivel to me.

"You're dating someone?" Keith, my stepdad, asks. "Since when?"

"Since a couple of weeks ago."

Jackson groans. "Not another right swipe, I hope. That last one was such a tool. The last several, if I'm being honest."

"No, actually," I say with the appropriate amount of snotty-sister tone. "He's an architect. I met him through work." I shoot a grin at the parental units. "Like back in the olden days."

Mom was working in medical equipment sales when she met Dr. Keith Dreux in his chiropractic office. She sold the young-ish widower a roller massage table, and then he took her out for dinner that night. Two months later, we had our first family outing with all the kids. Six months after that, they got married. The way they're looking at each other now would make you think they're newlyweds, but when they got married, Adam, Jackson, and I were in second grade, and Mikayla and Cassie were in fifth and seventh. I barely remember a time Keith and the gang weren't an important part of my world.

"What's this guy's name?" Jackson asks, his thumbs poised to type it into a search bar.

"Grant Covington."

"Sounds snooty."

"You're snooty."

He snorts. We both know he's the furthest thing from snooty, but it was the expected sisterly response, and I had to say it.

"Huh. He *is* an architect."

"Duh. I said that already."

"His feed is all buildings." He scrolls some more. "Oooh. There's one with a *gir-l*," he singsongs as he angles the phone toward me. "The ex?"

I look at the pic. "Tap it. See if she's tagged."

"Jealous?"

Am I? "Just curious."

He taps the screen. A tag appears. "Rae Covington Price."

"Ha! That's his sister. Lemme see." Jackson hands me his phone. I scroll through Rae's feed, finding tons of pics of her three kids and some pics of dogs, nature, and well-plated food. Finally, I come upon a pic of Grant. He has a goofy, happy look on his face, and three kids are hanging off him.

Those kids are super cute.

Their uncle isn't half bad either.

"Oh, my. Allie, you really like this guy."

I startle and meet Mom's gaze. "What? No, I don't. I mean, I do like him. He's fun. We're not dating seriously, though. Only for the winter."

"I think otherwise," Keith pipes up. "Your mom is right. I know that look. That's how your mom looks at me."

"Gross. Stop. There are cute little kids in the picture. I'm a sucker for cute little kids. Kindergarten teacher, remember?"

Keith frowns. "Oh."

"If that's what you say," Mom says, but it's clear she isn't convinced.

"What do you mean you're only dating for the winter?" Jackson asks, taking his phone back. "Are you truly that commitment-phobic that you've already decided when it's over?"

"I'm not commitment-phobic. I'm just not looking for anything serious right now. Grant isn't either. But it's nice to have an automatic date for stuff over the holidays. Grant and I both wanted a short-term relationship for the winter, so that's what we're doing."

"Please tell me this isn't like that *No Strings Attached* movie." Mom sounds worried.

Jackson puts his fingers in his ears. "La-la-la-la-la . . ."

"Or that other one," Keith says, his frown deepening. "What's it called? *Friends with Benefits?*"

"Guys. Please." I smack Jackson's chest with the back of my hand. He stops la-la-ing. "It's not like that. At all. And second of all, I am twenty-nine-and-a-half years old." My kindergartners would be so proud of me for adding the half. "And I wouldn't exist if two certain friends hadn't gotten drunk back in the 90s and had them some 'benefits.'"

"Guilty as charged." Mom's laugh isn't the least bit sheepish. "Do as I say, not as I do?"

A chuckle rumbles from Keith's chest.

"But honestly"—I do my best to look grossed out—"what are you two doing watching R-rated movies about casual sex? Aren't you a little old and married for that?"

"Please do not answer that question." Jackson groans. "Shut up, Allie. No one wants to hear their parents talking about sex, even movie sex from the 2010s."

"That's true. Forget I asked. Here's the whole story."

I lay it all out, from my just-for-funzies, winter boyfriend dreaming aloud moment at the cocoa club to Grant's multimedia presentation. And then I tell them how it is going great so far, and that there is no hanky-panky going on whatsoever.

"Hanky-panky?" Jackson sputters through a laugh. "What are you, eighty?"

"Shut up. I'm trying to talk to the old people. Speak their language."

"Old?" Mom says. "I'm only seventeen years older than you."

Adam and I arrived in the world approximately nine months after two high school besties raided my grandparents' liquor cabinet and then had—oops—a little bit too much fun. They've remained good friends and co-parents since, but they never married each other.

"I'm old," Keith says.

"You're only sixty-one, honey."

"You keep me young." His smile fades a little when it turns my way. "With age, comes wisdom. I know you're almost thirty, Al, but you still need to guard your heart, kiddo. They're pretty fragile organs."

"I hear you," I say. "I do. But don't worry. Grant and I aren't dating to fall in love. We're dating to date. We both know we're not compatible long-term, and we don't want to date each other long-term. It's the perfect winter plan."

It totally is. I'll prove it to them.

Chapter 13

GRANT

I've never gone Black Friday shopping in person before. I've seen the news reports—crowds of grumpy people operating on too little sleep and Thanksgiving hangovers, fighting each other for some stupid appliance or trendy toy—but I've never understood the allure of being an active participant in that retail nightmare. I can find great deals online, at a reasonable hour, in the peaceful quiet of my own home. But since I gave Allie my word that I would *happily* participate in any winter dates she planned, I'm showered and dressed at 4:30 a.m., peering out the side window next to my front door and waiting for Allie to pull in the drive.

A yawn pulls my mouth wide, and my eyes beg to close, if only for a moment or two. Between yesterday's big meals at Mom and Dad's and then driving home, I feel like a zombie. Even though I tossed back an espresso shot right before I got in the shower at 3:45, I'm not feeling it in my brain quite yet.

Headlights.

I laughed when Allie texted that she would be here at 4:32 a.m., but a glance at my phone proves she's exactly on time. I slide it into my back pocket, grab my coat and gloves, and head out the door.

"Happy Official Start of the Christmas Season!" she chirps as I slide into the front seat of her car. It's a white four-door sedan, probably five-to-seven years old, and I can't help but appreciate how clean and well-kept it is. It smells amazing. Bright and lemony.

"Good morning," I croak, and then clear my throat. "Sorry. I haven't used my voice yet today."

"No worries." She taps one of two insulated mugs in the cupholders. "Hot lemon water with a liberal squeeze of honey. It's how I start every morning. If you don't like it, don't feel like you have to drink it. But since I was making my own . . ." She trails off while she reaches in the backseat. She hands me a piece of paper. "Here. Our schedule. But before we go to the first stop, are there any particular stores or sales you hope to catch? Sorry, I probably should have asked you that way before now."

"Nope. I'm just happily along for the ride."

"Awesome. That's a relief, honestly." She taps the paper. "We have to keep pretty tightly to that schedule."

"So . . ." I pull out my phone and shine the flashlight on the page. "What is it you are specifically shopping for today?"

"Christmas cheer." She backs out of my driveway. "If I find any good deals on gift items, I guess that's a bonus. But that's not the goal today. I'm planning to do most of my Christmas shopping on Small Business Saturday this year in Sterling Grove. And maybe a little on Cyber Monday."

I'm confused. "You're going Black Friday shopping but not shopping?"

"Not intentionally." She laughs. "But it's gonna be great. You'll see."

She turns up the stereo, and Christmas music fills the space. "Want to do a little singalong?"

I take a sip of the hot lemon water that actually tastes a lot better than I thought it would. "You go ahead. My vocal cords haven't quite woken up yet."

Allie has a nice singing voice. Not the type of voice a trained musician would rave about, probably, but she's easy to listen to in a comfortable way. She's not off-key or pitchy, but she's also not so awesome that you feel like you can't join in because you'd sound like trash next to her.

I don't know if it's her peppy Christmas playlist that helps the espresso shot soak into my brain or her bouncy dance-driving, but I feel much more alive than I did ten minutes ago. This is nice. Even at 4:45 a.m.

We pull into the parking lot of the first big discount store on the list. The lot is packed. Cars and people everywhere. Allie eases down one lane . . . and then the next, and the next. Finally, we both spot reverse lights.

"There!" we say in unison.

She puts her blinker on. That's unexpected, but I appreciate her parking lot etiquette. We wait. Allie sways to the tune coming through the stereo. As soon as the other car has cleared the opening, she guns the gas and swings into that spot like a stunt driver.

When I start breathing again, I try to casually drop my hands back into my lap. They'd unconsciously braced.

She laughs. "Sorry. There was another car coming down the lane. Had to make my move."

"It's fine." I swallow. "Ready?"

She grins. "I am soooo ready. Let's go get after that Christmas cheer."

I kind of doubt she's going to find it in a big chain discount store at five a.m. on Black Friday, but . . . sure.

On the way in, I notice a jingling sound coming from Allie's direction. Keys in her pocket? Or maybe she has one of those ugly Christmas sweaters on under her coat. One with jingle bells affixed to it. After only a few dates, I know I've only scratched the surface of who Allie Hayes is, but I'd put money on Allie wearing jingle bells.

Inside the store, it's a zoo.

No, zoos have more crowd control. And the animals are way better behaved. And in some cases, more hygiene aware. Many of the people here look like they literally rolled out of bed in the parking lot. Some wear slippers and pajamas. A steady hum of voices is punctuated by the occasional bark of dismay or outrage. Small children cry. A few downright wail. Why did their parents think it was a good idea to wake them up early and bring them here?

The majority of shoppers are bleary-eyed; those wearing coats are obviously sweating. I suddenly wish I'd left mine in the car. I see a few smiles, but most of those who aren't outright scowling look a little dead inside.

Allie is one of the few exceptions to the rule. She's bright, bouncy, and smiling like it actually is Christmas morning. Her blond waves have been tamed into two braids that look adorable coming out beneath her red stocking cap, which has a shimmery white ball of fluff on top. I haven't noticed that she wears a lot of makeup normally, but she's definitely wearing it today. And wow, does she sparkle. It wasn't noticeable in the interior dome light of her car or in the dark parking lot, but under these industrial fluorescents, she has a certain fairy-like quality about her.

Eyes, cheeks, face . . . even her braids sparkle. Wow. Obviously, there was a lot of glitter involved in her morning routine today. What time did she get up to be able to look like that?

Allie's coat reaches down to her bright green boots, but the coat itself is a rather nondescript black button-up. At the neck opening, silver sequins glimmer like a mysteriously hidden disco ball.

I lean down to her ear. "It's five a.m. How do you look so amazing?"

She beams up at me. "Thanks." She grabs my hand. "Ready to enter the fray?"

"Lead on, Christmas Fairy."

"Housewares, aisle fifteen, here we come."

That was . . . specific. But now that the espresso has finally hit my brain, I think I recall that precise location being on the schedule.

Aisle fifteen is a mix of small kitchen gadgets and serving ware. It was a bit of a squeeze to get here because the lines to the front register go down all the center and major side aisles, clear to the back of the store. She pauses just inside the aisle.

"Okay," I say. "What item can I help you find?"

She holds up one finger and pulls her phone from her pocket. "Two minutes." She lets out a sound somewhere between "*Eeep*!" and "*Whee*!" while clenching her shaking fists over her heart. "Grant, if I were to toss you my coat, would you mind holding it for me?"

"Not a bit."

"You're the best." She starts unbuttoning her coat but keeps it on and pulled closed.

I do the gentlemanly thing. "Need help?"

"Not quite yet." She's grinning so wide she might need a cheek muscle massage later.

Allie peers behind me and gives someone a little wave and a nod. I turn. Ah, it's Lexi, the young music teacher from the cocoa club. Huh. She's wearing the same hat as Allie. I wave. Her eyes go wide.

"Attention, shoppers." A voice comes over the P.A. system. "As you know, it's the official start of the holiday season. We know you're tired. Your feet probably hurt from standing in line. We can't make the lines any shorter, but we sure can make them merrier."

"Here!" Allie's coat flies toward me.

She wasn't kidding about tossing it to me. I catch it. By the time I have it tucked over my arm, much louder music has started coming out of the P.A. system than the faint, barely noticeable Christmas carols of a moment ago, and Allie is obeying the vocalist's instruction to clap her hands.

"Is that the 'Cha-cha Slide'?" I ask. But something about it is different. "Are those jingle bells?"

"Yes, and yes." Allie grins as she detaches two jingle bell-covered mini maracas from a lanyard around her neck. "It's the Christmas Remix."

Allie moves back toward the center aisle. She's wearing candy cane-print leggings, and those bright green boots are topped with white faux fur I couldn't see earlier due to the length of her coat. I was right about the silver-sequin top. It's a skin-hugging show-stopper—so bright it almost hurts to look directly at it.

On second thought, I probably shouldn't be looking quite so directly at it.

Her eyes are up north, Covington. But, dang. As she walks past me, my gaze follows her, and my man-brain gives a low whistle.

Wow. If all the Christmas elves in the North Pole look as good as Allie Hayes does in that crazy outfit, Santa must really be a saint.

She looks over her shoulder while she slides to the left. "C'mon!"

I follow her.

In the main aisle, several other people are sparkling as brightly as Allie. Including Lexi. And Dylan. *What*? I laugh out loud. He's wearing the same hat as they are but with bright red sweatpants. His long-sleeved, oversized red t-shirt has silver sequin buttons and fur trim sewn on to make it look like Santa's coat.

When we reach the center aisle, where people are waiting in a long check-out line, I see more sequins. More red hats. With each new part of the song, more coats come off, and new sparkling Christmas elves join the ongoing choreography.

Soon, there are dozens of dancers, all dressed alike. They are *everywhere*, doing the "Cha Cha Slide" through the crowd, and shaking those handheld jingle bells at the appropriate times in the song. It sounds like Santa's reindeer are about to come in for a landing.

Oh my. This is . . . this is a . . .

Allie didn't bring me here for Black Friday shopping. She brought me here for a Black Friday flash mob.

A loud laugh expels from my chest. This. Is. Amazing.

Scowls are transposing into smiles. People are laughing. Some bystanders join in the dancing, while others pull out phones to film this sparkling spectacle of merriness and Christmas spirit.

I can't help it. Pretty soon, I'm sliding to the right, the left, and back. I'm hopping, tapping one foot and then the other. I'm cha-cha-ing, crisscrossing, and clapping my hands along with all these other now-merry party people.

It's just after five o'clock in the morning in a crowded, previously grump-filled discount store on Black Friday, and I'm having the time of my life.

But just like that, it's over.

"Quick!" Allie says. "Coat."

I fumble a little and then hold her coat open, the inside facing her.

She turns around and slides her arms in. "Wow. Thanks, Mr. Gentleman." She quickly buttons up, stuffs her hat in the front of the coat, and then looks at me, exaggerating a wince. "Still willing to be seen with me?"

I'm smiling wider than I knew was possible this early in the morning, vaguely wondering if we'll *both* need our faces massaged later. "Ohhhh, yeah." I nod, slowly. "That was *awesome*."

"Really?" She squeals. "I was hoping you would say that." She arches a playful brow. "And don't think I didn't notice your sweet dance moves when you joined in."

I offer my hand, and she takes it. We move toward the exit. "So, you like my moves?"

"Most definitely." She squeezes my hand.

Wait. Did she think I meant . . .?

"And if you're willing," she continues, "I have a spare set of jingle bells *and* an extra costume that should fit you out in my car."

I wasn't ready for that, but I did promise to happily participate in the dates she plans, so . . .

"Sounds like fun."

And then we're off to find somewhere I can do a quick change of clothes.

Chapter 14

ALLIE

"Ow!" I hiss at Raquel. I've lost count of the number of times her foot has connected with my calf during this Thursday night committee meeting, but I'm fairly certain it's equal to the number of times Grant has glanced my way and smiled.

"So, if no one has any other questions," Grant says, his unflappable professional confidence on full display, "that's all we have for tonight. I'll have some preliminary drawings for you all to look over next time. Have a wonderful week, everyone." Grant's smile spans the room, lingering a bit when it lands on me. The second he looks down and starts packing up his stuff, Raquel kicks me again.

"Dude, come on." I groan. "I'm gonna have a bruise."

"That's so sad. Maybe you can find someone willing to offer a calf massage," she says in the sort of low tone that's generally reserved for juicy gossip and double entendre. "Hope you shaved your legs this morning."

"Jealous?"

"Not a bit." Raquel twinkles her left hand my way, where her diamond solitaire is joined by a wedding band. "But watching you guys silently flirt for the past hour sure has me hoping for a 'calf massage'"—she makes air quotes—"of my own. What are the odds that Rob will have the kids in bed and sound asleep by the time I get home?"

"Slim to none."

Raquel sighs. "I love my family and all, but doggone. Kids can totally kill a mood."

"Up for some cocoa? It cures all the ills."

"Not tonight. I need to get home and finish my classroom newsletter, remember?"

"Right." That's one reason we drove separately. The other reason is that Grant offered to pick me up, and I accepted.

We both pitch in to help move the chairs and tables back to their original places.

When the room is set to rights, Raquel grabs her coat off the back of her chair. "Don't overdo it on the, uh, cocoa tonight." She gives me two exaggerated winks and leans in close, whispering, "Or do. It's the holiday season after all. Make merry."

I laugh. "Go home to your husband, hornball."

"Hey." She elbows me in the ribs and inclines her head to the front of the room, where Norma has Grant almost literally cornered. "Looks like he might need rescuing again."

I tune in.

"That sounds fun, Mrs. Kellogg," he says, "and I'm sure she's lovely, but I have a girlfriend."

That's me. I'm his girlfriend. His winter girlfriend, that is.

I'm blushing a little. What is that about?

"Would you look at that," Raquel says. "You rescued him again without lifting a finger or telling a single poop joke."

"It's a gift."

"Okay, duty calls. See ya tomorrow."

"Good luck on that newsletter. And that other thing too," I add, giving her an extremely exaggerated wink of my own.

With a laugh, she's heading for the door.

I pack up my own stuff. As simple as it might seem, I can't help but smile at Grant referring to me as his girlfriend. We've been on four super-fun dates together—five, if you count him coming over Sunday afternoon to help me set up my Christmas tree. He's proven himself to be an exceptional winter boyfriend. And against everything I assumed from the outset, I truly enjoy his company.

I hope he feels the same. Because honestly, I don't feel like I'm holding up my end of our bargain. If any guy doesn't need a dating-skills refresher course, it's Grant Covington.

I can't help but notice how nicely Grant fills out his wool dress coat. And he pulls off that scarf like he just closed a big deal and is waiting for his personal driver to pull a long black car to the curb. I don't know many men who can properly loop a scarf, but Grant did it without even looking, and that's kinda hot.

"He has a girlfriend, hon."

"Huh?" I blink and turn my gaze to Norma Kellogg. "Sorry. I was spacing off." Oops. Busted.

"Daydreaming, more like." Norma pats my arm. "And I don't blame you. He's a cutie."

She's not wrong.

"You know I think the world of you, sweetheart, but I have a sense about these things, and you two would never work." She shakes her head and gives me a sad smile. "Even if he was available, I'm sorry. I just don't see it." She pats my arm. Again. "There may still be someone out there for you. Somewhere. Don't give up hope."

A soft touch, low on the center of my back barely precedes Grant's arrival at my side. "Did you need to stop off at your classroom before we head out, Allie?"

"I do, actually." I don't, actually. "Thanks for reminding me." I know Norma would never intentionally insult me, but dang.

"Oh, sorry, Mrs. Kellogg." Grant winces, but it's an exaggerated wince, and it doesn't reach his eyes. "Was I interrupting?"

"Not at all, dear."

"Great. I hope you don't mind if I steal Allie away." He tugs me closer and then looks at his watch. "We'd better get going while the night's still young."

Norma's gaze darts between Grant, me, and Grant's hand, which has now slid around my back and rests at my waist. Confusion swirls across her face. "When you said you had a girlfriend, I didn't realize . . ."

Grant removes my coat from the back of my chair and holds it out. I slide my arms in like we've done this move a million times. While I'm zipping my coat, Grant cranks it up a notch, setting his hands on my shoulders and then rubbing down and back up my arms until they rest on my shoulders again.

Nice. I could get used to this.

And maybe I should. I mean, he's mine until the new year, so why not enjoy it?

"We'd better get going." I aim a bright smile at Norma. "Have a good night."

She nods, blinks a few times, and then says a quick, "You too," and shuffles out the door.

I let out a sigh.

"Not to steal your material," Grant says, "but you looked like you might need a rescue."

"Thanks. I kind of did."

He gives me a quick squeeze and then steps away. "I overheard a bit of that. I apologize if I was pouring it on too thick with the possessive thing, but wow."

"No, it was perfect. I appreciate it."

Grant shakes his head, looking in the direction of the door. "She's a piece of work."

"Nah. She's a good egg, for the most part." I take a deep inhale and exhale. "I don't know about you, but I could use a stiff cup of cocoa. Let's go."

"Sounds great. Didn't you need to stop at your classroom first?"

"Nope. Let's blow this popsicle stand."

At Cocoa & Froth, our usual table is taken by interlopers—how dare they—but our cocoa club, minus Raquel, awaits us in the big corner booth. After dropping off our coats, we order our cocoas.

He reaches for his wallet. "I've got this."

"Next round on me?"

His brow furrows, then relaxes. "Sure."

There's just enough room for me to slide in next to Paula, with Grant on the end next to me. When our order is called, he goes to retrieve it.

"Looks like the winter boyfriend thing is going well." Paula nudges my shoulder with her own. For the record, it's a much gentler nudge than those soccer-player kicks Raquel kept up during the meeting.

"It is. Grant's great, and we're having a lot of fun."

Lexi glances toward the counter and then leans across the table to whisper, "Is he a good kisser?"

"I wouldn't know."

She shares a glance with Dylan. "That's actually kind of a relief," she says. "As cozy and comfy as you guys seemed at breakfast on Black Friday, we were kind of worried that things were moving too fast for you not to get hurt when the new year rolls around." She leans back, and her gaze moves to Grant, who is approaching with our cocoas in hand. "Ooh. Is that the new s'mores cocoa? I haven't been brave enough to try that one yet."

"That's mine," I say. "Grant's having the salted caramel."

Grant sets our cocoas down and then slides in next to me. "I love salted caramel, but now I'm kind of regretting I didn't get the s'mores. But since I'd already stolen one of your moves tonight, I didn't want to be too much of a copycat."

"Here, I'll let you have the first sip." I scoot the mug his way as I explain: "Grant rescued me from Norma."

"Oh, good grief." Paula rolls her eyes. "I thought she'd decided to stop trying to find you a match ages ago."

"Oh, she did. Imagine how surprised she was to find out Grant won't be letting her set him up because he already has a girlfriend." I laugh, thinking about her shock. "Me."

I feel a squeeze at my shoulder. When did Grant put his arm around the back of the booth—and me? It feels nice. Cozy, just like Lexi said.

Being with Grant is so easy. He's never acted like he wishes I would rein in my personality around him, and it's refreshing to date someone . . . comfortable.

But I guess that makes sense. Since neither one of us wants this thing to last, the pressure's off, and we can relax and be real. Even if my particular brand of energy ends up wearing on him after a while, the knowledge that he only has to put up with it for a few more weeks should help him tough it out. And should I find that one thing about him that annoys me to the break-up point? I can simply shrug it off and look forward to a happy new year of being single again.

Norma Kellogg might not agree, but we're a perfect wintertime match.

Chapter 15

GRANT

Midway through Monday morning, I'm headed to the break room for a cup of coffee when Wallace Forsyth hails me from his office. "Grant, do you have a minute?"

"Sure."

"Come in. Go ahead and close the door." His voice has an odd tone I can't quite name. "Have a seat."

I do as asked. "What can I do for you, Wallace?"

"I've noticed a bit of a bounce in your step lately." He smiles. "Word around the office is that you're spending quite a bit of time with that gal you're seeing."

"The office gossip is correct."

"How's that going?"

"It's . . . awesome." I can't help but grin. "But we've only been dating a few weeks, and we're purposefully keeping it casual. As planned."

"You're getting out there and having fun. That's what we want to see." Wallace nods, and his expression turns a bit more serious. "You've always been a real go-getter, but all work and no play makes Jack a dull boy. I'm glad you're finding time to make a life outside of the office. It's important to have some balance."

"I can't argue with that." Allie's enthusiasm for life in general has infected me with a sense of relaxation I haven't known in a long time.

"I understand this young woman is a teacher in Sterling Grove and on the community committee for the new elementary school design."

"She is. That's how we met."

"I see. I see." Wallace presses his lips together. "Grant, you're a skilled architect, and under other circumstances I wouldn't even mention this. But considering you are the primary architect working on the Sterling Grove project, your romantic involvement with a committee member—especially one who is also a teacher who will work in the building you design—raises some concerns about a possible conflict of interest."

"O . . . kay. Could you elaborate on that?"

He nods and leans forward, tenting his fingers on the desk. "When you're personally involved with someone who will benefit from your design choices, it's natural that you would favor them. Obviously, when that person is your client and the one footing the bill, that should be happening."

"I would certainly hope so."

"Exactly. If you were designing a home or, say, the wing of a hospital that was being funded by a specific, singular donor, the client's interest wouldn't conflict with your design because theirs would be the only interest of import. But in this case, you're dating a teacher whose preferences and opinions could influence your design, whether you're conscious of showing favoritism or not. Therefore, it does present the potentiality for a problem."

"I get what you're saying." I do. "But I assure you that is not an issue with my design. Allie—my girlfriend—teaches kindergarten. The only request she's made was to inquire about colored toilets for the in-room kindergarten bathrooms, which she backed off from when she saw the cost. If I had to line-item the design requests from people on the committee, I'd guess I've tweaked at least twice as many design elements to accommodate the needs of the upper elementary wing as the lower grades."

"Mm. Yes." Wallace looks out the window for a moment before meeting my eyes again. "This has been an unusual project from the start, from the way it's being funded to this unexpected possibility of a conflict of interest."

I hum an agreement while the wheels in my brain spin. Was I wrong to join the after-meeting cocoa club? Is this going to negatively impact my chance at making partner?

Before I can ask for clarification, Wallace says, "You're a gifted architect, Grant. And I've always considered you to be a reasonable and ethical man. But I would not be doing my due diligence as a partner in the firm if I didn't investigate when concerns such as this are brought to our attention."

"I understand."

"Good. You do still plan to make a partnership bid, correct?"

"I do." I give one slow, solid nod. I thought jumpstarting my dating life would help me become a partner. Will my relationship with Allie—and some wrongly inferred conflict of interest—put that bid at risk?

"I'm glad." He smiles, and my stomach unclenches a bit. "As a future partner in this firm, this is the sort of thing you need to keep in mind for yourself as well as for those who work with and for you. Iverson-Forsyth Architectural Associates has earned a reputation for our quality architectural services and our commitment to ethical business practices. When Howard retires, I expect that reputation to remain in place, and to outlive my own tenure at this firm."

"As do I," I say, and take a deep breath. "I appreciate your candor and your leadership. If you're not busy, why don't we head down to my office. I'd appreciate your input, evaluating the design from a conflict-of-interest perspective. If Howard's available, I'd like him to take a look, as well."

"Wonderful idea." Wallace smiles, and it's genuine.

"The blueprints aren't final yet, but they're getting close. Before we reach that final stage, I think it would be a wise move—for all of us—to know the school is designed without prejudice."

"You're a good man, Grant." He stands. "Let's grab Howard and go see those plans."

I don't think I've shown favoritism. But what if I have, unconsciously?

Chapter 16

ALLIE

Either meteorology is a bit more guesstimation than science, or the weatherfolk are evil tricksters trying to ruin my weekend.

Yesterday, my weather app showed a 95% chance of our first measurable snowfall. I went to bed last night with the curtains open so I would see that sparkling fairy dust floating down the second I woke up. But it's after 10 a.m. on a Saturday that was supposed to be a full-on marshmallow world, and not *one* flake has fallen. Bah. Humbug.

All week, Grant and I have traded ideas for how to best take advantage of our first measurable snowfall. It wasn't supposed to be super cold—just cold enough for the good hearty snowfall that seemed like a sure thing. We'd decided to go sledding. Sledding! Now what?

The phone vibrates with a text from Grant:

> *Don't worry.*
> *I have a backup plan.*

Of course he does.

My phone vibrates again.

> *How do you feel about*
> *baking Christmas cookies?*

Excited!

I sit up, suddenly energized.

What if you can't eat them?

I pause on that question, my enthusiasm fizzling a bit. Finally, I type:

Conflicted.

Do you trust me?

Yes

I blink a little at how fast I typed and sent the answer to that question. But my surprise doesn't change the original answer. I do trust Grant. He's a good, solid guy. I might have had my heart set on going sledding with my winter boyfriend, but it's no surprise Grant has a backup plan. My guy is a planner, and as it turns out . . . I don't hate it.

*Would you rather bake
at my place, or yours?*

The busyness of the week didn't allow for a lot of housekeeping, and I'm not really in the mood to spend the time between now and my date cleaning. Besides, even though I know where Grant lives, I've never been inside his condo, and I'm curious.

> *Yours.*
> *What time should I be there?*

Around 2?

I glance in the corner of the phone screen. It's now 10:21. Plenty of time.

> *Need me to bring anything?*

I only have one apron.
Do you have one you
could bring?

I try to picture Grant in an apron, and the picture that pops into my head is so ridiculous that a bark of a laugh tosses me back into my pillows.

> *Full disclosure:*
> *I just woke up.*
> *My brain conjured an image*
> *of you in one of those*
> *sexy French maid costumes.*
> *HA!*

Three dots appear, disappear, and reappear, only to disappear again. Hmm .
. . I hope I didn't offend him.

> *Sorry about my brain.*
> *I'm sure your apron*
> *is super dude-like,*
> *and you look totally*
> *manly in it.*

> *I have an apron.*
> *I'll bring it. No worries.*

Three dots appear, disappear, and reappear again.

> *Now I can't help but*
> *wonder what kind of apron*
> *YOU will be wearing*
> *this afternoon.*

I snort and then respond to his carefully flirty text in kind.

> *Won't it be fun*
> *to find out?*

When I pull into Grant's driveway at 1:58 p.m., it's fifty degrees, the sun is
shining, and the sky is bright blue without a cloud in sight. I grab my bag from
the passenger seat and, as I walk up the steps to his front door, consider deleting
the worthless weather app from my phone, if only out of spite.

"Shake it off, Al," I tell myself. "Snow will come, eventually." It will. It always does. Still, I lift my hands and do a few quick finger twinkles to chase the negativity away and make room in my brain for good vibes.

That's better.

Grant answers the door with a smile. He leans down to kiss my cheek, and an electric shock surprises us both.

He jumps back, pressing his fingers to his lips. "Uh, welcome. Sorry. I didn't mean to do that."

"Holy cow." My hand lifts to my cheek. "Did you rub a balloon on your head or something before you answered the door?"

"No." He chuckles. "But maybe I'll try that next time. Come on in."

"Was there a spark?" I ask as he shuts and locks the door.

His head swivels my way, and his sideways smile has *flirt* written all over it. "Oh, yeah."

"Smooth." I laugh. "I meant, like, visibly, Romeo."

"You can't blame a guy for trying. But to answer your question, I didn't see one, but there almost had to be, right? That was . . . something. Here, let me take your coat."

He hangs it in the small closet by the door.

"Want the tour?" he offers, much like I did when he came to my house to help me put up my Christmas tree.

"Of course." I was hoping he'd offer.

"Obviously, this is the formal foyer. This hall" —he gestures to the right— "leads to the powder room and the laundry." Both doors are open. Both rooms are spotless.

"There's a chandelier in your laundry room? That's so cool."

He laughs. "Yeah. My sister's idea. Something she saw on Pinterest." He shrugs. "I was skeptical, but I don't hate it."

The powder room is a decent size and the same greenish-blue color. There's an architectural drawing on the wall. "Did you design that?"

"I did. It's my first large-scale design that was actually built."

"What is it?"

"A community center. It's over in Richland City."

"Cool."

I follow him back down the hall and through the foyer into the living room. A huge world map—one of those artsy ones with the words in Latin—graces one wall, framed in black. A dark brown leather couch is set in the center of the room, facing a modern gas fireplace from which blue flames dance out of chunks of glass. Between the fireplace and couch, an oversized ottoman takes up a huge amount of space. There's a black wooden tray on it with some cork coasters. I'm guessing the ottoman doubles as a coffee table. It's centered between matching sets of two chairs, upholstered in a darker shade of the teal walls in the laundry and powder rooms. Above the fireplace, a huge flatscreen TV hangs. Built-in bookshelves are arranged like something out of a magazine, with neatly stacked books, a few black-framed photos, a small globe, and some sort of antique tool thingies interspersed throughout.

"Are these your nieces and nephew?" I ask, walking over to examine one of the pictures.

"Mm-hmm." He points at the kids, one by one. "Charlotte, Leo, and Ava."

"They're sooo cute." They totally are. "How long have you lived here?"

"About six years, I guess?" He shrugs and starts toward the stairs.

Six years? But everything seems brand new, like in a model home meant to be marketed to people who don't really know how to kick back and relax. Except for that couch. I'd happily let that leather couch swallow me whole.

Upstairs, there are two bedrooms, separated by a loft-type area that overlooks the living room.

"Oh my gosh. Are those beanbags? They're huge!"

"Yep. My nieces love them."

"May I?"

"Sure."

I flop down into one of the couch-sized, bean-shaped pieces of nirvana. It's filled with some sort of body-hugging material that makes me want to find out where he bought it and replace my old hand-me-down sofa right now.

"Oh, wow." I wonder if they come in pink. Or bright yellow, maybe? "Wow. This is amazing." I let out a contented sigh. "But I'm going to need a hand getting out of here."

"Right?" Grant steps up and offers his. "I feel like a clumsy oaf every time I have to haul myself out of one of these."

The tour resumes. The two bedrooms each have their own en suite bathroom—though his bedroom and bathroom are definitely larger, and swankier.

"Wow. That's a lot of of shower spigots. Does water come out of all those things?"

"Yeah." He shrugs, looking down as if he's embarrassed. "It was kind of a splurge, and I thought I'd use the options more than I do. But every once in a while, it's . . . nice."

The scent of his cologne, a fresh and spicy citrus scent with just a hint of woodsy musk, lingers like it lives here and likes it.

I like it.

Everything is tidy upstairs, but it has more of a "lived-in" feel than the main level. There are more personal touches up here. More family photos. A sweatshirt thrown casually over a chair by the window. Several baseball caps stacked the slightest bit haphazardly on the dresser.

His decorating style is not my taste, but it suits Grant. We head back downstairs, through a formal dining room, and into the—

"Whoa." The kitchen island must be at least eight feet long. Dark stainless appliances. White cabinetry, topped by black countertops that sparkle under the lights. "This kitchen is ginormous. You could host a whole flippin' cooking show in here!"

"I don't know about that . . ." he says. "Is it obnoxious?"

"Not at all. This is a dream kitchen." It totally is. And would be totally wasted on me. "So, what kind of cookies are we baking today?"

"Christmas cookies, with a twist." His grin is a little sheepish. "They're for dogs."

"You have a dog?" I turn around, bending side-to-side, searching for evidence of a canine companion.

"No. I haven't had time for a dog during Phase I. But I'll get one after—" He abruptly cuts off, and his jaw moves. "I hope to have time for a dog one day."

"Let me guess. That's part of Phase II? Wife, kids, and the perfect golden retriever behind that white picket fence?"

"Uh . . ." Grant rubs the back of his neck as color rises in his cheeks. "That probably sounds terribly boring to you."

"I love dogs. And kids. And if you recall, my house actually does have a white picket fence. No judgment, my guy." I nudge him with my elbow. "But if you don't have a dog, whose dog are these cookies for?"

"They're for a charity auction, actually," he says. "One of the firm's partners' wives is on a local no-kill animal shelter's advisory board. My firm designed the shelter a few years ago, pro bono. Anyway, Claire Forsyth chairs an annual gala to help raise funds to keep the shelter running. Usually, I attend and bid, but I thought it might be fun to offer something for others to bid on this year." He clears his throat. "The auction is next Saturday."

"Won't the cookies be stale by then?"

"I picked a recipe that is freezer-friendly, and I cleaned out the freezer last night to make sure there was enough room."

"Of course you did." I laugh. "Is there anything you don't plan?"

He tilts his head, like a dog who just heard his favorite word. "Uh . . ."

I take a step back and cross my arms. "Okay. Here's what I'm gonna do, Mr. Perfect Planner. Right now. I'm going to reach deep into your brainstem, and I'm going to find that forgotten little nubbin at the base of your skull that secretly longs for spontaneity and risk. And then you know what I'm gonna do?"

"I've no idea."

"I'm going to tickle that nubbin until it starts giggling like a three-year-old with a cup of powdered sugar and a spoon."

His lips twist to the side as he tilts his head the opposite direction. "I thought the brainstem was all about fight or flight."

"Oh, fine." I groan with an exaggerated slouch and eye roll and then straighten. "I'll see your brain science and raise you one whimsical interpretation." I spread my arms wide and turn a full circle.

Stepping toward him, I take hold of his hands, lifting our hands until they're spread as wide as I can reach, at my shoulder height.

Our bodies are nearly touching. As I take that last tiny step forward, Grant's citrusy-spice scent envelops my senses. A happy little spark dances in the pit of my stomach. "Sometimes," I say, looking up at him as I guide him into a slow spin, "you need someone else to *fight* for you so you remember how to *fly* by the seat of your pants."

A slow smile blooms across his face. "So, you're the fight, and I'm the flight, huh?"

"Mm-hmm," I increase the speed of the spin. "But in a good way."

"How do you feel about formalwear?"

Our spin comes to a halt. "Swerve much?"

He shrugs, but his smile is a little ornery. "Maybe I'm just being conversationally spontaneous."

"Look at you, thinking you're getting out of your flying lessons that easily. That's adorable." I make a little "*awwww*" sound. "Formalwear. Hmm. It's fine, I guess? Outside of occasional bridesmaid duties, it's not something I've had to think about much since my senior prom."

"Allie, would you consider accompanying me to the dog shelter's black-tie gala next Saturday night?"

Ooh . . . fancy. I bet Grant looks amazing in a tux. "I'd love to."

But *oof*. I will need to go shopping, stat. Good thing I'm an experienced thrifter. Formalwear that fits a teacher's budget is hard to find.

His face lights up. "Really?"

"Absolutely." Then it hits me. I squeeze my eyes shut in a wince.

"What's wrong?" He steps back but keeps hold of my hands. "Second thoughts already?"

"Next weekend is the weekend before Christmas. It's my family's Christmas weekend."

"Oh, right. I'm sorry. I should have remembered. Don't worry about it."

"I think . . ." I pause to do some time gauging. "I think it could still work. Is the auction nearby?"

Grant nods. "It's at the Belvedere Lake Resort. But seriously, don't sweat it. That's sacred family time. I understand."

"No, that's perfect. The house we rented for the weekend is literally right on Belvedere Lake. You could even pick me up there. And the auction will only last a few hours, right?"

"It starts with dinner at seven. The auction starts at eight, and when it's finished, there is dancing until midnight or so. But you really don't have to—"

"I know I don't *have* to. I *want* to."

Grant looks at me for a long moment. "You're sure?"

"One hundred percent."

"Okay, but we leave right after the auction, and I get you back to your family."

"Or . . . we play it by ear," I say. "Oh! I have an idea. You should bring an overnight bag."

"What? Why? It's barely a thirty-minute drive from my condo to Belvedere Lake. In traffic."

"But I might need your help with a project back at the house."

"What kind of project?"

He has the most adorable head tilt. His Phase II woman is gonna fall hard for that. "The kind where I utilize your architectural skills while also helping you locate those wings hidden somewhere on the seat of your pants."

He laughs. "I'm intrigued, but I don't think imposing on your family Christmas after taking you away from it will make me very popular among your relatives."

"You only say that because you haven't yet experienced the beautiful chaos that is our family Christmas."

"But doesn't it feel a little like a serious relationship thing for me to stay with you and your family over the holidays? I don't want to give them the wrong idea."

"Pfft. I've already told some of them about you being my winter-only boyfriend, and I can let the rest know before you get there. It will be fun. I promise."

"You'll double-check with everyone to make sure it's okay?"

"I promise. So, are we on for next weekend, to be totally formal and totally informal, all in one day?"

He scrutinizes my face for a long moment. "Only if you're sure."

"As previously stated." I boop his nose. "Now, we'd best get to baking these dog treats. Besides, I'm dying to see your apron."

He opens a tall cupboard and pulls an apron from a hook inside. He holds it up for my inspection.

It's your basic dad apron, emblazoned with "King of the Grill."

"Not quite as fun as a sexy French maid costume, huh?" He grins. "I got it during an anonymous gift grab at a party a few years ago."

"Is it accurate?"

"I'll let you in on a little-known secret." He leans down beside my ear and whispers, "I don't even own a grill."

Chapter 17

GRANT

For the record, fresh-baked dog treats smell amazing. But they taste horrible.

When the first batch exited the oven, Allie insisted we taste-test them. I didn't argue. Not tasting them seemed like an opportunity, willfully missed. We broke one in half to share.

Who would have thought something that made the entire house smell like fresh-baked peanut butter cookies would taste like warm, chewy cardboard?

We baked, we tasted, we spit in the trash, and then we baked some more. After the dozens of cookies cooled, we decorated them with the recipe's guidance for sugarless frosting—which we also tasted, and Allie rightfully declared "nasty"—and then we stacked them in my freezer until it was full.

Six hours later, we're on my couch with our feet propped on the ottoman and a big bowl of pizza rolls between us. I've given control of the remote to Allie, and as she clicks through streaming services, trying to find something for us to watch, I stew over how to bring up the thing that's been bugging me for several days.

"Have you received any blowback because you're dating me?" I finally ask.

"What do you mean?"

"Has anyone accused you of, you know, dating me so I would design better features for the kindergarten classrooms?"

Her entire body stills. She opens her mouth, closes it, and then turns to face me directly. "Is that what you think I'm doing?"

"Me? No! Absolutely not. This whole thing was my idea."

"Yeah, but . . . do you think I agreed because of that?"

"No. I don't. Sorry. I wasn't clear." I take a deep breath. "There was a flaw in the winter dating plan I crafted. I didn't see it at the time, but it became obvious after my boss called me into his office for a chat earlier this week." I tell her about my conversation with Wallace Forsyth. "I just got so excited about the idea, and then about crafting the perfect plan that would meet our dating needs, that I didn't think how dating someone on the design committee might look in regard to my job."

She stiffens. Visibly. "Why should the people you work for have any say in who you date?"

"Here's the thing. Even though it's not your money on the table, you have a vested interest in how the kindergarten classrooms are designed, and you could benefit from me showing you favoritism through the design."

Her head swivels to me. "I would never expect that from you."

"I know. I'm not saying you would or have. But I probably should have talked to my bosses or, at the very least," I continue, "our HR person before asking you out. And then I should have insisted you do the same."

"*Insisted*? As in, ordering me to do something that should be my choice?" Her shoulders contract away from me, pulling her posture straight. "Wow."

I replay my words in my head and wince. Yeah, that's what it sounded like.

"Let me rephrase," I double back. "I should have given you the opportunity to talk to your boss or HR rep, if you thought it necessary, before giving me an answer."

Her eyes narrow on me, and I hold her gaze.

"Nice save." There's still a bit of tension in her posture as she leans forward and takes another pizza roll from the bowl. "Here's the thing, Grant. I wasn't sure I should even be on the design committee since my br— Wait." She shifts in her seat. "How much do you know about how the new school is being financed?"

"Very little, other than this project is out of the ordinary," I admit. "Generally, public schools are financed by something like a bond or special tax that a community votes on. The Sterling Grove project is different in that the new elementary school is being built by a private foundation that will then donate the building to the school district once it is completed."

"Mm-hmm." She nods. "And how much do you know about the foundation?"

"I know it's headquartered out on the west coast, and whoever's in charge seems to have bottomless pockets and a strong desire to help the Sterling Grove community thrive."

"Oh. Okay." She looks down at her lap, but her cheeks are a slightly pinker shade than they were a moment ago. A mixed bag of frustration and something near embarrassment crosses her face before her expression relaxes. "Wait." She frowns. "You're not actually doing up the kindergarten areas better than the rest, are you?"

"No. I showed the drawings to Howard and Wallace, the senior partners. After looking over the plans and my meeting notes, Wallace agreed that the upper elementary classrooms definitely had more tweaks-by-request than the lower grades. He actually suggested I add a few details to spiff up the lower grades' classrooms." I grind my teeth. "And then Howard suggested that perhaps I was subconsciously trying *not* to show favoritism and, by doing so, may have shortchanged the lower grades a bit. And I think . . ." My eyes slide shut briefly before I meet her gaze again. "I think he was right."

"Yeah?"

"Unfortunately. I over-allocated both committee meeting time and design hours to the upper grades."

"If it helps, I sure didn't notice."

"Thanks." I sigh. "I'm glad no one's been giving you a hard time."

We each grab another pizza roll, and she keeps scrolling for a movie.

"Oh, look. *The Holiday* is streaming. Have you seen it?"

"I have, actually," I say a tad sheepishly. "At least twice."

"You and every other person with good taste. Don't you dare act embarrassed about having multi-watched this classic holiday rom-com, Grant Covington." The scowl of her mouth is canceled out by the laughter dancing in her eyes. "Are there a few bite-sized bits that haven't aged extremely well? Sure." She shrugs. "But overall? Can't be missed. What's your favorite part?"

"I like that there's no cheesy villain."

She blinks at me.

"Oops. I probably answered that question way too quickly. Are you going to revoke my man card?"

"*Oof*." She cringes and shudders. "Talk about a concept that hasn't aged well."

"Oh, uh . . . right."

"I'm kidding. No, I'm not. But go on."

"Well . . . okay. I like that there's no big bad guy. No scheming ex trying to break people up, or co-worker trying to ruin anyone's reputation, or crazed serial killer out to kill the couples for kicks."

"Wow. That took a dark turn." She chuckles. "But there are messy exes in the picture."

"Yes, but they're not villains trying to sabotage the new relationships. They're just jerks who've left some scars on the leads."

She nods thoughtfully. "That's true."

Allie's gaze has sharpened—not in a dagger-ish way, like when she thought I was ordering her to talk to her HR rep, but in a way that makes me think she's found a path into my brain, my soul. And that she doesn't hate what she sees.

"Should I press play?"

"Go for it."

We're both quiet for a bit, watching events unfold and relationships grow on the screen.

"Grant?"

"Hmm?"

"Tell me if I'm overstepping here, but . . . do you have an ex who left some wounds behind?"

"At my age, I suppose I probably should, but no."

"Says who? You've been living your life, doing your thing, your way. Nothing wrong with that."

I love the passion behind her sentiment, but my bosses would disagree. "How about you?" I ask, truly curious. "Do you have some romantic wounds?"

"Romance would never be so rude as to scar me." She winks. "Not when I'm such a dependable consumer."

We both laugh. I love how she isn't embarrassed about her past dating disasters.

"Sure, I may have had one relationship that took a little more time to get over than some others," she admits with a shrug. "But I wouldn't say it wounded me. It just gave me a really good reason to take a hard pass on Norma Kellogg's matchmaking efforts."

Interesting. "The more I hear about Norma, the gladder I am that you rescued me that night. Otherwise, I may have ended up taking her up on it by now."

"Norma means well, but even if she was good at playing Cupid—which she most definitely is not—you wouldn't need her help. You're a solid guy, Grant. Once the new year rolls around, you're gonna be beating those ladies off with a stick. You've got it goin' on."

I tilt my head, feeling a smile tug the corner of my lips. "You're not so bad yourself."

Chapter 18

ALLIE

It's spitting snow as I ferry my students to the various buses and cars that will take them home for the night. I've been aching for a good heavy snow for weeks, but I need it to hold off just long enough for me to go shopping after school.

I've thrifted my brains out for a gown for Grant's gala thingy, but I've come up empty so far. As soon as the clock hits four, I'll dash to my car, speed the nine miles it takes to get to the nearest four-lane highway, and then speed about twenty miles more to the nearest town big enough to have a bridal boutique. There, I will—I *must*—find a dress that doesn't look too bridesmaid-ish, fits perfectly, and is blessed with a deeply discounted price. Once I find my dress, I will speed back to Sterling Grove for tonight's facilities committee meeting. All within a two-hour timeframe. And hopefully without a costly run-in with the highway patrol.

I'm nothing if not ambitious.

Except perhaps overly optimistic.

I wave to the last bus and then head back to my classroom to tidy up and look over my lesson plans for tomorrow. At 3:55, I put on my coat. My hand is on the light switch when the clock dings four, and I . . . am . . . outta here.

When I get to my car and pull up my hype Christmas playlist, however, I discover a text from my twin brother announcing his—and therefore *my*—change of plans.

Originally, Adam wasn't supposed to arrive until late afternoon tomorrow. His revised ETA?

5:05 p.m. Tonight.

Not even my slightly-unrealistic levels of optimism could find a way to make my shopping trip work in time to pick him up.

But if I play my cards right and the stars align, I may get another chance.

A quick jog back into the school results in the principal approving a personal day off for me tomorrow. It's a gamble since I've already had my Monday morning off-request approved for Big Family Christmas Weekend, but it pays off. Once back in my classroom, I call my favorite sub to make sure she's available and then type the sub request into the district's substitute-finding system. Within a couple of minutes, I see she's accepted the job.

Okay, this can work. It has to work. I only hope Adam doesn't mind making a couple of stops on our way up to the house on Belvedere Lake tomorrow so I can find a dress for the gala.

Less than an hour after receiving his text, I'm back in my car and on my way to a private airstrip ten miles west of Sterling Grove, where I'll await my twin's arrival via private charter.

Heaven forbid he'd fly commercial like a regular person. Or give someone more than two hours' notice when he needs to be picked up.

"Stop it, Al." I give myself a little shake. "That's not nice. Or even a little bit fair."

It's totally not. Adam has fifty billion extremely good reasons to avoid commercial flights. And I *am* excited to see him. I'm just a little hangry. And tired. And worried I'm going to embarrass Grant when I show up to his fancy gala in an ugly dress.

I glance at the dashboard clock. It's 5:09 p.m. Adam is officially late.

"Come on," I whine.

If it weren't for the dress stress, I would be bouncing in my seat, ready to jump out of the car and then tackle Adam in a hug the second his feet touched the ground.

My twin brother leads a fairly insane life, but when his schedule allows, he tries to fly in to spend some time with just me, his "favorite wombmate," as we call each other. Sometimes, like this year, it's kind of last minute.

I am excited to see Adam. I am. But what am I going to wear to the fundraiser gala?

I reach into the backseat and pull out my emergency snack stash. A protein bar and a partially frozen bottle of water isn't dinner, but it will have to do until later.

I skip a few songs on my playlist and then crank up the volume to a level that might put me on the naughty list. Not that I believe Santa would do that to me. He is, after all, a jolly old soul. I'm sure he appreciates a gal's need to get her Christmas carol on.

I distractedly sing along while scrolling Pinterest, trying to take my mind off the dress dilemma. It must work, because I don't notice that the plane has landed until it's come back around and taxied into the hangar.

Excitement bursts through my chest. Adam is here!

I can't get out of my car fast enough.

Once inside the hangar, the pilot takes a few minutes to open the hatch and release the stairs.

But I don't recognize the man coming down the stairs.

Long dark hair. A thick, dark beard. Definitely not Adam.

But . . . he walks like Adam.

The man pauses, as if looking for someone. His gaze finds me.

He *runs* like Adam.

The big, bearded guy picks me up and then spins me around in a giant bear hug, just like Adam.

Because, of course, it *is* Adam.

I gasp out a laugh.

"Gah, I've missed you so much." Adam gives me one more rib-crushing squeeze before setting me down. "I came straight from the set."

"Dude. This is next level." Adam usually has some sort of lame disguise to wear when we're in Sterling Grove. The sunglasses, ballcaps, and loose-fitting clothes have kept people in the dark about his celebrity status thus far, but this? There is nothing lame about this full-on transformation. I pull at his hair. "Is this even yours?"

"Some of it." He shrugs, grinning. "I didn't want to mess with a wig. They're hot and annoying. So they dyed my hair and added extensions. They have to touch up the roots about every third day, but it works."

"And the beard?"

"One hundred percent fake. I grabbed some spirit gum remover from my trailer and brought it with me. I was hoping you might help me remove it tonight?"

"Seems a shame. It looks totally real."

"That's kind of the point. But it's itchy."

"I bet." I take a step back and blink up at him. "We shared a womb for almost nine months, and I didn't even recognize you coming off that plane. You look . . . completely bizarre."

"So do you."

"Shut up." I punch his bulging bicep. "You look good, bro. But you sure don't look like you. You totally could have flown commercially like that. Even if you flew coach, no one would have recognized you."

Adam is something of an introvert, and while he loves performing, he has diligently protected his—and our family's—privacy from the very start of his career. Part of that protection includes the use of private planes and airstrips when he visits us. And while I'm sure his PR reps hate it, he somehow manages to keep even his charitable foundation under the radar.

A woman in uniform approaches. "You forgot your sunglasses, Mr. Cleary."

"Thanks, Kendra." He smiles at her, taking the sunglasses. "And thanks again for not being weird about signing the NDA."

If I discovered Adam has secret pockets sewn into the linings of his shirts just for storing nondisclosure agreements, I wouldn't be surprised. He always seems to have one handy when needed.

"My pleasure, Mr. Cleary," Kendra says. "We'll see you Monday morning for the flight back to Vancouver."

"See you then."

When our parents found out that their drunken oops resulted in twins, they decided that the first baby to come out would get Mom's last name, and the second would have Dad's. It caused a lot of confusion for our teachers and our friends' parents when we were growing up, but it's been kind of awesome for our family's privacy since Adam's acting career took off.

Besides my job interview right before graduating from college, I'd never visited Sterling Grove before moving here to teach kindergarten. Since I don't have any family here, and my last name has always been Hayes, no one connects that when I talk about my twin brother Adam, I'm also talking about A-list movie star Adam Cleary.

We all know it's only a matter of time before the bubble bursts. I can't imagine how weird it will be when the news hits the Sterling Grove gossip pipeline that Adam Cleary is my twin brother. Will sunglasses and baseball hats be enough? Or will he have to wear elaborate disguises like this every time he comes to visit me? The truth will be revealed, eventually. I only hope it doesn't ruin the town for him when it does, because from the first time he visited me here, Adam has been head-over-heels for Sterling Grove and the charming haven it presents.

Adam is traveling light, as usual. Just a backpack. But something's missing.

"Where's Tulip?" Adam almost always brings his elderly basset hound with him.

"She's at my house in Malibu. A friend of mine is in-between homes at the moment, and he needed a place to stay. He's dog sitting—and housesitting, I guess—while I'm on location over the next couple of months."

"Months?" I stare at him a full three seconds. "But Tulip goes everywhere with you."

"She used to." He nods, his forehead furrowing. "But she's not as young as she used to be. I wasn't sure her anxiety would do well with all the wolves on set."

"Wolves? Like, real wolves?"

"Yeah." He grins. "They're well-trained, but it's their nature to see an animal like Tulip as a possible snack. Not to mention what it would do to her anxiety to have me coming into the trailer every day smelling like wolves."

"Why would you need to be close enough to these flippin' wolves that you end up smelling like them?"

"I play a wolf conservationist going up against an organized group of trophy poachers. Since the storyline has the pack more or less adopting me as one of their own, I'm in close contact with those gorgeous beasts almost every day."

"That's amazing. And a little scary."

"Exactly. With her skin allergies, anxiety, and whatnot, my sweet little girl has enough problems to worry about in her old age. I didn't want to risk it."

"I meant scary for you, doofus. But poor Tulip, having to be away from her daddy at Christmas."

"It's not technically Christmas, Al. I'll be home with her for real Christmas. And we video chat almost every day."

I snort. I can't help it. "Of course you do."

It doesn't take us long to be back on the road to Sterling Grove, but even though I'm pushing the speed limit, we're running late.

"I hate to do this," I say, "but tonight is the last committee meeting before the new school design is presented to the board. It starts at six." It's now 5:56. "I'll let you in the house and then bolt. I should be back by eight at the latest."

"Oh. Huh." Adam falls quiet. Too quiet.

"You know what? Screw the meeting. I'll call Raquel and have her tell them I can't make it." I bite my lip. "I'm sure it'll be okay."

"No, you should go. What if . . ."

"What if . . . ?" I prompt.

He takes a deep, audible breath. "What if I just went with you?"

I'm shocked silent.

"Unless you don't want me there?"

"It's not that." I glance over and get another sharp jolt at his unfamiliar appearance. "Geez, Adam. If anyone has a right to be there, it's you. You're the one paying for the whole thing."

"It's not all my money. Other people have donated too. It's the foundation's money."

"Potato, tomato," I say. "But there will be teachers, parents, and community members there. You know, the public? And you're . . . you. You're Adam Cleary."

"Am I?"

I glance over at him again. He doesn't look anything like himself. Not like any role he's ever played before, and not like any photo—publicity or family—that I've ever seen of him. "Valid point. But don't you want to get that itchy beard off?"

"I've worn it since four this morning. I can manage another couple of hours." I feel his shrug in the air. "If it won't weird you out for me to infringe on your territory, I wouldn't mind seeing the plans for myself."

"Won't they send them to you for approval?"

"They'll send them to the foundation. And I'll get the email forwarded to me eventually so I can sign off, but I'm curious about the process. The committee and all."

"Oh my gosh." I slam on the brakes a little too hard at the first stop sign within the Sterling Grove city limits. "You want to meet Grant."

"Who?"

"Nice try, but you're not that good of an actor."

"Ouch." He laughs. "Okay, busted. I want to meet your winter boyfriend. Sue me."

"But his boss will be there tonight!"

"Technically, I'm his boss. He just doesn't know it yet."

"That's . . . awkward."

"You're awkward."

"Stop talking to your reflection in the window. I'm trying to have a conversation here."

He laughs. "Now, and for the rest of the weekend, I don't have to be *that* Adam Cleary. I can simply be Adam. Allie's brother. You picked me up from the airport and didn't want to be late, so you brought me with you. If anyone asks, that's all you need to say. Now drive."

"What if someone recognizes you?"

"You didn't even recognize me."

"I'm trying to protect you here. Besides, this is your downtime. And you hate being around strangers in your downtime."

"It's Sterling Grove, Al." His tone declares it's not only the sweetest town on the planet, but his hometown, even though he's never been more than an anonymous visitor. "I'll be fine. I promise."

A honk sounds behind me.

I put my foot on the gas and let out a long, labored sigh.

I guess I'm taking my brother, and his big ol' beard, to the meeting.

Chapter 19

GRANT

The door slams open, and Allie breezes into the school library, followed by some huge guy I've never seen.

"Whew! Made it. With one minute to spare," she says. "I had to pick my brother up at the airport." She jabs a gloved thumb over her shoulder. "Adam, this is everybody. Everybody, this is Adam."

This is Adam? Her twin?

I don't know what I expected Allie's twin to look like, but it definitely wasn't anything like the guy trailing into the meeting behind her. She said he was tall, but other than that, I assumed they would look at least a little alike. I see no resemblance whatsoever.

"I was cutting it close and didn't have time to drop him off at home," Allie explains. "Is it okay if he sits in? I made him promise to be quiet and behave." She laughs, but there's a nervousness to the sound I've never heard before.

"Of course," I say. "Welcome."

Adam gives me a typical bro nod as a familiar chorus of "sure," "good to meet you, man," and "welcome" goes through those gathered.

Allie fumbles with her coat, dropping it twice as she escorts her brother to the darkest, farthest corner of the room. She shoves a chair at him, saying, "Sit. Here." before practically running to her usual seat beside Raquel.

What in the world is going on? She hasn't told me a lot about her twin, but the few times she has mentioned him, it's always been with affection. Right now, she's acting like he has the plague.

Allie is a petite, blonde, blue-eyed cheerleader type—in a sweet way. Her dark-haired, full-bearded brother, however, looks years older and towers over her. Even in that dark corner, he looks big, and very much like the sort of guy you do not want to piss off.

And I'm dating his sister.

No pressure.

I give Allie's brother a nod I hope passes for friendly and welcoming and then decide that's the last time I'm going to glance his way until after the meeting concludes.

Speaking of which, now that everyone is here, I'd better get started.

"Welcome back, everyone." I reattach a smile. "I'm excited to show you some upgrades I've made to the school design. But first I want to introduce you to Wallace Forsyth, one of the senior partners at Iverson-Forsyth Architectural Associates.

"I first met Wallace when I was his summer intern during my undergrad years. He and Howard Iverson, the other senior partner, have been fantastic mentors for me to this day. I hope you'll join me in welcoming him to our final committee meeting."

I lead a soft round of applause, relieved when everyone joins in.

"Thank you, Grant," Wallace says and then addresses the group. "It's a pleasure to be here. After studying his latest plans for this building project, I couldn't help but want to come along to watch him present them to your group. This is one of the most creative and intuitive elementary school designs I've seen. I think teachers, students, and parents across every grade level are going to be pleased as punch with the latest additions to Sterling Grove's unique project."

"I can't take all the credit. I sought input from this committee"—I gesture at those seated—"and from a lot of other people too, Wallace Forsyth and Howard Iverson included. Let's take a look."

I click open my presentation. "Elementary-aged students need access to opportunities for physical activity and imaginative play. These activities help students foster creativity, develop leadership abilities, and learn important social skills, all while burning off the energy that builds up during sedentary learning. Outdoor recess is a wonderful opportunity for that. But where does that energy go when the temperature is too cold, too wet, or too hot for safe outdoor play?"

"To the principal's office, usually," a teacher jokes.

"You aren't kidding." Dylan groans. "Indoor recess is the devil. It's basically useless."

"A recipe for insanity," another teacher adds. "Mine."

Everyone laughs, nodding.

Exactly what I wanted to hear.

"I think you're going to like what I'm about to show you." I click to the next slide, zooming in on the additions. "I've designed three new areas to help alleviate the stress that pent-up energy can cause. Here, here, and here are grade-level-specific indoor recess rooms." I point out the locations and then click to a product picture. "Each indoor recess room will be furnished with easy-clean foam floor tiles that are replaceable individually, as the need arises."

I click back to the full design and point out the locations of the rooms, attached to the separate wings of the building. "This recess room will serve kindergarten and first grade." I move the arrow. "This one will serve second and third grade." I move the pointer to the final area. "And this recess room will serve fourth and fifth grade."

"That adds quite a bit of square footage," Paula says. "Is building indoor recess rooms the best use of our budget if they'll only be used occasionally?"

"Excellent question. Thanks, Paula." I appreciate how she provided my segue. "While primarily intended to provide indoor recess space, these spaces can be utilized at other times for so much more."

"The plan already provides state-of-the-art classrooms and an exceptionally well-designed gymnasium," Norma Kellogg says. "Couldn't those be used for indoor recess? It's not ideal, but it's been done that way for years."

Several nods and sounds of agreement round the room. But I planned for this objection.

"After looking through a few past-year schedules with your principal, it became clear that the gym is used for P.E. classes pretty much every hour of the day. And while I very much appreciate your compliments on the overall design, I think we all can agree that classrooms aren't always the best places for certain learning activities."

A few "hmm" sounds vibrate, but I can't tell whether they're open to the idea yet or not.

"I am not a teacher, but I believe teachers should be provided with the best possible physical environment to help them succeed in their incredibly difficult and often under-rewarded jobs." I take a breath. "I've listened to the concerns of the people on this committee—as well as those I've worked with on past school design projects. I believe we've designed amazing, hardworking classroom spaces for every grade level, but I believe we are in a unique position to provide even more for the students and community of Sterling Grove."

"That is the goal." This, from Paula. Her tone seems a little less skeptical than it did a few moments ago.

I click forward until I reach the desired slide and then continue my presentation, showing examples of imaginative play stations, functional storage, and indoor play forts.

I think the "Oooooh . . ." I just heard came from Allie and Raquel's table. I can't blame them. I found a company specializing in creative indoor play areas and then bounced ideas off some people I know who have elementary-aged kids to see what options I should include for each specific age group.

I click to the next slide. "All three indoor recess rooms will have sound-insulated dance areas, complete with non-strobing colored lighting, a full-length, shatterproof plexiglass entry wall for full visibility, and a screen to play carefully selected tutorials for all those internet dances the kids love to learn."

"I may be retired, but I'm not so sure how that will go over with parents," Norma interjects, and a slight tone of disapproval rides her words. "There are always a few who—"

"But imagine the epic after-school dance parties we could have as staff members," Allie pipes up and then ducks her head. "Sorry for interrupting. Go ahead, Mrs. Kellogg."

Norma sends Allie an indulgent smile before refocusing on me. "Sometimes, fun-sounding ideas turn into recipes for disaster. Or, at the very least, a hassle. There are always a few parents who object to certain curricula. Imagine how some of the more, ah, conservative folks in our community might respond when their kids come home and demonstrate how they learned to—what do you call it? Tweek?—at school."

I glance at Allie. I have no idea what a 'tweek' is.

"Did you mean 'twerk,' Norma?" Allie shoots me a wink.

"Oh, yes. That's it. Thank you, dear."

"Ah. I see what you're saying," I concede. "In the absence of proper adult supervision and without the careful curation of available materials, yes, that could be a problem. But with a staff of such dedicated, child-centric people like we have here at Sterling Grove Elementary school, I don't see that happening."

A movement to my right turns my attention to Wallace. "The adults utilizing that particular technology would obviously need to curate access," he says. "And the use of any particular area within these indoor recess rooms would, of course, be at the discretion of the adult supervisor in charge at the time."

"As a music teacher, I don't have a lot to do with recess supervision." It's rare that Lexi speaks up at these meetings. Everyone tunes in. "Dance is such good exercise, and it's one of the best stress-relieving activities. It sounds like a perfect indoor recess activity to me."

"I love it," a parent on the committee adds. "They could boogie all the wiggles out before the car ride home."

Everyone laughs.

"Right?" Lexi laughs. "Anything that increases a child's positive engagement with music is awesome in my book. I would be happy to curate age-specific collections of music and dance for something like that."

"You'd be amazing at that," Allie says. "Don't you think Lexi would be great at that, Norma?"

"I suppose she's the natural choice for the job." Norma nods. "But I still worry it could cause some problems between parents and staff in the long run."

"Okay, I'm sure some of the teachers have already thought of ways they might use various features of these spaces as learning tools." I receive a few nods. "Would anyone like to share?"

"Moving the kiddos to a fresh space can inject energy into a lesson," Raquel offers. "A lot of us take our classes outside in nice weather. I like the idea of being able to change up the learning environment regardless of the weather."

"I'd love to be able to spread my students out to play some review games without the pain—and screeching noises—of moving desks and chairs out of the way and then back again," Dylan interjects. "That alone sounds amazing."

"Doesn't it?" I grin, nodding.

"Imagine teaching basic geometry," Wallace pipes up, "and demonstrating a concept like a right angle or an isosceles triangle by simply walking across the hall to look at the geometric aspects of a jungle gym." I love the enthusiasm in his voice. "Or let's say you're doing a science unit on the solar system, and—" Wallace cuts himself off, glancing at me. "Oh, you didn't get to that part yet, did you? Didn't mean to jump the gun on you."

"No worries." I'm one slide away from the feature Wallace—an astral photography hobbyist—was particularly enthusiastic about. I'd hoped to wait to bring it up until it seemed like the majority of the group was in favor of the recess room additions. I'm not sure we're there yet, but I think we're getting close.

"I discovered a company that makes ceiling tiles with LED lighting positioned as constellation maps." I click to the slide, showing a dimmed room view of the tiles in use. "Originally, this company custom-designed a single set of high-powered telescope images for use in a family's high-end home theater ceiling. They created a gorgeous night sky for that family to enjoy indoors."

It really is the coolest thing, and the "Ooohs" from the meeting attendees seem to agree.

"Once they posted pictures of the finished ceiling on their website," I continue, "they began receiving more requests. They've been mass producing these constellation-map tiles for about three years, and while they are pricey, I think these tiles would provide both an aesthetic and an educational value to the recess rooms."

"Those are so freaking cool."

My gaze, as well as everyone else's, flies toward the far dark corner of the library.

"Er, sorry," Allie's brother says. "I'm kind of an astronomy nerd." He waves a hand. "Carry on."

"No problem," I say while a part of my brain puzzles over why his voice sounds familiar. It's obviously nothing like Allie's, and I've never met him before, so . . . it must remind me of someone I know.

"As something of a night-sky nerd myself," Wallace says with a nod toward the back corner, "I was almost giddy when Grant introduced me to this company. Now, these ceiling tiles aren't cheap, and we will need to run the extra expense by the powers that be, but if this committee likes the idea, I will present the additional line item to the financiers for approval."

"How much are we talking here?" a parent asks.

This could go south, fast. "An additional fifty thousand dollars per recess room," I admit. "Give or take."

"For a *ceiling*?" This time it's Paula expressing dismay. "That's more than a starting teacher's yearly salary."

"I can vouch for that." Lexi cringes.

"It is really cool," Dylan says, "and I can see the educational value. But that does seem like a lot of money for a ceiling."

"I agree," Allie says, surprising me. "But unlike most public schools, it's not taxpayer money at stake here. If we all like it, maybe we should leave the decision up to the guy—" She winces. "Er, I mean the foundation people, who are financing this whole thing. If they think it's too much to spend on a ceiling, we can just have a regular ceiling and call it good."

"There is no way anyone is going to approve that expense," an older community member says. "It's outrageous."

It is a huge extravagance, honestly. I can see where she's coming from. "You may be correct. But there's always a chance they'll go for it."

"If the funding foundation did approve the expense," Wallace says, "would you—or this committee, rather—want to go ahead with it?"

The silence is not encouraging.

"I'd like to give you all a few minutes to discuss the idea of these indoor recess rooms amongst yourselves," I say. "Not just the ceilings, but the addition of the recess rooms, with or without them. There is always the option to return to the preexisting plan if that's the group consensus."

"Grant and I will step out into the hall for a bit and let you all talk it out, unencumbered." Wallace stands. "When we come back, we'll address any concerns that pop up and then take a vote on which plan we should use, moving forward. How does that sound?"

When everyone seems agreeable, Wallace and I move toward the door where, to my surprise, Allie's brother meets us and then follows us out, closing the door behind him.

I turn to introduce myself to Adam to find his hand already extended. I shake it. "Grant Covington. Pleasure to meet you."

"Likewise." He turns to my boss with a much wider smile. "Wallace. Good to see you again."

Wallace smiles, but his brow furrows as if he's scrolling through a mental contacts list while searching Adam's face. After a near-startle, he blurts, "Good heavens!" and the force of his handshake strengthens. "I didn't recognize— If I would have known you planned to attend the meeting tonight, I would have asked Howard to come along."

Allie's brother knows both Wallace and Howard? How . . . odd.

"It was kind of a last-minute thing," Adam says. "I came straight from work. I didn't know there was a meeting tonight until my sister picked me up at the airport." He glances at me, clears his throat, and returns his attention to Wallace.

"Considering all this"—he splays a hand in front of his face and makes two quick circles—"and the fact that my own twin didn't recognize me until I was right in front of her face," he says with a soft laugh, "I thought I could probably sit in on the meeting without raising too much of a fuss."

Wallace is positively beaming.

I am so confused right now.

"What do you think of Grant's design?" Wallace asks.

"It's great." Adam turns to me. "Nice job. The indoor recess room idea is especially cool." He frowns. "It sounds like there's some rough opposition, though. Especially to the ceiling thing. But I hope they go for it."

"Thanks," I say. "There's still the question of whether the organization financing the building will give it the go-ahead or not, but one thing at a time."

Adam's smile quirks up one side of his massive beard. "I don't think you'll have much opposition from that corner." He and Wallace share a chuckle. "If you will both excuse me, I think I might stretch my legs a bit. Be right back."

"Well, isn't that something," Wallace says after Adam rounds the corner and moves out of sight. "Howard is going to spit nails when he finds out he missed this."

"How do you both know Adam Hayes?"

Wallace frowns. "Who?"

"Adam Hayes." Is Wallace all right? Should I be looking for signs of a mini-stroke? "The man we were just talking to?"

"You mean," he lowers his voice to almost a whisper, "Adam Cleary?"

The library door bursts open, and Allie appears. She glances back and forth down the hall. "Where's my brother?"

"He needed to stretch his legs," I say automatically while trying to process who Wallace seems to have mistaken Allie's brother for.

"Oh. Right. Okay." She frowns toward the dark hall Adam disappeared down a couple of minutes ago.

"How's it going in there?" I ask. "Everyone keeping the gloves on?"

"Huh?" She gives her head a little shake and then gives me an odd smile. "So far, so good. Was he nice to you?" She winces. "Or did he do that obnoxious, 'if you hurt my sister, I'll break your kneecaps' thing?"

"Uh …" Is that on his agenda? I'm not a small guy, but Allie's brother is *built*. He could probably snap me like a twig.

But he didn't.

I take a breath, more aware of my intact kneecaps than possibly ever before. "He was perfectly polite," I reassure her. And myself. "We talked about the school design. The dating thing didn't even come up."

"Oh, good." Her whole posture relaxes. "Brothers can be so ridiculous about—"

"Pardon me," Wallace interrupts Allie, but then turns to me. "Am I to understand that the teacher you're dating also happens to be our client's sister?"

"Allie's brother is a client?" Is this yet another obstacle on my path to partnership? Obviously, Wallace is worried about an additional conflict of interest on my end.

But … how could it be? This is the first time I've met Allie's brother, and he's not *my* client. Apart from the Sterling Grove project, I've personally met all of my clients. Adam must be working with one of the other architects. Probably Wallace, since they seem so well-acquainted. I suppose that could technically be a conflict of interest since I work for the same firm, but … really?

"Which project?"

"Which project?" Wallace laughs, and Allie lets out a low groan. "This one, of course. Adam founded the organization funding Sterling Grove's new school." He beams at Allie. "Your brother is an extraordinary young man. As is this young fella here." He pats me on the back. "It's a pleasure to meet you, Miss Cleary."

"Hayes," Allie and I say in unison, though Allie's tone is one of resignation, whereas mine has at least two giant question marks attached.

Chapter 20

ALLIE

So . . . this is happening.

"Adam and I have different last names," I explain, "which has helped him stay anonymous when he visits." I give Grant what I hope is an apologetic smile. "Since neither of us is originally from Sterling Grove, I've tried to make it a place of escape for Adam. I want him to feel safe here when he visits and to not get mobbed by fans and paparazzi and stuff. I'm sorry you're finding out like this." I grimace. "But . . . yeah. My twin brother is a movie star. Can we please keep this to ourselves and not make it too weird?"

"Oh, dear." Wallace rubs his hand across the back of his neck. He looks at me, worry painted across every feature. "You didn't know?"

Grant shakes his head. "No."

"Grant and I have only been dating for a short time. It's not something I usually share this early in a relationship."

"Of course, of course." Wallace nods, still rubbing the back of his neck. "Have I just violated the NDA? Oh, dear. Oh, shoot."

"I'm sure it's fine. Grant works for you. He should be able to know who his client is, right? If Adam takes issue. . .? Well, maybe Grant would be okay signing a nondisclosure agreement too?"

"Sure." Grant nods. But he still looks confused.

Movement catches the corner of my eye, and I turn to see Adam coming around the corner.

"Hey, Al." When Adam meets my eyes, his smile falls. "What's up?"

I fill him in, and after Wallace's profuse apologies, Adam says, "You wanna grab the car keys for me?"

"Are you leaving?"

"No. I'd like to grab an NDA out of my bag, and it's in the car."

"Gotcha." I'm slightly shocked he doesn't have one on him, in a secret pocket or something. "Hold tight."

After retrieving the keys for Adam, I head back into the meeting at his urging, feeling a bit like my nerves are poking out of my skin. I don't often shy away from awkward situations, but I hate feeling like I've been lying to Grant. Not that I'd take it back. Adam's safety is a priority. But still.

"I like the recess rooms and the fancy ceilings," one committee member says as I take my seat. "Yes, it's a lot of money, but it's not taxpayer money. If the foundation is okay with it, why shouldn't we do it? Like my dad always says, 'don't look a gift horse in the mouth.'"

"That's a good point," another member says, "but even a free horse requires a lot of costly feed and care."

"Keep in mind," Norma cautions, "that the burden of upkeep will be on the district and the taxpayers."

"Sure, but imagine if you were thinking of moving your family to Sterling Grove and then toured our new school and saw something like that," Raquel adds. "I mean, come on. That would be a selling point for more than just our school. It would make the whole town look good. And heaven knows Sterling Grove needs all the help it can get drawing new people here."

The discussion swirls around for approximately seventy thousand more years, but I'm having a hard time paying attention. What is Adam doing out there? Is he playing the big brother card and being all intimidating? Is he giving Grant the third degree while he signs the NDA? I told him we are only dating for the winter. It's not like I'm gonna marry the guy or anything. But I really like Grant, and we've had some good times together. I don't want Adam to scare him off with only about three weeks left to go in our deal.

"Allie?"

"Huh?" I blink, and by the time my gaze finds Dylan, the person who said my name, I realize all eyes are on me. "Uh, sorry. Could you, uh, repeat the question?"

"I asked what you think about the recess rooms," he says. "You're being pretty quiet over there."

"Oh. Right. I'm all for it. Indoor recess is a pain in the butt, making it hard to reclaim the learning space afterward. I'd love having a place the kids could go." I glance toward the door. "I get what everyone is saying about the expense, but keeping something nice is a lot cheaper than building something nice."

"Exactly," someone else says.

The discussion continues. Finally, someone retrieves Grant and Wallace. Adam follows them back in. After the architects answer a few more questions, Grant suggests a vote by anonymous ballot.

When the ballots are counted, all but one vote is in favor of the plan's new features. Majority rules. We're getting those indoor recess rooms.

But as I try and fail to catch Grant's eye as he packs up to leave, I begin to wonder if after all this . . . maybe I won't need to buy a fancy dress for the gala after all.

Chapter 21

GRANT

I think I've recovered from the initial shock of learning Allie's twin brother is Adam Cleary—a man whose numerous movies I've seen on big and small screens. Taking advantage of a drop-in yoga class at my gym this morning might have played a small part in re-grounding my short-circuited brain. Even so, as I make my way out of town toward Lake Belvedere, I can't help but admit that I'm still a little stunned that the anonymous force calling the financial shots on the Sterling Grove project is not a boardroom full of suits, as I assumed, but a big-time Hollywood celebrity.

I've tried not to let myself dwell on how weird this is, but it keeps creeping into my thoughts. I signed the NDA, though, so it's not like I can talk it out with anyone other than Wallace and Howard, and they're no help. On the drive home from the meeting, Wallace seemed almost giddy about me dating our celebrity client's sister. He reassured me that there was no sign of favoritism in my design, but added—rather gleefully—that if anyone tried to claim I'd added perks for Allie's benefit, her being the twin sister of the financier would get me—and the firm—off the hook.

"If anyone should have a say in how a building is designed," Wallace had said, "it should be the client. And if the client wanted his sister's area to have special perks, we would, of course, fulfill that request as best we could. Not that we can divulge our client's identity, of course," he'd added, "or his relation to your girlfriend, for that matter. But it's a nice bit of personal reassurance that our ethical standard is still in play."

I wish I could be as confident as Wallace that this isn't somehow going to blow up in our faces. Having a celebrity client is unexpected. Having to sign an NDA should be kind of cool. But the fact that I've been unknowingly dating that client's sister for several weeks definitely ups the weirdness factor.

I'm dating an action hero's twin sister. How utterly insane is that? I've always assumed I make a decent first impression, but how do you impress a guy like Adam Cleary?

Now, I'm moments away from seeing him again, as well as the rest of their family. What will they think of me? Allie said she's told them all about our short-term dating arrangement. What do they think of that? What would I think in their place?

I do not care for the direction of these thoughts. I need to re-calibrate myself.

After a series of deep, cleansing breaths, my heart rate seems to normalize.

I don't want to act strange—or worse, starstruck—around Adam this weekend. Especially since Allie texted me last night, asking if I was angry with her and saying that she understood if I wanted to cancel our date for the gala. I assured her I had no intention of canceling.

Thursday evening was a lot to take in, but how could I be angry with Allie about who she's related to? If my sister Rae was famous, hounded by cameras and fans everywhere she went, I'd go full ninja bodyguard warrior to make sure she felt safe.

Was it a little embarrassing in front of Wallace that I didn't know my girl-friend's brother is the famous Adam Cleary, and the financial backbone of the project I've been working on for months? Well, sure. But I'm not mad about it. Allie hasn't shared Adam's celebrity identity with her co-workers—well, other than Raquel, I guess. I saw her chatting with Adam after the meeting, and it seemed like they'd met before. But Dylan, Lexi, Paula, and heck, even Norma have been in Allie's life a whole lot longer than I have. If she didn't tell them, why should I expect her to tell me? Besides, by this time next month we'll have gone our separate ways, and—

That's a sobering thought.

This time next month . . . no more dates with Allie Hayes.

I don't want to think about that yet. I really like her. So much more than I would have thought possible when I came up with the whole date-for-the-season plan. I'm not sure I'll be ready to let her go.

But we have an agreement, and that's that. I'll cross that bridge when I come to it, I guess.

The GPS announces I'm a quarter mile from my destination. After one final curve, I pull into a circular driveway lined with an array of cars, minivans, and SUVs.

Parking as close as possible to the front door, I turn on the seat warmer for the passenger side and leave the car running. I know it's bad for the environment, but I don't want Allie to have to sit in a cold vehicle. When I exit the car and face the house, however, all my overthinking rushes into the ether as pure awe forces me to take a step back.

Allie's description of "a big rental house on the lake" doesn't touch the scope, grandeur, and sheer presence of this structure. Before me, a symphony of concrete, wood, glass, and light sings clear notes of both large-scale coziness and precision.

I am head-over-heels in architectural love.

This home is an enormous, gorgeous love letter to architects like Arthur Erickson and Frank Lloyd Wright but it's also somehow unique in the warmth it exudes. This is the kind of home a Silicon Valley billionaire would build in Lake Tahoe and have decorated by someone specializing in Hygge home design. It's definitely not what I expected when I plugged the address into my GPS half an hour ago. I daresay it's not what anyone would expect to find built on some random midwestern lake near a mid-sized city most Americans may not recognize by name.

A blast of wind ruffles my hair. I take a moment to collect myself before moving toward the nine-foot-tall double doors.

After I straighten the lapels of my long wool dress coat, I clear my throat and then press the doorbell.

When the door opens, a cacophony of sound slams into me, and I'm once again amazed at the home's design and construction. I heard barely a whisper of noise until that massive door cracked.

"Hello." I offer my hand to the short-ish, slightly balding blond man who answers the door. "I'm Grant Covington."

"Ah." He gives my hand a firm shake. "Allie's winter boyfriend. I'm Martin Hayes, Allie's dad. Come on in. Al should be down in just a sec."

"Hey, Marty," a feminine voice rings from somewhere above us, "could you— Oh, hi!"

I look up to find an attractive, middle-aged woman with blonde hair peering down from a balcony loft area that overlooks the grand foyer.

"You must be Grant," she says. "Hang on. I'll tell Allie you're here." The woman disappears.

"That's Dawn. Allie's mom," Allie's dad says. "I hear you've already met our son Adam?"

"Briefly." I nod. "Just a quick hallway introduction during a meeting, to be honest."

"He seemed impressed with what you've done with the school design. When he described the indoor recess rooms, some of the older grandkids started begging their parents to move to Sterling Grove."

I laugh. "It probably doesn't hurt that their aunt lives there."

"The kids love her to pieces. Don't be surprised if you get the evil eye from a few of them for taking her away for a few hours."

I wince. "We don't have to go, really. I don't want to—"

"No, no. Don't be silly. It's fine. Adam and Jackson stepped up to take over the kid entertainment for the evening. The little ones may not like it when she leaves, but they'll barely notice her absence once those two fellas get things rolling." He grins, and it's so much like Allie's smile that I can literally feel the tension easing from my core.

"Besides," Martin continues, "our Allie doesn't get to be fancy very often. It'll be good for her."

"I suppose there aren't a lot of opportunities for formal events in Sterling Grove."

"It's a sweet little town. Emphasis on 'little.'" Martin chuckles. "We were all surprised when Al took the job there. Not in a million years would I have guessed she would stay there this long. I always figured our little spitfire girl would be some sort of jet-set adventurer, bouncing between cities and continents like the earth was her personal trampoline. Boy, was I wrong."

"Hey, Grant. Merry Christmas." Adam's massive beard is gone, and its absence has revealed an entirely different and much more recognizable Adam Cleary—although I'm more accustomed to seeing him as a blond and on a screen.

"Thanks. Same to you." I give him a nod and try to separate the man from the movie star in my brain. "You look a lot different without the beard."

"You had a beard?" Martin tilts his head up at his much taller son, squinting.

"Yep. Allie helped me get it off after we went shopping yesterday."

"Ah, I see," Martin says. "I was wondering how you managed that shopping trip."

Adam shrugs. "It was a big beard."

"It was," I concur. That wasn't the sort of beard someone could grow over a matter of weeks. It would take months. "That must have taken a while to shave off."

A laugh rumbles in Adam's chest. "No shaving necessary, well, not until after the beard was off. Just a lot of spirit gum remover."

I am so confused right now. And it must show on my face because he says, "It was fake. A prosthetic beard. I flew in straight from the set of the film I'm working on."

Ohhh, right. "It was entirely convincing. I would have never guessed."

"Thanks. My makeup artist is second to none." Adam pulls his phone from his back pocket, reads a message, and laughs. "Mom says Al's about to come down for her prom pics. I'll go get everyone for the big reveal."

"I'm sure Allie's told you, but we have a fairly large crowd for Christmas," Martin says as people start filing into the grand foyer area, and he then proceeds to introduce me to them, one by one, starting with his wife Michele, a lovely brunette with a dazzling smile. "Don't feel bad if you don't remember everyone's names," he adds when my brain is buzzing. "I occasionally call some of Keith and Dawn's grandkids by the wrong names. Heck, sometimes I call my own kids by the wrong names." He grins. "Everyone just rolls with it."

"Drumroll, please!" Dawn announces from the balcony above, and as she makes her way down the stairs, it's clear where Adam got his height. A breath later, an actual drumroll sounds from somewhere in the crowd that is Allie's family. Dawn laughs. "I was kidding!"

"Had it ready," a male voice says. "App on my phone."

Allie is an absolute vision as she glides down the curving staircase. Her wavy blonde hair is caught up in some sort of elegant hairdo that probably has a special name and took hours to achieve. Her lips are a glossy, icy shade of pink, and she's wearing a body-hugging, sparkling silver—no, pewter—gown that leaves one creamy shoulder exposed . . . and my mouth suddenly dry.

A chorus of "oohs" and "pretty!" and other exclamations of awe move through the people, but all I can say is, "Wow." And I'm not even sure I said it aloud.

I take a step forward, swallow, and offer my hand for her final two steps. "You are stunning."

"Thanks." Her shoulders bounce up as her chin tilts down. A little pink rises on her cheeks. "So . . . you've met everyone?"

"Yes."

"Great. Let's go."

"Wait!" Michele steps forward, waving her phone in the air. "We need to get pictures."

After seven-to-ten minutes of Allie posing both with and without her various family members and me, she says, "Enough! There are dogs' lives at stake here, people. We need to leave."

"And they say I'm the dramatic one," Adam deadpans.

"Shut up, loser."

Ah, sibling endearments. I'm quite familiar with the concept, and that helps humanize my girlfriend's celebrity twin a little more.

"You promised stories," a pouting little voice says.

"And she will deliver them when she gets back," one of her stepsisters' husbands says. "Remember, children who whine have early bedtimes on Big Christmas Weekend."

"Don't rush." Dawn bends down to give Allie's hair a little kiss. "Enjoy yourself."

"Have fun, kiddo," her stepfather adds. "We'll all still be here when you two get back."

Allie turns a beaming smile to me. "Ready to go be fancy heroes for some dogs?"

I grin back at her and offer my arm. "Your chariot awaits."

Chapter 22

ALLIE

I've heard a few people talk about this resort, but I'd never given it more than a passing thought. Now I want a billion excuses to take a mini vacation here. Not that I could afford it on my salary, but a girl can dream.

As we pass through the spacious lobby, I consciously close my mouth to keep the "oohs" and "ahhs" that echo in my brain from exiting aloud. It has the sort of woodsy vibe you would expect in a lakeside resort, but in an understated kind of way that feels clean, fresh, and almost ridiculously elegant.

Oh, wow. On second thought, the idea of a vacation here doesn't sound all that great. I'm anything but elegant. You'd think that wearing an amazingly expensive gown—thanks, Adam—and the comparatively pricy cashmere coat my brother insisted I needed to go over it, would make me feel like I fit here. It doesn't. This elegant space doesn't seem to welcome any sort of spontaneous tomfoolery, which is pretty much my number one prerequisite for any vacation.

But . . . I'm here with—and more importantly *for*—Grant, who absolutely looks like he belongs here. I need to figure out how to absorb the spirit of this dress into my body just long enough to make him happy he invited me.

Is he going to regret inviting me?

Good grief, Al. Pull yourself together.

The gentle pressure of Grant's hand at the small of my back somehow calms me. We move to a wide hall, following tastefully placed signs directing us to the fundraising gala's event space.

"I'll check our coats." Grant helps me out of mine before removing his own.

If I expected the ballroom to be any less impressive than the lobby, I was wrong. The same elegance reigns here, but with sparkling chandeliers and a string quartet adding to the ambiance. It's a large space full of glitteringly elegant people, all of whom look fully at home in their formal finery.

"They usually have a DJ later," Grant says, "but we'll be gone long before then."

"Oh. Too bad." A DJ? I kinda hate that we're gonna miss that. A DJ might chase the hush right on out of here. And doggone it, I haven't had an excuse to let loose on a dance floor in a long time.

But . . . this isn't about me having a good time. This is about me holding up my end of a wintertime dating bargain with a guy who's gone over and above for his part. This evening is for Grant, and I'm gonna do my best to elegant-ize the absolute crap out of myself so I don't let him down.

I take a deep breath to square my shoulders. "The string quartet is nice," I say. "Classy." I wince. It's probably not considered classy to call things 'classy.'

"Yeah, it's a fairly tame start to the night, compared to what happens after dinner when the open bar starts flowing." He smiles. "Ready to meet some people?"

"Always."

"I don't doubt that." He chuckles. "Come on. I'll introduce you around."

We mingle. I say hello to Wallace Forsyth, and when I'm introduced to Grant's other boss, Howard Iverson, and his wife Elizabeth, she grabs both of my hands and squeezes them.

"I am so pleased to meet you, Allie." Elizabeth gives my hands another squeeze before letting them go. "It's good to see Grant getting out and enjoying time with other young people. From what Howard says, you've breathed new life into him." She sends Grant a wink. "Not that you weren't perfect before, of course. But you know we just love you so much and want you to be happy outside of work too."

Grant smiles and kisses her cheek. "I know."

Wow. Grant has mentioned that he has a good relationship with his bosses, but this makes it sound like they've practically adopted him.

"Grant is pretty great," I say, because who could deny it?

She asks me about my job and about Sterling Grove. I ask her about her life and her and Howard's plans for their retirement. I know she's at least thirty years older than me, but she has a relatable, sisterly vibe about her.

Other people join the conversation, and I'm introduced to more of Grant's coworkers, their significant others, and a few other people Grant knows, but not necessarily through work. As we small talk our way through the room, I sense quite a few eyes on me, and I catch the odd person here or there seeming to size me up.

"Doing okay so far?" Grant asks.

"Yep." I give him a big, toothy smile that turns into a cringe. "Not to be weird, but . . . is my dress hanging funny or anything?" I do a little twirl.

"No, you look amazing. Why?"

"I just . . . I feel like people are staring at me."

Grant does a quick scan of the room and then frowns. I follow his gaze to find one of the coworkers he introduced me to earlier grinning from ear to ear, giving him two thumbs up.

Grant lets out a two-syllable breath that sounds like that guy's name—"Brenton"—and frowns. When he glances down at the floor before meeting my gaze, I'd swear a little pink rises above the white collar of his tuxedo shirt.

"This is the first time I've brought a date to a work event. I mean, this isn't really a work event, but it's work adjacent. I guess people are curious." He glances toward Brenton. "Some more overtly than others. I'm sorry it's making you uncomfortable. But then again . . ." He pauses, and his frown warms toward a smile. "I can hardly blame them when I've caught myself staring at you too. You're utterly captivating."

Now *my* neck feels a bit warm. "Wow." I swallow. "Can't say I've ever been called that before."

"Then all those other guys dropped the ball."

"None of those guys saw me wearing anything like this." I laugh, glancing down at the amazing sparkle-fest that is my dress. "Off the clock, I'm usually more of a sweatshirt and leggings type. As you know."

"The dress is great, Allie. But you're what makes it shine."

Cheesy, but I don't call him out on it. "I'm pretty sure it's the sequins."

"There are plenty of sequins here on other people." He's not wrong. There are sequin gowns up the wazoo of this place. "But only one Allie Hayes. Trust me on this. You are always captivating."

His gaze is intense and sincere. It makes me feel like my insides are made of electric sparkles and warm cocoa. I like it, but the intensity scares me a little bit.

Wow. I've been over here feeling like a stranger in my own skin, and I haven't yet told him how altogether yummy he looks tonight.

"Um . . . thanks. And you look absolutely yuh—" I cut myself off. Now that I almost said it aloud, I realize how out of place that word is here. "You, sir, are supremely dashing this evening."

Oh, barf. Why did I throw that weird British-y accent on there?

"You don't have to answer a compliment with a compliment." He gives me a little wink that is sweet and a little flirty but not at all creepy or weird like I probably made him feel with my goofy accent. "I wasn't fishing."

"I know that." Not his style. "But I was so busy absorbing all of your compliments that I forgot to say how fantastic you look. And wow, you really do. Well done with the penguin suit. It's a good look. I'm guessing it's not a rental?"

"No, it's not." He gives a little laugh that widens into a grin. "It's my very own penguin suit."

"Figures. Makes perfect sense that you would own a tux. Your tailor deserves a generous tip, by the way. And maybe your trainer. I mean, I knew you had great shoulders, but when you get all penguined-up?" I pantomime the chef's kiss. "Yummy."

His eyebrows shoot toward his hairline.

"Dang it. I didn't mean to say that aloud. Sorry. That was uncool. Oops."

He laughs. "Not sure I've ever been called 'yummy' before, but as it turns out . . ." He shrugs and gives me a sideways smile. "I don't hate it. Not from you."

We just stand there, stupidly grinning at each other until Claire Forsyth, event chairperson and wife to Wallace, sidles up to us.

"Oh, there you are, Grant. One of the donors brought a rather large item for the auction, and I need a couple of strong young guys to help get it in." She glances at me. "Would you mind if I steal him away for just a couple of minutes?"

"Not at all."

He glances at me, a question in his eyes.

"I'll be fine," I say. "Go flex those superhero muscles and save some dogs."

"I'll be right back."

I make my way over to a waiter holding a tray of champagne and take a glass. I've never been much of a wallflower, so while I await Grant's return, I mingle with some of the people I met earlier, only to discover—and not happily—that not all of Grant's coworkers are as nice as he and his bosses are. One, in particular, seems all too invested in the fact that my relationship with him isn't serious.

Chelsea is also an architect at the firm. Wearing a black silk gown with a red belt that shows off her hourglass silhouette, her sleek black hair is accentuated by a rhinestone clip holding it back on one side. She's gorgeous and clearly intelligent, but in that cold, snooty sort of way that makes you feel like she sees you as dowdy and simple, at best.

"You have no idea how much hope you've given us Iverson-Forsyth gals." Her smile makes me think she could step into any lineup of cartoon villains and fit right in. "He's been so untouchable, you know? But if you're just having a casual fling, maybe the rest of us will finally get our ch—"

"It's not a fling." That sounds so sleazy. "It's more like we're good friends who do date-type activities together. It's nice. Comfortable. Casual, but not in the way you're thinking. Grant would never—"

"Sure he would, with the right incentive. He's a guy." She takes a sip of champagne. "The question is, why wouldn't you? I mean, you have seen him, right? Grant Covington is prime rib in a sea of chicken nuggets."

She literally just compared Grant to a piece of meat.

Then again, I called him 'yummy' just a short while ago, so am I any better?

"If I were you," Chelsea says, arching one black eyebrow, "I'd grab a slice of that every time I had a chance."

"Yeah, umm . . . Oh, hey. I think Grant's looking for me." He could be. Or he could still be moving heavy objects. "Better go. Catch you later, Chelsea."

I spin on my heel . . . and walk straight into Grant's chest, but somehow manage not to spill my drink.

"Oh, hey," I say. "There you are."

"Hey yourself."

"Are people allowed to dance yet?" I ask. "Or is that just for later?"

"I'm not sure. Do you want to dance?"

"Why, Grant Covington! Are you asking me to dance?"

"I— Er . . ." A collection of expressions—mostly bathed in confusion—cross his face. "Yes?"

I set my glass on the tray of a passing waiter. "Of course I'll dance with you." And then I practically drag Grant over to a thinly populated area near the string quartet. I'm not sure if this is the intended dance floor, but since it's on the opposite side of the room from Chelsea and her Grant-as-meat metaphors, it'll do.

Chapter 23

GRANT

Well, this is awkward.

I've attended this gala at least six times, and as far as I know, no one has danced at all until dinner, dessert, and the auction are over. The dancing starts with the DJ. But here we are, near the DJ's empty booth, swaying to the strains of a string quartet.

Is this a waltz? Should we be swaying, or . . . what? I don't know how to waltz. I don't even know if this is a waltz. I just think of the word "waltz" when I think of string quartets.

"You feeling okay?" Allie asks.

"Uh, yeah. I'm fine. Why do you ask?"

"You have the sort of look one of my students might get about a minute before they blow chunks."

"Oh." I blink at her, trying to erase that visual from my brain. "Uh, sorry. I'm good."

"Cool, cool." She's clearly unconvinced. "Do you not usually dance at this thing?"

"Me? Sure. Later. When the DJ is here." Will she pick up the hint? "How else did you think I knew the 'Cha Cha Slide'?"

"We're almost the same age. Unless you spent your late teens and twenties in a cave, it's a fairly safe assumption. But I meant *slow danced*."

"Oh. Well, yeah. Sure."

"And do you always leave room for a third person when you slow dance?"

"Do I . . . what?"

Allie removes her right hand from where it had rested between my collarbone and shoulder and runs it back and forth between the eight-to-ten inches separating us. "You know. Like it's our first middle school dance and we're scared one of us might get pregnant if we stand too close to each other?"

I can't help the snort that sounds off from somewhere deep in my sinuses. "Sorry." I press my right hand into her back and pull her closer. Reaching my left hand for her right, I pull it from my collarbone and clasp it like we're a couple of grown-ups who actually like each other. "This okay?"

"Much better." She beams. "So, if you've never brought a date to this thing, with whom did the mysteriously single Grant Covington dance?"

Of course she had to ask that. "I'd rather not say."

"Oh, boy." She grins. "Now you have to tell me."

"Okay." I sigh. "Don't laugh."

"Sorry, I can't promise that."

At least she's honest. I sigh. "I danced with Claire Forsyth and Elizabeth Iverson."

"Your bosses' wives. I see." Her lips press together. Her eyes dance. "So . . . when was the last time you danced with a woman not old enough to be your mother?"

"I've been in a few weddings over the years where I had to dance with some bridesmaids, but—"

"Had to? You don't like to slow dance? The most purely romantic of all the dancing styles?"

"It's a little awkward with people you don't know very well. Or who are old enough to be your mother." Or when no one else is dancing.

A faint shadow of hurt crosses her face.

Oh, shoot. "Not that we don't know each other. I feel like we've gotten to know each other pretty well at this point. This feels . . . nice." I cringe. "Normal, I mean. Like we're two grownups who actually like each other, normal."

She chuckles, and I feel a little tension ease from her form.

"It's just . . ." I wince and decide to just come out with it. "It feels a little weird being the only two people who are dancing."

Her eyes widen, and she abruptly stops our sway. "I've embarrassed you, haven't I? I'm so sorry. I didn't think—" She bites her bottom lip. "I fly by the seat of my pants most of the time, so the fact that I don't embarrass easily isn't always great for the people I drag along with me." She keeps hold of my hand, but drops her other hand and backs up. "No more dancing. Do you want to mingle? Grab a drink? Go breathe into a paper bag in a dark corner? Or should I call for a ride so you can enjoy the rest of the night in peace? Be honest."

"Definitely not that last one. I'm fine. Really. I'd rather feel odd about dancing than be here without you." I look at my watch. "But maybe we should find our table. It's just about time for—"

I'm interrupted by the amplified voice of Claire Forsyth, telling everyone to please take their seats.

We weave through the people, greeting a few we haven't yet on our way to our assigned table. I pull Allie's chair out for her.

"Such a gentleman." She takes her seat. "You spoil me. Thanks."

We're the first people to show up at our table, but it isn't long before we're joined by an elderly couple and a local veterinarian and her husband. When there are two seats left at our table, one is soon taken by a man who introduces himself by saying, "I'm Jeff. No plus one for me tonight." And then a woman scoots out the chair beside him. My coworker, Chelsea.

Allie smiles at each new addition to the table, and once again, I see how a room full of five-year-olds would be happy to do whatever she asked just to get that smile to fall on them.

Something twists in my stomach to realize Allie and I are nearing the end of our dating season. This winter boyfriend thing has been a lot more fun than I expected. It's going to be weird—and a little sad—when our relationship's expiration date arrives. But arrive it will. And then I will have to start dating with purpose and focus on Phase II.

I take a deep breath and look over at my date, who throws back her head and laughs at something the elderly woman beside her just said. Allie glances at me and winks, nudging my shoulder with hers before turning her attention back to the woman. When I glance across the table, I find Chelsea's eyes on me. She lifts her glass and takes a sip, arching one eyebrow in a way that feels like an invitation.

I quickly look away. Was she . . . flirting with me? While my girlfriend sits right beside me?

Not cool.

Then again, when introductions went around the table, Allie and I didn't introduce ourselves that way. The other couples included things like "Audrey's husband" and "Daniel's wife" in their introductions, but Allie and I just gave our names and jobs. Chelsea might not realize we came here together.

But . . . wasn't Allie talking to Chelsea when I came back from helping Claire? If she's met Allie, how could her flirting—if that's even what she was doing—be based on innocent ignorance?

There's no way the office gossip chain hasn't reached her by now. Brenton has known about me and Allie dating for weeks.

Not. Cool.

I sense Chelsea's gaze on me, and it's making me feel like I'm under a microscope. My collar feels a little tight, almost like noticing her looking at me makes me guilty of being . . . I don't know. Unfaithful?

I don't like it.

I know my relationship with Allie is casual and short-term, but it doesn't matter. I am with Allie now. Not forever, but definitely now. And I am not that guy. I don't ever want to be the kind of guy who would let someone think he is single when he is not.

Time to put an end to it.

Chapter 24

ALLIE

Grant's arm goes around the back of my chair, and his hand gently, if a little possessively, cups the side of my exposed shoulder.

Not gonna lie, I don't hate it.

When he leans over to my ear and whispers, "I'm so glad you're here with me tonight," it's a good thing I'm sitting down because the shiver that travels across my neck goes hot, and I turn all gooey inside.

I'm not sure what's gotten into Grant since we sat down, but he's turned into a laser-focused Casa-freaking-nova, and I am, without a doubt, the luckiest girl in the room.

We've had a lot of fun together. But I didn't realize how much I've missed the warmer, snugglier parts of being in an exclusive dating relationship. When I'm comfortable with someone, I'm an unabashed cuddler. Not necessarily in a romantic way, I'm just big on physical affection in general. With my family, friends, and—when I've dated someone long enough—significant others. Grant and I have hugged, held hands while walking, and we've sat close to each other on the couch, but we haven't been super snuggly thus far. Until now, I hadn't given much thought to that aspect of our relationship because, let's face it, as relationships go, ours is destined to be fairly insignificant. Our dates are generally filled with activities—with doing, not just being. I wouldn't change a thing.

But I haven't snuggled with anyone for a long time. And the way Grant is acting tonight, I'd bet my favorite fuzzy blanket that he's a cuddler too.

Grant's thumb rubs back and forth on my shoulder, injecting glitter through my skin.

Oh, boy. I bet Grant Covington is an amazing kisser. I wonder . . .

I take a sip from my champagne flute to wet my suddenly dry throat.

We've been dating, officially, for several weeks, but Grant has never gone in for a goodnight kiss. Which is fine. We didn't discuss physical boundaries, and I'm cool with where we're at in that department. We're going our separate ways in a couple of weeks.

I take another sip. Grant's thumb rubs my shoulder.

Yeah, I'd also be fine with it if he kissed me.

Grant keeps his arm around me until dinner is served, and as soon as dessert is consumed, it returns. By the time the auction begins, we've both turned semi-sideways in our chairs, and I'm leaning back into his chest, content as can be.

Then again, I have consumed two full flutes of champagne, with a third in front of me. I'm not sure where it came from, other than that the waitstaff here is *fire*. For his part, Grant had one glass of champagne and then switched to water. "I'm driving," he explained to the waiter, and they've kept his water glass filled too, though I haven't necessarily seen them fill it.

Hmm. Maybe I've had enough champagne. I'm kind of a lightweight, and I don't want to confuse a cozy, comfy buzz from the bubbly with Grant making a move. I might end up embarrassing us both.

The auctioneer starts the bidding for our homemade dog treat cookies at $25, which is probably where it should have ended, in my opinion. They finally sell for $175.

"They know they're dog cookies, right?" I whisper up toward Grant's sculpted jawline. I'm leaning hard into his chest now. "The guy said that, right?"

"Yes. And if the bidders didn't hear it correctly when announced, the winner will know when they take them home."

"If they read the label."

"True. But if they don't read the label," Grant says with a shrug, "that's on them."

"Ha! True."

He tilts that jaw to aim his smile down at me, and I realize that if I turned my head just a little bit more and scooted up his chest just a tiny bit . . . I could totally kiss him. Right on his perfect mouth.

Whoa. *Whoa, Allie.*

I straighten enough to put my champagne flute back on the table where it belongs before settling back against Grant's chest once again. It's definitely time to cut myself off on the champagne, but I'll keep the Grant-related buzz going a while longer, thank you very much.

The auction concludes with cheers for all the money raised for the dogs. The overhead lights dim, only to be replaced by the DJ's flashing colored light show and a thumping bass I can feel clear to my soul.

"Ready to head out and get back to your family?"

I'm conflicted. Yes, I promised my family I'd be home early, but . . . I love to dance. "What time is it?"

He looks at his watch. "Eight-thirty."

That is the best news. "I think we could wait a little while." I glance out toward the dance floor where people are beginning to gather. "How do you feel about dancing, now that other people are doing it?"

"Pretty good, if you'll dance with me." He smiles. "What time do you want to leave?"

"If we leave by nine-thirty, we'll get back to the house before ten. That's about the time the kids will start settling down. Emphasis on start," I add with a laugh. "Possibly later, depending on sugar intake and how much Jackson and Adam get them wound-up."

He stands and then holds out his hand to help me from my chair. "Let's dance."

Chapter 25

GRANT

Regular-Allie is pure sunshine. Dance-floor-Allie takes uninhibited joy to a whole new level. Her joy is infectious and electric. One zap of that smile and you're drawn in with electromagnetic force.

At some point during the evening, she found out our elderly table mates danced to "Macarena" back in its heyday, twenty- or thirty-odd years ago. Before we left the table, she grabbed a pen out of her little handbag, scrawled the request on a napkin—a cloth napkin, unfortunately, although I don't think she noticed that detail in the moment—and handed it to the DJ as soon as we'd danced near enough.

When it came on a few songs later, she cheered, said, "Be right back." and proceeded to urge that older couple from their seats. It took them a bit to get started, but once they got in the groove, they showed us all how it's done.

After "Macarena," the DJ slowed things down, and the two octogenarians stayed on the dance floor, swaying in each other's arms.

"I love them," Allie says as I pull her close and start our own sway. "That right there? That's the good stuff."

"You made that happen," I remind her. "Maybe you're the good stuff."

"Nah. That's all them. Those two are golden years goals." She sighs and nuzzles her head at my shoulder.

I dip my head and press my lips to her hair. It's the second time I've kissed her, if I count that electric lip-to-cheek shock the day we made the dog treats, but I'm not sure she noticed. It probably doesn't count, anyway. Maybe neither kiss counts.

Allie's head fits perfectly into my shoulder. Her hair carries the faintest scent of coconut mixed with a brighter floral scent. I could get used to this.

Unfortunately, we need to leave after this dance.

We stay for one more dance—another slow one. I don't think either one of us is ready to go, but it's time.

When we walk into her family's Christmas rental house, we're greeted by a sonorous beast roar, followed by the gleeful shrieks and footfalls of what sounds like anywhere from five to five hundred children. They slip-slide through the foyer with one of Allie's brothers loping and roaring behind.

"See?" Allie laughs. "They didn't miss me a bit. Come on. I'll show you where you can change out of your sexy penguin suit."

She thinks I'm sexy?

Or maybe she thinks the tux is sexy. Yeah, probably the tux.

I toss my duffle over one shoulder and follow her up the stairs. It's not a bad view, three steps behind her.

Suffering a twinge of guilt, I aim my gaze higher.

Allie leads me to a bedroom with three sets of bunk beds built into the walls. All but one of the lower bunks look rumpled like they've been slept in.

"If you're still okay staying over tonight, you can have that spot. Adam and Jackson are in here, and a couple of the older little boys, I think. Here's hoping there aren't any bedwetters above you."

Umm, what?

"Kidding." She gives my shoulder a little nudge, but then her lips twist sideways. "At least as far as I know." She shrugs. "I'll go change in my room, and then whaddya say we meet out on the balcony and go back down together?"

I nod. "Sounds good. Are you sure your family is okay with me being here?"

"Totally." She turns, only to turn back and take two quick steps toward me. She rises on her tiptoes to kiss my cheek. "Thanks for inviting me to the gala, Grant. It was . . . perfect."

"My pleasure." I fight the urge to reach up and touch the spot on my cheek her lips touched. "I mean that."

With a smile that looks strangely shy—especially for Allie—she ducks her head and then exits the room. But not without looking back one more time as she closes the door behind her.

I stare at the door for the better half of a minute before I give my head a little shake and toss my duffle on my assigned bed.

I unpack my tux's garment bag first and lay it out, removing the hangers for easy access, and then pull out some sweats and a t-shirt—as per Allie's wardrobe instructions.

Once I've dressed, I hang my tux bag in the closet and zip it up. I'm surprised to find Allie out by the balcony already, waiting for me.

She's washed off her makeup, and her hair is different. Still up, but . . . differently. She's now wearing the same leggings she wore for the Black Friday flash mob and an oversized white sweatshirt with the word MERRY emblazoned across it in fat, red letters.

She looks amazing.

How did she accomplish all that in the time it took me to change? I don't think I took a long time packing up my tux, but . . . did I? Probably. Why? It's going to the dry cleaner on Monday. I could have wadded it up and shoved it in my duffle.

No, I couldn't. Even the thought makes me cringe.

She tilts her head. "Everything okay?"

"Perfect. Have you been waiting long?"

"Nope. I didn't want you to have to wait on me." She smiles. "I may have rushed a bit. I yanked quite a few hairs out with those bobby pins."

"Your hair still looks good."

"Pfft." She wrinkles her nose, lifting a hand to her head. "I can do a messy bun in my sleep."

A chorus of gleeful shrieks again pass below us. Another roar sounds, followed by a deep voice, growling, "Uncle Bear is hungry for . . . toes!" More shrieks.

"That would be Jackson." Allie grins. "He invented the 'Uncle Bear is Hungry' game back when there were only a couple next-gen kiddos, and it's been a part of our family get-togethers ever since."

Downstairs, we stop in the kitchen to grab bottles of water and then make our way to a soaring great room with floor-to-ceiling windows flanking an immense fireplace on the far wall. I expect the room to be full of people, but distant shrieks and growls prove Jackson has chased the little ones to another part of the house. Only Adam occupies the large space, and he's sitting on the floor by a coffee table with his phone held in front of his face.

Adam looks up and smiles. "Hey, you're back. One sec." He looks toward his phone. "You be a good girl now, sweetheart. Daddy loves you. Bye-bye." He sets his phone down. "How was the gala?"

Allie never mentioned that Adam had a daughter.

"I had so much fun." Sincerity rides on Allie's voice, and I'm glad to hear it. "How's Tulip?"

"Those eyes." Adam groans. "She's killing me. It's like she knows I've been cheating on her."

Wait. *What?*

"I'm sure she doesn't."

"You didn't see her face."

"She's a dog, Adam. I know you miss her, but you're doing this to protect her, remember?"

Ohhhh. Okay.

"Yeah. I know." He sighs and seems to relax.

"Hey. I have a plan for later," Allie says, "and I'll need your help to build it. Jackson too, if he's willing. But we can't start until all the kids are tucked in. You in?"

Adam nods. "Sure."

"What are we building?" I ask, intrigued.

"It's a surprise." She puts a finger to her lips. "I'll fill you in later."

"Does this have anything to do with those giant suitcases you made me leave out in your car?" Adam asks.

"Yep. And if you're super nice to me, I'll let you use those big muscles of yours to go out and get them."

"Wow. What an honor," Adam deadpans.

"Thanks, bro." She bats her eyelashes at him a few times. "You're the best."

The next thing I know, a flock of flush-faced children are herded into the great room by a very sweaty Jackson. Or should I say, *Uncle Bear*.

"Aunt Allie's back!" he announces. "Time to jam out!"

Jam out? I thought they were going to settle down for bed.

As several kids make dismayed sounds, Allie raises her voice over the groans. "You heard Uncle Bear. It's time to brush your teeth, go potty, and get those jams on. And if everyone does an extra good job jamming out, I might be convinced to read you a story."

Ah, pajamas. Got it.

When the room has emptied of children again, Jackson jumps over the back of the sofa Adam leans against and stretches out. "Can you imagine having to do that every day? I love those little idiots, but they're freaking exhausting."

"To be fair," Adam says, "I don't think any of their parents do the Uncle Bear thing. At least not every day."

"That's why I'm everyone's favorite. Works for me! All the fun, with none of the diapers and everyday drudgery." Jackson lifts his head from the couch cushion and aims his gaze my way. "You have any rug rats, Winter Boyfriend?"

"Grant." Allie grabs a throw pillow from a nearby chair and wings it at Jackson's face. "His name is Grant."

"I know." Jackson grins, tucking the pillow beneath his head. "Just messin'
with you, man. So . . . no kids?"

"No. My sister has three kids, but I don't have any of my own."

"Smart man. Hey, Al, gimme a sip of your water."

She hands Jackson her bottle. "No backwash, please."

He takes a long draught and keeps drinking. He hands the empty bottle back
to her. "No backwash."

She expels a sigh that seems more put-on than serious. "I'm gonna go grab
another water, since mine is strangely empty."

When Allie returns, she's brought three water bottles. She hands one to each
of her brothers and then checks that mine is still mostly full before cracking hers
open and chugging half of it.

"Where did everyone else go?" I ask. With a group this large, I can't imagine
everyone else is asleep already or even could be with all that "Uncle Bear" game
noise.

"There's a killer theater room in the basement," Jackson says. "They're all
down there watching a movie, trusting us to keep their kids alive and unharmed.
The fools." He lets out a comically evil laugh.

There's a relaxed vibe with Allie's brothers, and I can't help but be relieved
I'm getting eased into the group a little at a time instead of thrown in all at once.
They ask me about my job and my work on Allie's school. We trade basic life
info. Adam shows me several pictures of Tulip, his elderly basset hound, as well
as one of him on the set of his current film, grinning in between two wolves he's
using as armrests. When they question Allie about the fundraiser, she becomes
animated, sharing how someone paid $175 for those disgusting dog treats we
baked and how the elderly couple cut a rug.

"Oh, and there was this unbelievably bold diva chick at our table." Allie leans
forward. "A hardcore model-type. A little villainesque. You know the type."
Her brothers nod. "She's actually an architect, not a model, but you get the
idea." She brushes a hand through the air. "She had the audacity—the absolute

au-da-ci-ty—to make bedroom eyes at *my boyfriend* while I was sitting right beside him."

Oh, dear. "I didn't think you'd noticed."

"Kindergarten teacher," she says. "Full-spectrum awareness is a life necessity."

"Sorry about that."

"Why? It's not like you encouraged it." She snorts. "Wait. Oh my gosh. Is that why you got all cozy and snuggly with me? To make her stop?"

I sense a shift in the easy vibe as two pairs of apex predator eyes assess me as possible prey. I open my mouth, close it, glance at Allie's brothers to confirm the danger, and then, finally, I speak. To her. "Initially, yes."

"Initially." Allie says, but I can't read her tone.

"Both Chelsea and Jeff came without a plus one," I explain. "When introductions went around the table, we didn't introduce ourselves as a couple, so I guess it's possible that the flirting was innocent on her part. But—"

"Oh, she knew. She and I had a whole conversation about it before dinner."

"Right. Okay. Well, regardless, we *are* a couple, and I wanted that to be clear."

"For how much longer, though?" Jackson grunts when Adam's elbow connects with his ribs. "I just mean that if this Chelsea person is hot, and interested in you, you might want to date her after this winter boyfriend thing is over. Why not keep that door open?"

"I'm in a relationship with Allie now," I say, feeling my hackles rise. "I've made a commitment to her. Regardless of the timetable, I honor my commitments."

"Right answer," Adam says, just as the first pajama-clad child returns.

"But considering this whole winter boyfriend thing," Jackson says, "which is bizarre, by the way, I—"

"And it's their business," Adam says. "Stay out of it."

Jackson lifts his hands in surrender. "Just sayin'."

One by one, the little kids filter back into the room, finding homes on laps. When all the familiar laps are taken, one little guy in footy pajamas comes up to me with a blanket in one hand. He stares for a moment and then raises his little arms. I lift him up and set him in my lap.

I glance over at Allie, who is flipping through a stack of children's books one of the kids must have brought with them. When she looks my way, her smile warms with affection for the little fella.

And maybe a little for me?

When Allie turns the last page, the parents collect their respective children and carry them off to bed. The oldest generation announces they're turning in for the night as well. When the room is clear of all but Allie, Jackson, Adam, and me, Allie sends Adam to bring the mysterious suitcases from her car.

I offer to help, but he waves me off. "I've got this."

By the time Adam returns, Allie is practically bouncing in her seat.

She jumps up, unzips the first suitcase, and lets it fall open, revealing what looks like miles of string lights. When she unzips the other one, she exclaims, "Look at all the sheets I brought!"

"Uh, why?" Jackson asks. "The beds had sheets on them when we got here."

"For the past year," Allie says, rubbing her hands together with pure glee, "I've scoured thrift stores and discount racks, seeking the biggest, brightest bedsheets I could find, all with this singular night in mind. Gentlemen— Oh, and Jackson." She sticks her tongue out at him. "We are about to embark on an epic blanket-fort-making adventure."

"We're building a blanket fort?" Adam laughs. "Cool."

"Yep. And with the unexpected benefit of having a real-life architect in residence, we shall create the most amazing blanket fort in the history of blanket forts! Ready?"

If my grin remotely mirrors those dawning on the other faces in the room, I'd say we are.

Chapter 26

ALLIE

We decide the theater room in the basement is the best place for our blanket fort. It will give the kids a cool place to watch *Elf* tomorrow night, as is the tradition on our last night of family Christmas weekend before everyone heads home on Monday morning. Since this spot is away from the main areas of the house, it will allow for a perfect "big reveal" in the morning.

After several fails and a lot of laughs, my bright collection of thrifted bedsheets is draped, positioned, and secured to various anchor points around the room, with a big opening by the movie screen.

By the time it's all set, it's after midnight; Adam and Jackson are both fighting yawns. They don't argue when I dismiss them to their beds. But even if they had, trying to work around the anchor points on the edges of the room has become a bit of an acrobatic event, and there's not much maneuvering room left on the outside of the fort. Besides, it's kind of nice having only Grant here to help me string up the lights.

I've just crawled into the fort with the first string of lights when Grant says, "Draping the lights over the top of the fort would be safer. You know, with cords and electricity and stuff."

"I should have thought of that." I back out of the fort. "Keeping little kids safe is kind of in my job description."

"Mine too," he says. "Technically. From a bit more of a distance."

Together, we squeeze ourselves around the fort's various anchor points, finding wall outlets to use while Grant keeps us mindful of the UL cord warnings not to exceed the number of light sets connected to each other. In the end, we only use about a third of the lights I brought. I may have gone overboard on the light buying.

Standing in the theater room doorway, we survey our work.

"What do you think?" Grant asks. "Is it everything you hoped it would be?"

"It's kind of a mess, to be honest," I say and then beam up at him. "But I love it. And I think the kids will too."

"So . . ." Grant begins, "are we going to stand here and stare at it, or are we going to crawl inside and see how we did?"

"Oh, we're definitely going in there. But there's one more thing we have to do first. Up for a stealth mission?"

He tilts his head and then breathes out a quiet laugh. "Sure."

After several stealthy trips up and down the stairs, we've transferred every available throw pillow and throw blanket from the great room to the theater room. Once our pile of comfort is complete, Grant and I become human bull-dozers, pushing the pillows and blankets down the fort's passageways on our way to the movie screen.

Somewhere in the middle, I lose my balance and face-plant into a pillow.

Grant is behind me. "You okay?"

"Yep," I reply into the pillow. Laughing, I roll over, sprawling onto my back. "Oh . . ." I breathe. "Grant. Get over here."

"Need some help?"

I pat the carpet beside me. "C'mere."

It takes a sec in our close quarters, but soon he's lying beside me, looking up at the light trails strewn over our colorful canopy.

"This is the coolest blanket fort ever," he says. "I should make one of these for my sister's kids the next time they come over."

"I'm thinking I need a permanent blanket fort installation in my living room," I say through a yawn. And I might even mean it. "Or maybe in my bedroom so I could sleep under the stars every night." I scoot closer to Grant. "Thanks for helping with this."

His arm goes up and around me, and I tuck myself in as he pulls me close. "My pleasure. Thanks for including me."

We're quiet for a while, enjoying our cozy fort. I'm positive whatever buzz I had from the champagne at the gala wore off a while ago, thanks to the combination of lots of water, lots of activity, and a few hours in between. But Grant smells amazing, and my blood rushes with the fresh and woodsy, citrusy-spice high of his nearness.

I've always been weak in the presence of a nice men's cologne. But a yummy cologne on an extremely attractive and super nice guy is definitely a recipe to turn my knees to jelly. Good thing I'm already lying down.

But that's also a bad thing; if I accidentally-on-purpose snuggle just a little more into Grant, I might end up rolling far enough over to kiss him, and . . . I'm not sure he wants that.

But I do.

Boy, do I.

Should I?

I'm not sure that's a line he wants to cross. Not with me, anyway.

I get it. He wants to keep things casual. Simple. Fun. We're a couple now, but we're not the kind of *couple*-couple who wonders if this could be "the one." Nope. We started this thing with a break-up plan. With a spreadsheet, for Pete's sake. A spreadsheet!

That word alone should cool my romantic-moment jets.

It does not.

Spreadsheet, spreadsheet, spreadsheet.

I repeat the word in my head, but it keeps getting overwritten by the memory of snuggling with Grant during the auction. And dancing with him. And that moment when I thought he kissed my hair but wasn't sure, so I didn't acknowledge it.

He probably didn't. He probably just bumped me. Softly. With his lips. Accidentally.

I'm his dating refresher course. That's all.

Grant is my boyfriend for a season. That's all. He's the sweet guy with whom I get to do fun, romantic, wintery things without the pressure of wondering when the axe will fall.

That predetermined expiration date is a gift. I don't have to worry about when he'll decide I'm just a little too all-over-the-place for him or when I'll finally discover that one thing I can't stand about him. We already have a plan to break up, and that takes all the pressure off.

Not that I've found that one thing yet.

And he's been such a good sport when it comes to going along with my somewhat erratic flow.

Even the spreadsheet thing is kind of adorable, now that I've gotten to know him.

My breath catches. I did *not* just think that. Nope, nope, nope.

There is nothing cute about a spreadsheet, I remind myself. *Spreadsheets are the spawn of an unholy union between math and pure evil.*

Grant takes a big breath in, and as he lets it out, he turns onto his side, near-to-facing me.

This could be it.

I angle a bit nearer him and tilt my head up as his other arm comes around me, pulling me close. His head tilts down . . .

I lick my lips, my gaze on his already-closed lids. Finally. *Finally*!

Grant's forehead rests on mine, a sublime moment during which I suspect this might go down as one of the best kisses of my life thus far.

We stay like that. Foreheads touching but lips still too many millimeters apart.

When I can finally hear his breathing apart from my own slightly elevated respirations, I realize it's a deep, even sound.

No way. No freaking way.

You've got to be kidding me.

Is Grant . . . asleep?

Chapter 27

GRANT

I'm not sure if it's a sound or the sudden tickle to my nose that wakes me up, but when I open my eyes, Allie is squirming out of my arms and scrambling to a sitting position while whisper-shouting, "Just a sec!"

"What's going— Where . . .?" It takes me a moment to get my bearings in the dim, twinkling light. "Right. Blanket fort. Sorry. I must have dozed off. What time is it?"

Allie pulls her phone from a side pocket in her candy cane-print leggings, wakes the screen, and then looks at me with wide eyes. "It's almost eight o'clock."

"A.M.?" I ask stupidly.

She nods, and her messy bun—which has tilted off to one side—bobs. "And our absence has been noted."

"By . . .?"

"Your friendly neighborhood stepbrother," an adult male voice announces from somewhere nearby, but outside the blanket fort. "You two kids better get your clothes back on before Adam gets down here. Grant's bed was clearly not slept in, and I can only hold him back so long."

"Shut up, Jackson," she hisses and then adds, "Nobody's naked, you perv. It was late. We fell asleep admiring our fort."

"Likely story." Jackson laughs. "Good luck convincing Adam."

"Adam can mind his own beeswax," Allie growls, "and so can you, you big dumbhead."

I can't help but smile at her kindergarten-approved verbiage, even while wincing over the thought of what a large action hero might do to the guy he thinks has taken advantage of his sister.

Allie shoves her phone back in the side pocket of her leggings. "I'm just gonna apologize in advance for anything anyone says about"—her gesture encompasses our sleeping space—"this."

"No worries."

I may have a few worries. Most involving flashes of scenes from movies in which I've seen Adam Cleary beat the absolute crap out of the bad guys.

"Uh, should we finish getting all these pillows and blankets closer to the movie screen before we go upstairs, though?" I ask.

"Good thinking." Allie starts gathering the items that didn't make it past this area of the fort last night.

It only takes a couple of minutes to get everything set for the big reveal, and then we crawl out of the fort.

"Good mornin', lovebirds. Or should I say, 'winter lovebirds?'" Jackson stands in the theater room doorway, grinning like an ornery little brother who is about to get his sister in big, big trouble. "Ready for your walk of shame?"

"The only thing I'm ashamed of is having to walk into a room with a big dumb jerk like you," Allie shoots back at him, sticking her tongue out.

Jackson returns the gesture, then laughs. "Aww, come on. I'm just messing with you." He puts an arm around her shoulders and leads her toward the stairs. "Adam was still asleep when I got up. Being the awesome stepbrother-slash-wingman I am, I was kind enough to rumple Grant's bedding to make it look like his bed was, in fact, slept in last night."

Relief washes through me, and then I feel like a wimpy sixteen-year-old kid for feeling it. I make a mental note to remake that bed before I leave.

"You're a pest." Allie punches Jackson's side for emphasis. "But also . . . thanks, I guess. Except for the part where you implied we were down here getting our freak on in a space designed for *children*. That's nasty, bro."

I accidentally inhale saliva and have to cough a couple of times. *Getting our freak on?*

"You okay?" Allie glances back at me.

I cough again and clear my throat. "I'm good."

When we reach the main floor, we bypass the kitchen where it sounds like breakfast preparations are underway, and head upstairs to get ready for the day. After a quick shower and a much-needed tooth-brushing, I put on a fresh t-shirt and the same sweatpants I unintentionally slept in. When I return to the bedroom to repack my toiletries, Adam is awake and rummaging in his backpack.

"Hey, Grant," he says. "Sleep well?"

"Surprisingly, yeah." I decide to err on the side of honesty. "But I didn't actually sleep in here. Allie and I accidentally fell asleep in the blanket fort."

He stares at me for a few seconds before saying, "I know."

I'm not sure what to say to that, and since my brain is as-of-yet uncaffeinated, I can't think of a response. Luckily, the pause isn't too long.

"My phone must've fallen out of my pocket somewhere down there last night," Adam says. "I didn't realize it was gone until I woke up around five this morning. When I went down to look for it, I crawled inside the fort and found you two. You looked . . . cozy."

His tone isn't threatening or anything, but I think there might be a question implied.

"One minute we were admiring our work, and the next I woke up to Allie informing me it was morning. Nothing happened that you need to worry about."

"You're both adults. Not my business," Adam says. "The lights look cool though. You guys did a good job."

"Thanks." I like the real Adam a lot more than the slightly scary picture Jackson was trying to paint. I'm not sure he believes me about Allie and I literally *sleeping* together, but I appreciate his attitude about Allie's privacy. Not to mention how much better it is to feel like a man in his thirties instead of a teen caught in the act. "It was fun."

"She likes you."

"Yeah?" If anyone could discern the truth of that, it would probably be her twin. "I like her too."

He nods, looking at the floor. "Allie comes off as pretty carefree, but she has a lot more capacity than she admits. Even to herself. But . . . she's not bulletproof." Adam looks up, meeting my gaze. "I know you two have a deal to break up, and that's fine. But the word 'break' is still in there, and I wouldn't be a good brother if I didn't worry at least a little bit about how she's going to take it."

"Probably a lot better than I am."

Adam's eyes widen.

Uh . . . did I say that out loud?

A slow smile parts his lips. "Interesting."

"I, uh . . ."

Adam grins, takes a step forward, and claps a hand down on my shoulder. I almost don't flinch.

"In that case, carry on." One solid, grinning nod later, he's out the door.

Okay. So . . . I think we're good? He didn't kill me, which is nice.

I want Allie's family to like me, to approve of me. All things considered, it probably shouldn't matter so much to me, but it does.

Once I have all my things packed, I take my bags downstairs and prop them near the front door.

"You're not leaving before breakfast, are you?"

I look up to where Allie is standing at the balcony. "No, but probably soon after. I don't want to infringe on any more of your family time."

"You're not infringing." She starts down the stairs. She's changed into black leggings and a fuzzy red sweater that looks like it was knit from glitter-coated yarn. Her hair is a magical mess of pale waves around her face. "But I get it. We're kind of a lot."

"I think your family is actually kind of awesome."

"We totally are." She laughs and then gathers her hair into a fluffy ball on top of her head, securing it with a hair tie she pulls off her wrist as she continues down the stairs. "But it's a lot of awesome all at once for an initiate."

About halfway down the stairs, she pauses. "I guess 'initiate' implies you'll level up, doesn't it? And since we're only dating for the season . . ." She gives her head a little shake and continues down the stairs. "I don't blame you for wanting to duck out early, but my mom will skin me alive if I let you leave before she gets to feed you. You'd better at least stay for breakfast."

Something stirs in my stomach, tightening it. It's not like I expected Allie to beg me to stay longer, but . . . if she had asked, I would have said yes. It's a fun group. How could it not be with Allie in it?

But she's not going to ask. As she said, our relationship has a ticking clock. There's no leveling up, no reason for me to get to know her family any more than I already have. It's a rather raw truth, and it's oddly disappointing.

"Breakfast sounds great." I follow her into the kitchen.

Chapter 28

Allie

I'd taken a half-day off to avoid having to race back to Sterling Grove from the rental house Monday morning, which was nice. But it's already Wednesday, and I've yet to recover from the events of the weekend. We're less than forty minutes away from the official start of winter break, and I'm not sure I've ever been more excited for a school day to end.

My class of kindergartners is staying surprisingly on-task, considering we're in the home stretch to winter break. As I walk around, giving "Nice job" and "Wow, that's a creative use of color" compliments to the snowman pictures they are coloring, I'm struggling to be fully present.

I wonder how Grant's doing? We're supposed to hang out tonight and "do something wintery." His words. But for some reason, I keep expecting him to cancel.

I glance at the clock again. Thirty minutes to go. Thirty minutes until I can send the kids home and check my phone to see if Grant has, indeed, canceled our date. He hadn't yet when I checked during my lunch break, but . . .?

Ugh. I hate this feeling. Why can't I shake this?

"Do you like my snowman's nose?"

I blink myself back into the moment and lean down. "Very nice, Libby."

"It's purple because it's an *heirloom* carrot," she says.

Libby is one of my most precocious students. "That's very cool."

"My mom got some heirloom carrots in a prescription box."

It takes me a sec, but . . . "Oh, a subscription box?"

"Yes. A subpictionary box."

"Nice." I should probably correct her until she gets it right, but we are now twenty minutes from dismissal, and I don't have the energy. "Were the purple carrots as yummy as they were pretty?"

"No. They tasted like carrots," Libby says. "I don't like carrots. But I *love* purple."

"I like purple too. And your snowman's nose is perfect." I move on to the next table.

Maybe I was imagining that strain between Grant and me on Sunday morning. Maybe he was just all peopled-out and needed to get away to save his sanity.

He's done a spectacular job putting up with my electrically-charged confetti personality—much better than any other guy I've dated this long. But any outsider would be overwhelmed when faced with my whole crazy family in one place, and I could hardly blame him if that's what made him go so quiet. If that's the case, all will be fine tonight. We'll have a fun time doing whatever wintery thing he has planned, plus we'll have over a week of wintertime date possibilities left.

But . . . what if it wasn't my family that exhausted him? What if it was me? Then what? Do we cut our losses and move up the expiration date?

I don't want that. I actually still like Grant. I enjoy being around him, regardless of the setting or the people in it—which is rare for me, this many weeks into a dating relationship.

Like, super rare.

But what if the only reason I still like him—and want him to like me—is because I know I don't have to like him much longer?

Hmm. Yeah, that's probably it. And that's fine. Soon, I'll go back to my perfectly lovely life with a ton of sweet memories from my time of having a just-for-the-winter boyfriend.

Meanwhile, Grant will dive into his Phase II thing. He'll find his dream woman, and they'll make beautiful spreadsheets together forever, occasionally having spontaneous fun because his just-for-the-winter girlfriend taught him how. It's fine.

Better than fine. It's exactly what we signed up for. Goal achieved.

I'm excited to see what Grant has planned for the final week and a half of our relationship. He's gone over and above what I expected from him in the "fun wintertime dates" department. But did I teach him how to be more spontaneous?

Did I need to? He's happily gone along with every idea and activity I've sprung on him. Is being able to initiate spontaneity even that big of a deal for someone so otherwise awesome?

Grant is smart, sweet, and exceptionally attractive. He's kind, and he's respectful, dang it. I can't deny it: he's kind of the full package. An organized, tidy package of spreadsheet-loving but otherwise gooey chocolate chip cookie dough goodness. He's a certifiable catch.

Not my catch, of course. We have more of a catch-and-release thing going. Besides, Grant Covington is not looking for someone like me. I have to remember that. He's looking for someone like *him*. Someone with whom he can bask in the predictable routines of weekly menus, monthly budgets, and filling up retirement accounts. He needs someone organized and steady. Someone whose idea of a vacation is quietly reading literary memoirs under a beach umbrella in between visits to hushed-voiced museums, with all activities completed according to a scheduled itinerary.

I would *hate* that.

And that's why we're dating for a limited time. We came into this knowing we're only compatible short-term.

"Miss Hayes?"

But what if . . .?

Nah.

"Miss Hayes?"

A tug on my sleeve jolts the connection between my ears and my attention. "Yes, Libby?"

"Miss Hayes, Cale said purple is ugly, but that's a lie. Purple is beautiful, even if it tastes like carrots sometimes. People should never lie, right Miss Hayes?"

Back to work.

Once I've solved the purple debate—at least temporarily—I glance at the clock.

Finally. The big hand and the little hand are exactly where I need them to be. "Okay, class. It's time for cleanup."

Once the supplies are stowed, the kiddos start getting coats and backpacks on, and then I escort my class to the buses and carpool lines, wishing them all, "Happy Holidays!"

Back in my classroom, I check my phone. Still no cancellation text from Grant, so all must be well, right?

After I tidy all that still needs to be tidied, I put on my coat and—hello, winter break!—head for home.

When I pull into my driveway, my favorite neighbor is outside, sprinkling ice-melt on his sidewalk. I roll down my window. "Do you think it's finally going to snow?"

"Flurries tonight," he says, "but there's freezing rain forecasted for our overnight. Do you have some road salt on hand? Might be good to throw some out."

"Um . . ." I try to mentally categorize the contents of my garage, but it's about as organized as the kitchen junk drawer. "I don't know."

Dennis laughs. "I have plenty. Stocked up as soon as Bill got his first shipment in at the hardware store. I'll come over and do yours when I'm finished here."

"You're the best." I blow him a kiss, complete with the *mwah!* sound.

"You better save those kisses for your fella. How's that going, by the way?"

"It's been great." I told Dennis all about the winter boyfriend plan shortly after Grant's presentation of the idea. "I've had so much fun. It's kind of a shame it's almost over."

Dennis tosses another handful of salt on his sidewalk. "Maybe it doesn't have to be."

"We have a deal." I shrug. "Besides, I'm not his type. Grant is calm, focused, and driven. I'm like confetti in a wind tunnel."

Dennis frowns. "Did he call you that?"

"No." I laugh. "It's facts, my friend. Hey, what's a bag of road salt cost? I'll pay you back."

"Don't be silly."

"I was born silly." I click my garage door opener and make a mental plan to bake Dennis a batch of cookies soon. "See you later, sweet neighbor."

"Get in your home, Christmas gnome."

I laugh. "That's a new one."

As I pull into my garage, I reflect on just how good my life is. Having a winter boyfriend has been like the sprinkles on top of a frosted sugar cookie. Sure, sprinkles add a little color and texture, but the cookie is just as tasty without them. I have awesome friends, a loving family, my dream job—most days—and my happy little house. It's a good life. And it will be a good 'normal' to come back to in the new year.

My phone vibrates, and I pull it from my coat pocket. My heart leaps into my throat when I see the text is from Grant. I open it.

My mouth relaxes into a smile. He's not canceling. He's on his way.

Chapter 29

GRANT

I'm glad I've had a few days to rewire my brain before seeing Allie again. I know she could tell something was up with me on Sunday morning.

The truth is, I wanted more time with her. I wanted her to ask me to stay. I know it was outside the bounds of our original relationship agreement. I know it was selfish of me. But I wanted to stay.

I can't pin down exactly when it happened, but at some point over our last few dates, the hard-drawn lines of our plan have blurred a little for me. Without permission, the expiration date morphed from being a concrete ideal to a deeply flawed concept.

I like Allie. A lot. On my drive home Sunday morning, I realized I was thinking of Allie as my girlfriend in an open-ended, long-term way.

Clearly, she isn't on the same page. That's okay. I'm a man of my word, and I can stick to our agreement. But it would be a whole lot easier if she was a little harder to be around.

When I get out of my SUV at Allie's house, my feet crunch against rock salt on the driveway and all the way up to her front door. As disappointed as she's been at our lack of measurable snowfall so far this season, I wouldn't have expected Allie to prep her driveway to repel snow, but it's not the first time she's surprised me, and it probably won't be the last.

When she opens the door, she's already wearing her coat. "I'm ready. Let's go!"

"I haven't even told you what we're doing yet."

"Doesn't matter. I'm sure it'll be amazing."

"You have a lot more faith in me than you probably should. That being said, I do think tonight's date will be fun. In a low-key sort of way."

"You haven't disappointed me yet, sir, and I don't foresee that happening anytime soon." She steps outside, locks the house, pockets her keys, and then slides her gloved hand into mine. "Lead on, winter boyfriend."

Yep. I needed that reminder.

"Our first stop is dinner," I tell her. "I thought we'd try out that bar a couple doors down from Cocoa & Froth. Dylan said it's the best place for a hearty bowl of soup in the winter."

"O'Daire's Pub." Allie nods. "They do have a strong soup game. Just don't let the owner hear you call it a bar. She's not a fan of that word, and she will absolutely let you know it."

"Thanks for the tip."

Inside the pub, we're greeted by the low hum of conversation. There's an enormous stone hearth off to one side, and the fireplace is ablaze. I see a table for two near the hearth and usher Allie toward it.

Shortly after we're seated, a man at the next table leans over and, after greeting Allie by name says to me, "First time here?"

I nod. "I've heard good things."

"They're all true," he says as our waitress approaches. "This is the best bar in town."

As the waitress passes him, she smacks the back of his head.

"Ow!"

"How many times do I have to tell you, Gary? This isn't some crusty old bar. This is a fourth-generation, local institution. Call it a pub. Call it a restaurant. You could even call it a tavern," she says, her bright red lips drawn into a pointed scowl. "But don't you dare call my great-grandfather's dream come true a *bar*."

"Sorry, Rainey." The man ducks his head. "Won't happen again."

"Look at me over here, not holding my breath," she grumbles in a dry, exasperated tone and then turns her attention our way. "Sorry about that. Hiya, Allie." She lifts her chin at me in a half-nod greeting. "Allie's friend."

"This is Grant Covington," Allie says. "He's the architect designing our new elementary school. Grant, meet my friend Rainey O'Daire. She owns this amazing establishment."

"Architect, huh?" One of Rainey's coal-black eyebrows arches toward her matching hairline as she aims her question at Allie. "The one you texted to warn me about back around Halloween?"

Excuse me?

Allie tips her head back and laughs. "I'd almost forgotten about that, but yes. This is the guy Norma wanted to set you up with."

Oh . . . right. I smile, remembering how Allie rescued me from Sterling Grove's apparently cursed matchmaker via colored toilets.

"So this is a work thing? You two hammering out some design stuff for the school?"

"Nope." Allie grins. "We're on a date."

"Yeah, I figured." Rainey's smile has the timbre of an inside joke between friends.

I don't recall Allie ever mentioning a friend named Rainey before. But then again, I've yet to meet anyone in Sterling Grove Allie Hayes wouldn't consider a friend.

"I'd heard you two were dating," Rainey says. "News travels fast in Sterling Grove. I figured you'd make your way over here eventually."

"Nice to meet you," I say. "Your pub comes highly recommended."

"Thanks." She glances over her shoulder. "You taking notes, Gary? This is how to ensure I don't water down your whiskey again." She turns back to us. "Tonight's soups are Cheese and Ale, French Onion, and Colcannon, which is a creamy potato soup that comes with an optional side of crumbled bacon. We also have vegan chili if that's more your style."

"I'll have the French Onion," Allie says. "Extra croutons."

"Got it. And for you?"

"The potato one sounds good. What was it called?"

"Colcannon. Did you want the bacon with that?"

"Oh, for sure."

"That's what I'm talkin' about. And to drink?"

Allie orders a hard cider, and I opt for a craft beer. In no time, our drinks and soups are on the table, as well as a heaping bowl of hand-cut croutons Allie insists I try, which prompts me to wave Rainey over to order my own bowl full.

"Rainey's aunt makes them fresh every day," Allie says. "Aren't they the absolute best?"

By the time our soup is gone, the croutons are too. After paying the check, I reveal my plan for us to drive around and look at Christmas lights, and we head outside.

"Oh . . ." Allie's voice is a hush of delight. "Look, Grant. It's snowing."

"Is it?" I squint into the darkness. "Oh, I guess it is spitting a little snow."

"The perfect addition to our date." She spins a circle with her arms spread wide. "I've been making myself wait to go light-looking in case you wanted to do it together."

"I'm sorry I didn't plan to do it sooner."

"No, it's fine. I decided that if you didn't plan a Christmas lights-viewing date, I'd save it for something to do on Christmas Eve or Christmas night."

"You're staying home—in Sterling Grove—for Christmas?"

"Yep."

"I guess I just assumed you'd be traveling somewhere."

"Not this year. The parental units are all going on a cruise together. They fly out tomorrow. My stepsiblings all have their own family things going on."

"What about Adam?"

"He flew back to Vancouver Monday morning. He'll have a couple of days off for Christmas, but he needs his alone time. Especially coming off our big family Christmas. Adam is a major introvert, if you couldn't tell. If he's going to avoid a big crash, he needs some time alone with his dog, his pool, and his gaming systems."

"Ah. That makes sense."

Once we're in the car, Allie says, "Mind if I turn on some Christmas music?"

"Please do."

We drive around, singing along with Allie's Christmas Oldies playlist. After about forty-five minutes, we've driven down every street in Sterling Grove—several of them twice. It's still spitting snow, but I'm not sure whether it's snowing more or only looks like more due to the headlights. "Feel up for some cocoa?"

"I'm *always* up for some cocoa."

The barista greets us both by name, and when I reply with, "Hi, Josie," I momentarily question whether I've developed a hot cocoa addiction. We pick a booth, and when our order is ready, I collect two butterscotch cocoas topped with whipped cream and crushed butterscotch candy sprinkles.

"You know when we were in the blanket fort, admiring our handiwork with the lights?" Allie asks as I slide into the booth opposite her.

"Mm-hmm. Oh, I forgot to ask. How did the kids like it?"

"It was a huge hit. They played down there all day."

She drags her bamboo spoon through the crushed-candy-topped whip on her cocoa and pops it in her mouth, closing her eyes a moment as she savors it.

"But back to when we were in the blanket fort," she says. "Before you fell asleep, I kind of thought you were going to, you know, make a move."

"You mean like—" I inhale through my nose and then exhale. Does she mean . . .? "What kind of move?" I take a sip of my cocoa, trying to be cool.

"What kind of—" Allie's singular laugh is somewhere near a squeak and a snort. "Right. You haven't dated anyone in a while. Let me explain."

Allie presses her palms to the table and sits up straight, studying me with a spark in her eye that seems like it's either trouble or fun. Maybe both.

I take another sip of cocoa.

"Hmm. How do I explain . . ." She joins her splayed palms in front of her face and taps her fingers together. "Okay, it's like this. Sometimes, when a man and a woman like each other, or find each other physically attractive, they experience certain natural . . . *urges*."

I choke on my cocoa and sputter into my mug, sending a froth of whip over the rim and onto the table.

Allie cackles, tipping her head back with a hoot. "Oh my gosh. Your face." Still laughing, she reaches for a handful of napkins to help wipe up my mess. "I'm kidding about the urges. It's a real thing, of course. Basic sex ed. Unless . . ." She snorts. "Wow. You may need more of a dating refresher course than I am qualified to present. Ha!"

"I . . . er . . ."

"Relax. Forget I said that last part. What I meant—before I went way off track, that is—is that I really did think you were going to kiss me in the blanket fort. Just kiss me. That's all." She laughs again but then sobers. "And just for the record, I was okay with that idea."

She was? Does that mean . . .?

Could Allie's feelings for me be growing in the same direction mine have grown toward her?

Chapter 30

Allie

If the deer-in-the-headlights look on Grant's face is any indication of how much I should not have brought up the-kiss-that-wasn't, perhaps I should not have brought it up.

"Relax," I say again, hoping I've managed a soothing tone, because this is not going at all how I thought it would. "You don't have to kiss me, Grant. It's okay."

How can I salvage the conversation?

I have no idea.

Might as well dive back in.

"Since I don't recall anything about, you know, kissing and stuff, from your very thorough multimedia presentation," I begin, "and, well . . . since kissing is generally an accepted—and frankly, sometimes expected—dating practice, I just thought I'd put it out there. Unless . . ." I pause "Shoot. Was that on one of those slides I didn't get to see?"

"No, I didn't make a slide about kissing, or anything like that. It didn't occur to me." Grant offers a wobbly smile. "As noted, I've been out of the dating game for a while. But I've apparently been in the obtuse nerd game for far too long."

Oh . . . I get it. Duh.

Grant is apprehensive about kissing me because it's been so long since he's kissed *anyone*. He's probably worried that he doesn't remember how. Oh, how precious. How utterly sweet. Oh, this guy. My adorable, spreadsheet-loving winter boyfriend is afraid he's not a good kisser.

I've had so much fun with Grant this winter. He's checked so many items off my romantic wintertime dates list. But from Grant's perspective, this winter boyfriend thing was supposed to serve as a dating refresher course. Can I claim I've held up my end of the bargain if I send him out to find the future Mrs. Covington with rusty kissing skills?

No, I cannot.

Put me in, coach. I'm ready to play.

Wait. In this scenario, I'm the coach.

I may have to ease my soon-to-be star player into it, though.

"Let's say you've been dating again for a while and dating the same woman exclusively for six weeks. You with me?"

He nods.

"Do you think you would have kissed her by that point?"

He takes a deep breath and stares down at his cocoa. "I would certainly hope so."

"So six weeks is an acceptable amount of time for you to feel comfortable enough to kiss your girlfriend?"

"More than enough."

"You've been dating me for roughly six weeks. Do you feel uncomfortable around me?"

"No. It's not that." He presses the heel of his hand to his forehead for a moment and then reaches for his mug but doesn't take a drink. "If I would've thought to make a slide about this sort of thing back in the beginning, we could have established how we wanted to handle . . . that. Set up some expectations." His eyes meet mine and go wide. "No, not expectations. Gross. That sounds entitled. Sorry. Boundaries. I meant boundaries."

"I know what you meant. But since we didn't have that conversation back then"—I reach across the table to rest my hand on top of his—"we could just talk about it now."

"Sure. Go for the mature adult option." He takes a deep breath through a wobbly smile. "Okay. Let's talk about it."

"Cool. Here's my hot take. If you want to kiss me, you can kiss me."

He blinks at me. "And?"

"And nothing." I shrug. "I like you. I'm attracted to you." And I am soooo freaking curious to find out if Grant is as amazing at kissing as I think he might be. "Correct me if I'm wrong, but I think you kinda like me too."

"I do like you, Allie." His vigorous nod is short-lived. "So much. Obviously, I'm attracted to you. Everything about you."

Oh. Wow. The way he said that. So earnestly. Almost reverently.

"Thank you." Am I blushing? I think I'm blushing. *Stop it, skin.* "But consent goes both ways. Let's say I want to kiss you. Should I?"

"Absolutely."

Whoa. My guy was quick with that answer. Interesting. Does that mean he needs me to make the first move? Fine. I can do that. Maybe that will help me feel like I'm holding up my end of our deal a little more. Dating refresher course achievement . . . unlocked.

"See how easy-peasy that was? Now, if, at some point before January first,"—I wrinkle my nose at our expiration date—"one of us decides to make a move, we can know both of us are cool with—"

Grant slides out of the booth and to his feet so abruptly that a wave of cocoa and whip sloshes out of both mugs.

Grant pulls his wallet out of his back pocket and drops a few bills on the table, only to swipe them back up. "What a mess." He replaces the singles with a twenty-dollar bill. "I'm going to order two more of those"—he gestures to our mugs—"but in to-go cups. Then, I'm going to take you—the woman I've been dating for six weeks and counting—for a romantic walk in the snow. Be right back."

"It's still snowing?" I scoot to the edge of the booth and peer over toward the wide front windows. "Oh my gosh! It is." It's even starting to stick a little bit.

I skip off to the ladies' room while Grant orders our cocoas. After washing my hands, I breathe into my hand and take a quick sniff to check my breath. I think

I catch a pleasant hint of butterscotch but, thankfully, no noticeable French onion soup.

Our to-go cups sit on a dry corner of the table where Grant stands, wearing his coat and holding mine. As we step out into the light snowfall, I take a sip and then lick my lips, hoping to leave a little bit of that butterscotch behind. As soon as the opportunity presents itself, I intend to transfer a bit of that sweetness to my winter boyfriend's lips and help boost his dating confidence.

Chapter 31

Grant

With my right hand holding my cup and the fingers of my left hand interwoven with Allie's—or as interwoven as they can be when both people are wearing gloves—I stroll down Maple Boulevard, trying not to be too obvious as I check every lamppost and doorway for mistletoe. Truth be told, I don't actually know what I'm looking for. It's probably green and probably hung in a way meant to create a place for a couple to kiss. I assume.

Maple Boulevard paints a picturesque scene, perfect for a romantic walk in the snow. A wide strip of grass, at least as wide as each stretch of pavement to either side of it, separates the traffic paths through Sterling Grove's business district. Within it, mature maple trees share the grassy space with paved crosswalk paths, decorative lamposts, and the occasional bench. It's a bit like having a long, narrow park dividing the street into halves.

There aren't very many people out, which isn't surprising for 7:30 on a small-town Thursday night. Besides the pub and the cocoa shop, there are still lights on in the hardware store and the hair salon, where two of the three salon chairs support foil-headed women and what looks like a lively conversation. The sign over the storefront windows says *Me-ow! Beauty Studio*.

"That's where I get my hair done," Allie says, nodding toward the salon.

"Do they also do pet grooming?"

She laughs. "You wouldn't be the first to ask, but no. It's a play on the owner's name, Caterina Payne. She goes by Cat."

"Clever." Though it would probably suit a pet groomer better.

A closed sign is evident in the floral shop's window, but there's movement in the back.

"Oh, there's Bill." Allie points her cup toward the hardware store. "Looks like he's closing up a little early." She chuckles. "He must be heading over to Paula's place. You go, Romeo."

Ah, so that's the famous ceiling fan man I keep hearing about at the cocoa club meetings.

Both sides of the boulevard are decorated with an abundance of white lights, wreaths, and other various holiday decor items, but even though the street is well-lit, I don't see anything resembling mistletoe.

According to nearly all the small-town Christmas romance movies I've seen, there should be random sprigs of mistletoe in oh-so-convenient places, ready as needed. Did Sterling Grove not get the memo? I'm trying to do a thing here. A romantic thing. But can I locate the one thing I need to give Allie—who seems to be moving toward the idea of us being more than just a wintertime couple—the Christmas movie kiss she deserves?

No, I cannot.

I look over at Allie. Snowflakes dot her bright pink stocking cap and rest on her hair. She closes her eyes, takes a deep breath in through her nose, and then looks up at me as she exhales.

Enchanting.

After another short block, Maple Boulevard turns into an undivided residential street. We cross at the intersection and head back down the other side of the boulevard. Maybe the businesses on this side will prove those Christmas movies right.

A block or so ahead of us, a woman stands waiting as her dog sniffs around the base of a lampost.

Still no mistletoe.

"Everything okay?" Allie asks a few strides later.

"Yes." I pause. "Why do you ask?"

"You were scowling pretty hard at that office. Did that company raise your car insurance rates or something?"

"No, they just disappointed me." I let out a long sigh. "In fact, every storefront we've passed has disappointed me."

Allie stops walking, and when I turn her way, her expression moves from shock to something like offense. "I know Sterling Grove isn't as fancy as some places, but I think we do pretty well with what we have." She pulls her hand from my grasp and looks away. "I'm sorry if my town doesn't live up to your stan—"

"Hey," I interrupt her. "Sterling Grove is great. I wasn't insulting the town. The thing is, all those Christmas movies we've watched have implied that mistletoe would appear when—and where—we needed it. Now I need it, but not one of these stores bothered to include it in their holiday decor."

A slow smile dawns on Allie's face. "Here. Hold my cocoa for a sec."

I take it.

"Okay, now turn toward the street."

I comply.

"Don't move."

After a few rustling noises, she emits a little "oof" grunt. "Okay, set the cups down on the ground and then turn around."

I do as instructed to find Allie standing just beneath a recessed doorway, dangling a glittery star over her head.

"Did you pull that off a wreath?"

"I'll put it back in a minute," she says. "It's fine. Buck's an old softy. He won't mind."

"Buck?"

"Herb Buckley. His friends call him Buck." She points up to the illumined sign above the window that proclaims this to be the office of Herbert Buckley, Attorney-at-Law.

"And you, of course, are his friend."

"Of course. I've had two—no, three of his grandchildren go through my class." She wiggles the glittery star. "My arm's getting kind of tired, Grant. I know it may not look like mistletoe, but if you're willing to tap into the holiday spirit corner of your imagination, we could pretend."

I take a step closer. And then another, until I'm looking down into her eyes. I reach up and wrap my hand around the hand holding the star and bring it between us. With my other hand, I trace the curve from her forehead to her jaw, trying to ignore the wave of nervous energy coursing through my blood.

"I've wanted to kiss you for a while now," I whisper. "But I didn't know if you—"

Allie rises on her tiptoes and pulls my face toward hers. My breath catches. I'm not sure if it's Allie or me who closes that final millimeter between us, but one electric breath of a moment later, her lips are pressed against mine.

Our heads tilt perfectly, like they know what to do without an awkward attempt to choreograph the movement. I pull her closer. My shoulders drop, and all tension seeps away as something deep within me relaxes.

In my arms, Allie softens, fitting against me like she was molded for that purpose. Our kiss is gentle, but not tentative. It's warm and sweet, and it feels like . . . home.

As our lips slowly separate, Allie rests her head in that space between my shoulder and my neck. "That was nice." Her sigh sounds more contented than surprised.

As first kisses go, I'd say it was better than nice.

It was perfect.

Chapter 32

ALLIE

As we stroll back toward where Grant parked his SUV near the pub, I keep stealing glances at him, only to have to hold back my giggles at his ever-widening I-just-conquered-the-world grin.

If my neighbor Dennis had written our first kiss with his Rosalie romance hat on, he'd accurately describe it as "sweet with promise" or something like that. That first kiss was closely followed by kisses two and three, which were every bit as sweet and tender. To look at Grant's jubilant smile now, though, you'd think he'd just rounded the bases for his first home run.

He squeezes my hand. "Want to cut across the grass?"

"Sure."

We're standing on the brown grass of the boulevard's wide, park-like median, positioned between two bare maple trees, when Grant stops and turns. "Have I mentioned how utterly enchanting you look, all dusted with snow?"

"No, but I'll accept that compliment." I brush a few snowflakes from the lapel of his wool coat. "I don't think I've ever been called 'enchanting' before. But I have to give a little credit to the atmosphere because it set me up with a good backdrop." I aim my face toward the bare branches above, enjoying the feeling of tiny snowflakes whispering wonder down on my face. "Tonight has been the definition of a perfect wintertime date," I say. "Thank you, Grant."

"It's not over yet." He reaches inside his coat. "One sec."

And then he pulls out his phone and starts scrolling.

Um, *what?*

"There it is," he says, finally. "Hang on. I need to turn the volume up."

He slides the phone back inside his coat just as the music starts playing, and a man's voice speaks some sort of old-timey-sounding intro.

"Is that . . .?" The voice is so familiar, but I can't quite place it.

"Bing Crosby," Grant supplies.

"The king of Christmas music."

"He is that. But this isn't exactly a Christmas song. I hope that's okay." He holds out his hand. "Allie, would you dance with me?"

There's a sharp intake of breath, and it was me who made the sound. "Grant Covington, are you asking me to dance with you in the falling snow?"

"I am. But it's kind of a short song, so . . ."

I slip my hand into his. He rests his other hand on the small of my back, pulling me close. I tuck my head between his shoulder and chin, our clasped hands resting at his chest, over his heart.

As we begin to sway, I sigh. The pure romance of this snowy, spontaneous moment is bliss.

And that it was Grant who initiated it? Even better.

The music is a bit muffled, pressed between us as it is, but not too badly. "I don't think I know this song," I say after a minute or so of swaying to the soft, slow rhythm.

"It's called 'A Kiss to Build a Dream On,'" Grant says. "When we were little, my sister and I would spend two weeks every summer with our grandparents in Minnesota. Every night, my grandma would sing us to sleep with songs that weren't necessarily lullabies but worked just as well. This was one of her favorites."

"Awww." It's a sweet story about a sweet song, both of which are absolutely on-brand for my sweet winter boyfriend.

Grant presses a kiss to my hair, and I tilt my face up. His lips melt into mine.

This kiss is different than before. Still soft, but something about it seems more confident. When the kiss deepens, it happens so naturally that I don't realize we've unclasped our hands until my hat falls off from the movement of his fingers through my hair.

Our lips separate just long enough for me to catch a glimpse of something fiery and somehow raw in Grant's eyes before we crash together again.

Delicious warmth surges through my veins. My back meets the trunk of a tree, and I reflexively bunch his coat in my fists.

Ohh. Oh, my.

This. Man. Can. *Kiss.*

My hands slide up toward his shoulders; his hands are in my hair as he presses ever closer.

The best kind of dizziness sparkles across my brain and then travels through every inch of my body. I grab a fresh handful of his coat—not necessarily to stay upright, but also maybe to stay upright?—because if Grant let me go right now, I would collapse into the snow. No question.

His lips trail across my cheek and then down my jawbone to my throat. A little gasp escapes me.

He pulls away. "Too much?" His breathless voice carries a trace of worry. "Am I moving too fast?"

"Oh, heck to the no," I say, my own voice lacking air.

His lips find mine again, but softer now.

"Oh, my goodness!" A woman's stark surprise breaks through my bliss. "Good heavens."

My stomach jumps like I'm a teenager caught in the backseat of my boyfriend's car. I peek around Grant to see a woman standing, frozen in place as her little dog squats a few yards away doing his business.

"Oh hey, Norma," I say, unable to suppress a little giggle.

"Allie? Oh, hello. And— Of course. Mr. Covington. Yes. Well. My, my. My goodness." Her eyes dart back between us. "This is . . . something, running into you two kids."

"Sure is," I reply. "Beautiful night, isn't it?"

She glances at her dog and then pulls a little plastic bag out of her pocket. "So sorry to have interrupted your, uh, evening." She picks up what her dog left behind and ties the bag closed. "We'll be off and just let you get back to your . . . uh— Bye!"

Norma scoops up her dog and practically jogs away.

Chapter 33

GRANT

Allie giggles all the way back to the car, even snorting a couple of times. I'm glad she's taking it so well, but I am mortified. I'm not sure if it's due to being caught making out with my girlfriend in a public space or from the realization that I just went from a romantic mistletoe moment to full-on make-out madness with Allie Hayes in under five minutes. In public.

If Norma's interruption wasn't the vocal equivalent of a cold shower, I'm not sure what would be.

On the short drive back to her house, my brain runs laps around a bucket of self-reproach.

In her driveway, I shift into park. "Allie, I owe you an apology."

Her head swivels to face me, and she wrinkles her nose. "What for?"

"I think I may have let things get out of hand back there. I'm not a public displays of affection kind of guy, and—"

"Could've fooled me." She smirks. "Sorry, go ahead."

"Er, uh, yeah. What I'm trying to say is that it wasn't my intent to maul you. I guess I got carried away and turned what was supposed to be a romantic walk in the snow into . . . whatever that was."

"You don't hear me complaining, do you? Shake it off, my guy. It was just Norma. It's fine."

Maybe I'm making too much of this. Allie is my girlfriend, and we are adults.

"Hey, do you want to come in? We could find a cheesy Christmas movie to stream. Unless you need to get home. I can sleep in in the morning, but you probably have to get up for work."

I glance at the dashboard clock. It's only a quarter to nine. "If I'm on the road by eleven, I'll be fine."

As soon as we're inside, Allie runs to her room to put her phone on the charger. By the time I've hung up my coat and scarf, she's plopped down on the blue velvet sofa—a plush, vintage piece she says she found in a thrift shop in college and had to buy because, in her words, "They don't make 'em like they used to." She must be right, because it somehow looks almost new. And totally Allie, thanks to the collection of bright, jewel-toned pillows she's layered on it.

She tosses a pink pillow to the floor and pats the spot beside her. "Take a load off."

After a little bit of scrolling through Christmas categories, we land on a made-for-TV movie featuring a rich and beautiful vineyard owner destined to fall in love with a handsome, down-on-his-luck dairy farmer who is trying to market his farm-to-table cheeses for wine-tasting events. Since it promises both literal and figurative cheese, we decide it's perfect.

Between the dialogue, the over-acting, and the set backdrops of a clearly fake vineyard, it is *so far* from perfect—which is exactly what *makes* it perfect. We have to pause it several times because our commentary on the movie is so much better than the movie itself, and we scroll backward to replay the worst bits just to laugh at them again. By the time we reach the end, we've snort-laughed at dozens of melodramatic longing glances, cringe-worthy lines, and the oh-so-predictable "surprise" snow on Christmas Eve.

As the credits roll, the corner of the screen lights up with a recommendation for something called *Twelve Drummers Drumming: a Christmas Band Camp Romance.*

"Oh, this I've gotta see." Allie clicks it, but then presses pause. "Unless . . . are you all cheesed out?"

"Not even close. Let's do it."

"A movie title like that requires popcorn. If only to have something to throw at the TV as necessary. Do you prefer your corn with or without Milk Duds?"

"With, of course."

"Grant Covington, you are a man after my own heart."

"And to think, I could have just shown up with Milk Duds and skipped all that pesky dating stuff."

"What can I say?" She stands up. "I'm a simple woman. Be right back."

Being with Allie is so comfortable. So easy.

Too easy, maybe, if my earlier public performance is any indication. But since Allie doesn't seem concerned about it, maybe I should take her advice and shake it off.

At least she knows where I stand. And which direction I'm falling.

On her.

No, not on her, *for* her. I'm falling *for* her.

I am so glad I did not say that aloud. *Wow, Covington. Just . . . wow.*

I drop my head into my hands and groan. These cheesy movies must be melting my brain.

On the coffee table, my phone lights up with a notification. When I glance over, I see it's from the office—a reminder about next week's staff holiday party—but the bigger numbers above that notification steal my attention. How did it get to be so late?

It's almost midnight. I still have to drive an hour home and then be at work at eight tomorrow morning. As much as I want to stay, I need to go.

I head to the kitchen where Allie has just set a bag of kernels in the microwave. "Time got away from me. I should probably take off."

She glances at the microwave clock. "Oh, shoot. You wanted to leave by eleven."

"Could we put that movie on the watchlist and save it for another night?"

"You bet."

I put on my coat, and as I'm sliding on my gloves, I remember my phone is still on the coffee table. I go grab it, which reminds me of the email notification from work.

"Are we still on for the company holiday party next week?"

"You'd better believe it." She comes over and tugs the lapels of my coat. "I wouldn't dream of missing the Iverson-Forsyth Architectural Associates party. Where else will I get a chance to see paper chains made out of strips cut from old spreadsheets?"

"Hardy har har." I kiss her cheek. "Can I call you tomorrow?"

"You'd better." She rises to her tiptoes to press a quick kiss to my lips. "Text me when you're safely home, okay?"

"Will do. Do you want to hang out tomorrow night? I could bring some Chinese takeout, if that sounds good."

"I dunno. Hmm." She wrinkles her nose and twists her lips sideways. "I'll need to check my schedule."

Not where I saw that going. "I don't want to suffocate you or anything, so if you need a breather, that's fine."

"I'm kidding." She jabs my bicep with her fist. "It's winter break, my guy. I have no schedule. Chinese takeout sounds divine. Now get out of here before you turn into a pumpkin or whatever."

I step out onto her porch, and a blast of cold air hits me. I bet the temperature has dropped a good fifteen or twenty degrees since we took our walk. As I reach the steps, I glance back to where Allie is standing in the open doorway. The warm glow of her home creates a full-body halo around her, like pixie dust around a Christmas fairy.

When this whole thing started, it never occurred to me that I might fall for her. But here we are. "Even out of the snow, you're still enchanting."

She laughs and shakes her head. "Get outta here, Casanova."

As I step out from under the porch roof, snow—no, sleet—hits my face. It stings a little. A moment later, my feet fly out from under me. My back hits the sidewalk, knocking the breath from my lungs.

"Grant! Oh my gosh. Are you—"

A squealed "Eeep!" later, the breath I've just recovered is knocked out of me again when Allie lands on top of me.

Both groaning, we try to get up but slip and fall back down. I roll off the sidewalk into the crunchy, ice-covered grass, pulling her with me.

Struggling to our knees, we face each other, blinking sleet out of our eyes.

"Well, that was something," she says. "I totally forgot there was freezing rain in the overnight forecast."

I didn't know there was, but I should have. "I could have sworn my shoes crunched on rock salt on our way to your door earlier."

"Yeah, Dennis tossed some out for me. Ow! This stings." She wipes at her face. "I guess either it wasn't enough, or maybe this stuff has been coming down hard for quite a while."

"I'm going with the second one."

Allie shivers. "Think we can make it up the steps without cracking our skulls open?"

I glance over at my car. The streetlight reveals a glaze of ice. "I'll help you back in and then remote start my car, but as soon as the windshield's clear, I should get go—"

"Oh no you don't. Do not even suggest you could drive home in this, Grant Covington," she says, full-on teacher voice in effect.

"I have four-wheel drive." I blink the stinging sleet from my eyes.

"Which means absolutely bupkis on ice, you stubborn man."

She's not wrong.

"Accept facts, Grant. You're staying over tonight."

Chapter 34

ALLIE

It's only 6:15 a.m., and even though I don't have to go to work today, there's no going back to sleep for me. Not when my winter boyfriend is sleeping just down the hall.

Or is he? Did he already get up and drive home so he could get to work on time?

Surely not. As bad as it was icing up last night, there's no way the roads are clear yet.

I pad to my squeaky bedroom door and open it as quietly as I can. A peek down the hall reveals the guest bedroom door is still closed. Unfortunately, that does not answer my question. I tiptoe out to the living room and hazard a glance out the window.

The sun hasn't risen yet, but the world is bright with freshly fallen—and still falling—snow. At some point during the few hours I slept, the freezing rain and sleet transformed the world into a beautiful, magical snow globe.

Light from a streetlight dances through the falling confetti. No footprints have yet marred the marshmallow perfection, and Grant's SUV is still in the driveway, looking almost like an oversized wedding cake, frosted white and sprinkled with diamond dust sugar.

He's still here. Good.

And also . . . weird.

In the eight years I've lived in this town, the only men to sleep over have been my brothers and my dad. I know I'm almost thirty years old, but it still feels a little naughty that Grant stayed over. I won't deny that was one WOWEE-WOW-WOW kissing session we had on the boulevard, but nothing particularly 'naughty' happened last night, regardless of how our PDA shocked poor Norma. Right after we struggled back up the icy steps and into the house, I offered him some shorts Adam left in my dryer the last time he was here and showed him to the guest room. Where he still is.

I take a quick shower, brush my teeth, and get dressed in appropriate snow-day attire: black leggings and an oversized, fleece-lined sweatshirt. As my stomach growls for sustenance, I make a quick rummage through the linen closet in search of the little plastic bag the dentist sent home with me from my checkup a few weeks ago. *A-ha!* Found it. I remove the still-in-the-packaging toothbrush, toothpaste, and floss and set them on top of a fresh towel and washcloth on the bathroom counter, all ready for Grant when he wakes up.

But what will he wear? The same clothes as last night? Or will he stay in the clothes he slept in?

I open my closet and stare at the contents, wondering if anything of mine will work for him.

Doubtful.

When my gaze lands on some bright green boots, however, inspiration rings giant jingle bells in my brain. With a silent giggle or three, I lift up the panel to the crawl space, climb down, and dig through a storage tote. Soon, I'm back up the ladder and laying clothes out on the bathroom counter next to the other items.

Still giggling a little, I head to the kitchen to make myself a cup of hot lemon water and some toast.

While my bread is toasting, I retrieve my phone from the charger to engage in some mindless scrolling until Grant appears. But my mind keeps wandering to those kisses on the boulevard last night, and it's all I can do not to wake him up for a live reenactment.

I take my toast and lemon water to the living room and position myself by the window. As the rising sun dances across the snow, the world takes on a beautiful, pinkish-orange glow.

A door creaks down the hall. Grant's awake.

When Grant walks into the living room, with Adam's shorts hanging low on his waist, his abs are on full display. I have to stop myself from counting them. Reluctantly, I lift my gaze.

Grant's dark brown hair is sleep-mussed, and my mouth is suddenly dry. That feeling of being caught doing something naughty returns, heating my collar and erasing all other thoughts from my mind.

"Good morning." The low, subtle gravel of his morning voice makes me melt a little more.

"Good . . . morning." I have to swallow, because this man is as smokin' hot as the devil's front porch.

"My boss texted early this morning. The office is closed due to the weather. I checked the highway patrol website, and it looks like pretty much every road in this half of the state is 75-100% covered."

"And it's still snowing." I nod toward the window.

"Yeah." He runs a hand through his hair. "My weather app says high winds are supposed to move in before noon."

"It's gonna drift. Big time."

"Sounds like it. I don't want to impose, but . . . I think you may be stuck with me until tomorrow."

"You say stuck, but I call it the perfect opportunity to watch that Christmas band camp movie." I rise from my chair and give him a good morning hug. "You're welcome to stay as long as you need." His arms encircle my back, and he pulls me in close until my face rests just above one of those sculpted pecs of his. I sigh. "Dang, boy. I could get used to this."

But I won't. I can't. The timer on this relationship is counting down.

He pulls me in tighter.

Would it hurt if I let myself enjoy it while it lasts, though? Nah.

I mean . . . maybe?

I drop my arms, and he releases me.

I step back. "I laid out a towel, some toiletries, and some, uh,"—I try to keep a straight face—"fresh clothes for you. They're on the bathroom counter."

"Awesome. Thanks."

"Do you want me to make you some coffee?"

"Yes, please." Relief rides on his tone. "Wait. You have a coffee maker? I thought you didn't drink coffee."

"I don't. The French Press is one of many things I keep on hand for my brother's visits. Trust me, Adam needs his morning coffee, and he's super picky about it. I'll get a pot started now." I turn away but blow Grant a kiss over my shoulder.

He pretends to catch it.

I laugh. "Get out of here, nerd."

As I get the coffee started, I try to remember what he took from the huge breakfast buffet my mom prepared last Sunday. Just to cover my bases, I scramble two eggs, make some toast, and set out some butter and a couple of different flavors of fruit spread. By the time that's finished, I hear the shower stop.

I warm up my lemon water in the microwave and sit down at the kitchen table to scroll while I await Grant's reappearance.

When he finally returns, I look up from my phone . . . and burst out laughing.

Grant is wearing the flash mob costume I left in the bathroom; the same one he wore on Black Friday and then had dry-cleaned before returning it to me. He looks deliciously, ridiculously festive right now, and his grin is the absolute personification of flirtatious holiday cheer.

This is shaping up to be the best snow-in ever.

Chapter 35

GRANT

After breakfast, Allie searches the internet for a hot cocoa recipe. The one we end up making fills an entire slow-cooker, giving us an excuse for all-day refills. As it simmers, we putter around in the kitchen mixing up a big batch of cookies to go with it.

Allie is so easy to be with. Even when our conversation pauses, it's without tension. This relationship has turned into quite a surprise.

When I proposed the winter boyfriend idea to her all those weeks ago, I saw her as the furthest thing from what I hoped to find in a partner for Phase II and beyond. But now that I've gotten to know her, it's hard to imagine anyone else could measure up.

We play cards while the cookies bake, after which Allie puts on her flash mob costume so we match and, with the help of some YouTube tutorials, we learn a couple of new line dances, and then try learning a basic Foxtrot.

We're not half-bad at it. In fact, we're a pretty good pair.

When the wind picks up, as predicted, I suggest we light a fire and gather some candles and flashlights. With the amount of ice on the trees, a few strong gusts could take out some powerlines.

"Were you a Boy Scout?" she asks, and I decide her laugh is my favorite sound.

"No, but I'm a lifelong Midwesterner, and I like to be prepared."

Later, as we're snuggled under a blanket fort watching a couple of nerdy trombone players get makeovers meant to—hopefully—make the studs in the drumline fall in love with them, the lights flicker twice and then go out.

"Oh no!" Allie whines. "How will I be able to sleep tonight without knowing if Margo and Jenny's new flat-ironed hairdos made their Christmas Band Camp dreams come true?"

"Right?" I agree, laughing.

"You have to admit, though," she says, "as ridiculous as the storyline is, the acting isn't half bad. The only time I threw popcorn at the screen was when that bonehead with the big bass drum took Margo's trombone and then emptied the spit valve on her head."

"Same. That bonehead deserved it. But I have a feeling he'll get what's coming to him."

"Yeah. It's that kind of movie, for sure."

When Allie rolls onto her side, I can't stop myself from pulling her close.

"I knew you'd be a world-class cuddler." She snuggles into me. "Good call on the fire, by the way. Hopefully, the power won't be off too long."

The power comes back on before midnight, and we're relieved to learn the bonehead bass drummer does, indeed, get what's coming to him. Meanwhile, Margo and Jenny realize they're too good for the cocky drumline guys and end up falling for a pair of nerdy-but-sweet tuba players. No further popcorn is thrown at the screen.

By the next morning, the wind has given way to bright sunshine in a clear blue sky. We suit up and spend the morning uncovering my car and shoveling Allie's driveway. While Allie digs around in her garage for some rock salt, I shovel her neighbor's sidewalk and drive. He invites us over for lunch.

Dennis Rose makes a mean pot of chili, and he's an excellent conversationalist. I can see why Allie likes him so much.

Allie's quiet, letting Dennis and I get acquainted. He's an animated storyteller, and it's no surprise he's been a writer of one sort or another his whole adult life. Every once in a while, I catch Allie watching me, biting her bottom lip on one side. I've never seen her do that before, but . . . it's cute.

Around two o'clock, we head back to her place. When I check the highway patrol's website, it says the roads are clear enough for travel. It's been an idyllic couple of days being snowed in with Allie, but it's probably time for me to go home.

With my coat on, I pull her into my arms. "Pack a bag and come with me to my parent's house tonight," I say into her hair. "Tomorrow is Christmas Eve. I hate the thought of you being alone for Christmas."

"I know turnabout is fair play," she says, dropping her arms. "But if not for the gala, you wouldn't have had to meet my family. There's no good reason for me to butt into the Covington holiday bash."

I let go of her and step back. "I want them to meet you."

"I . . ." She bites the side of her bottom lip. At Dennis's house, I thought it was just one more adorable Allie quirk, but here, now, it's registering more like discomfort. "Why would they want to meet me?"

"Because you're my girlfriend?" I didn't mean to phrase it as a question, but that's how it lands.

"Only for another week, give or take. And then you're on to Phase II, remember?"

I open my mouth, but no sound comes out.

I thought we were on the same page. I assumed our expiration date was a thing of the past. I thought—

"Besides," she continues, as if she didn't just pull a rug out from under me, "Jackson texted this morning. I guess the pipes froze at his uncle's place last night. They had to send everybody home. He's coming here instead. I won't be alone. No worries."

"Oh. Well, that's . . . good."

Maybe we're okay. Maybe this is just about her spending Christmas with her stepbrother.

"For the record, I enjoyed meeting your family." I hope she doesn't think otherwise. "And I think you'd get along really well with mine."

Allie's brow furrows, and something in her posture stiffens. "I'm sure they're great. But I told Jackson he could come, so . . ."

"I wasn't trying to pressure you or anything." Why does this feel so weird all of a sudden? "Sorry if it came off that way."

"Don't sweat it." Her stance relaxes. "Hey, don't forget to stop by Dennis's place on your way out. He was going to pack up some chili for you." She puts her hands in her pockets and rocks back on her heels. "I guess I'd better go strip the guest bed and get it ready for Jackson. Have fun with your family."

"I will. Thanks." That feels like a dismissal. I can take a hint. "Tell Jackson hello. We can hash out the details about the office party after Christmas."

"Sounds good. Drive safe, okay?"

I give her a quick kiss—on the cheek, because that's where my lips land when she turns her head—and then take my leave.

"Don't forget the chili from Dennis," she hollers out the door when I'm almost to the driveway.

I pause. "Since I'm going to my mom and dad's place tonight right after I get packed at home, it probably won't get eaten. Why don't you and Jackson enjoy it."

"Are you sure?"

"Positive. Tell Dennis thanks for me though, okay?"

"Will do. Drive safe."

And with that, she goes back in her house, shutting the door behind her.

What. Just. Happened?

Chapter 36

ALLIE

Inside my house, I lean my back against the front door, waiting for the crunch of Grant's tires to announce that he's finally leaving. When the sound comes, a deep exhalation deflates my body, like one of those Santa inflatables that just got unplugged. I slide down the door until I'm sitting with my legs flat against the floor.

This morning, Grant and I shared kisses in the blanket fort we'd camped out in all night. We chatted about everything from past vacations to college memories to childhood friends, and I was fully at peace. But sometime between shoveling the sidewalk and taking that first bite of chili at Dennis's house, everything changed. Out of the blue, being cozy and comfortable with Grant started feeling . . . wrong.

No, that's not the correct word. It's more like I realized everything felt too *right*.

Shortly after we left our little snowed-in couple bubble, the danger of the warm and fuzzy feelings I too eagerly enjoyed these past two days slapped me upside the head.

It probably felt a little abrupt to Grant, but I had to take a step back—for his sake as much as mine. Grant's been super about going along with every random enthusiasm grenade I've thrown at him, but his tolerance armor must be paper thin by now.

Sure, Grant valiantly hung in there through the snow-in, and his desire to spend even more time with me felt utterly genuine. But I don't want to press my luck and risk his enjoyment of my company fizzling out before we reach our expiration date.

There may not be many days left before the new year rolls in and we go our separate ways, but there are plenty of fun wintery date occasions still possible within that short span.

For one, we finally have snow, which opens up a host of outdoor activities. It's kind of crunchy and pokey with that ice on top at present, but still: snow. Not to mention his firm's holiday party next week and New Year's Eve a couple of days after that.

If this were a conventional relationship, its days would be numbered already—if it was still even a thing—and I wouldn't care so much. But we're in the final stretch of what's been an amazing run. I can't risk his apparent affection for my wilder quirks turning into some form of agonizing endurance just yet.

Been there. Done that. Not fun.

To go from zero dating to dating someone like me had to have been a shock to Grant's system. And although that jolt probably provided a sweet *survive-or-die* adrenaline rush, he's been riding that high for weeks. He's surprisingly adept at navigating those surges, but he must be nearing his Allie-exhaustion point.

The sad thing about adrenaline rushes? Eventually, they end. At least for most people. And if my past relationships have taught me anything, it's that even Grant Covington can't avoid that inevitable crash.

I give myself a couple more minutes on the floor and then get up, dust myself off, and get to work stripping and remaking the guest bed to get it ready for Jackson. Once that's done, I disassemble the blanket fort, because I can only imagine Jackson's sassy implications, and I won't give him the opportunity.

About the time I'm finished with that, I check my phone, only to find that I received a text from Jackson several hours ago. Apparently, his grandparents offered their home in Madison for the family celebration, and so he's heading north instead. He doesn't need to come to my house for Christmas after all.

Figures. And after I'd already turned down an invitation to spend Christmas with Grant.

No. Bad Allie. If I intend to exit this relationship with the same good vibes we've had all along, declining Grant's invitation was the right thing to do. I'll be fine on my own. I have five streaming services, a ton of cookies, and I can always whip up another big batch of that hot chocolate Grant and I demolished yesterday. I'll be fine.

Mmm. A cup of hot cocoa sounds good right now. Cocoa made by a professional, however, sounds even better. Maybe I'll see if Dennis is up for a trip to Cocoa & Froth this evening. That would help me pass a little of the time I thought I'd be with Jackson. I need to go get that chili, anyway.

I throw some cookies in a baggie and then put on my coat and boots to head next door.

"Well, hello neighbor!" When Dennis greets me at the door, he's wearing his coat and holding his keys.

I hold up the baggie. "I brought you some cookies. Grant is on his way to his family Christmas, and he didn't want your chili getting lost in the shuffle and not eaten. But if you're still looking for someone to take it off your hands . . ."

"You're more than welcome to it." Dennis chuckles. "Why didn't you go with him?"

"We're breaking up in just over a week, remember? I don't want to confuse the issue."

One of Dennis's eyebrows lifts. "For whom?"

"For everyone." I shrug. "Going to someone's family Christmas is kind of serious-relationship stuff, and we're not that. Definitely not that."

"Definitely, huh?" His eyes narrow, and then he nods. "I see. Did he invite you?"

"Yeah, of course. You know how nice he is."

"He does seem like a decent young man. Smart. Kind. You could do worse."

"Oh, and I totally have." I laugh. "Anyway, I thought maybe you'd be interested in going on a cocoa outing with me, but it looks like you've already got plans."

"Unfortunately." He nods. "The nursing home called, and it seems my mother is rather agitated today. They thought perhaps I could calm her down."

"Oh, I'm sorry." Dennis's mother is in her mid-90s and in the memory-care unit of a nursing home a couple of towns over. "Is there anything I can do?"

"Thanks, but no." He takes the baggie of cookies. "I bet she'll like these, though."

"Need more? Grant and I baked a huge batch yesterday. I was going to send some with him for his family, but I forgot. There's no way I can eat them all myself."

"Maybe tomorrow? I should probably get going. I'll grab that chili for you first, though."

He comes back a moment later with a sealed container filled with enough chili to feed me twice a day for the next three or four days.

"Yeesh, Dennis. Save some for yourself."

"Oh, I did. You know how hard it is for me to make a small batch of soup."

It's true. As soon as cooler weather arrives, I am a regular recipient of all kinds of "extra" soup. This is a lot, though. I may have to freeze some of it.

"I like Grant," he says, but something tentative rides on his words.

I nod. "What's not to like?"

"It was obvious he's rather fond of you."

"He's a gem like that."

"You're a gem too, Allie."

"If you want more cookies, just ask. You don't need to butter me up."

He doesn't laugh like I expect him to. Instead, he frowns. "Have you ever considered renegotiating your agreement? Why stop seeing Grant if you like him so much?"

"Oh, come on. Someone like Grant could never be happy with someone like me."

"Maybe you should let him decide that."

"We're too different. We both know it."

"I've heard it said that opposites attract."

"Says the romance novelist."

"I can't deny the charge." He smiles. "But the funny thing about that trope, my friend, is that the two people at its center generally come to realize that perhaps they're not as opposite as they once thought." He looks at his watch. "I would love to talk about this some more, but I really should get going. How about we plan to have a good, long chat over cocoa one day next week?"

"Sounds good. I hope things go okay with your mom."

As I walk back to my house, I make a mental note to come up with something other than my winter boyfriend to talk about when I meet Dennis for cocoa.

Chapter 37

GRANT

It's nearing eight o'clock when I finally arrive at my parents' house. After that drive home from Allie's, with my mind whirring at least as fast as my tires, I needed some time alone at home to process.

It wasn't enough, apparently. Within thirty minutes, my sister corners me.

"She broke up with you." Rae's statement is laced with a promise of vengeance.

"No." I shake my head. "We're still planning to date until New Year's."

Rae takes a step back and crosses her arms. She's nearly as tall as I am, and although we used to share the same hair color, she started dyeing hers a dark, cherry-red shade in law school and never went back. Her hair is almost as short as mine. She calls it a "pixie cut," but I don't think any fairy creature could pull off that style or color like Rae. It gives her a take-no-prisoners look that I imagine intimidates a whole lot of witnesses in court.

Especially when combined with the squinty, suspicious lawyer expression she's wearing right now.

"You texted Mom. You asked if you could bring your girlfriend," she says. "Girlfriend. Not winter girlfriend. Reportedly, you implied that the win-ter"—she makes air quotes—"part of your relationship was no longer in play. So?" Her chin tilts down, and her eyes narrow. "Where is she?"

I should have known Mom would tell Rae.

Yesterday, when replying to a text from my mom, I stupidly shared my excitement over what was, apparently, a major misinterpretation of relationship status.

"It's complicated."

"Oh, please." Her head tilts back until she faces the ceiling. "Not the 'it's complicated' thing. That's so ten years ago." She straightens. "What. Happened."

I wish I knew. "I guess I misread some signals."

"Like what?"

"Enough with the cross-examination, okay?" I huff out a breath, raking my fingers through my hair. "I don't know what happened. Everything seemed fine, and I felt like we were on the same page. And then she got kind of quiet, which is not like her, trust me. I didn't think much about it, though, until she reminded me that we're breaking up at the end of next week and then practically shoved me out the door."

Rae blinks a couple of times, looks off to the side, and then meets my gaze. "Sounds like she got spooked."

"Huh?"

"Either that or she was on the defensive."

"What do you mean?"

"You look like a big, dumb puppy when you tilt your head like that."

"I'm aware." Only because she's been telling me that most of my life.

"So . . . did you tell Allie how you feel?"

"I thought I'd made my feelings clear. I thought she felt the same. I mean, we—"

"But did you actually say the words?" Rae demands. "Did you say, 'Hey, girl. Let's dissolve the terms of our original agreement and keep dating into the new year' or anything like that?"

"Well, no. But I thought—"

"You can't think your feelings into somebody else's head, Grant."

"I know, but—"

Rae's husband crosses the room, looking ready to join the conversation. Good. I could use some backup.

"Maybe she's not the problem," Rae continues. "Maybe the problem, little brother, is *you*." She jabs a finger into my sternum. "I bet you dialed in to that infuriating verbal ineptitude so common among the males of our species and made Allie think you weren't actually into her."

I glance at Jamie. He raises his hands in surrender and silently backs away. Coward.

"I guess that's possible, but—"

"On the other hand," Rae says slowly, "it makes more sense that maybe you came on *too* strong and spooked her, as I said first." She frowns. "You really like her though, right? Like, a lot?"

"Yes."

"Do you think you might love her?"

"I don't know. Love is a big word." I rub a hand over the back of my neck. "Maybe not yet, but . . . I don't think it would take much to push me over that ledge."

"Alrighty then." Rae brushes her hands together like there are crumbs to remove from them. "Tomorrow is Christmas Eve, so counting that, I guess you've got . . . eight full days to figure out how you feel about this woman, tell her how you feel, and then give her a good reason to want to keep you around." She turns away, only to look over her shoulder and snap the back of her hand against my chest. "The clock's ticking, buddy. Figure it out."

Chapter 38

ALLIE

I know I made it kind of weird when Grant left after the big storm, but I think we're okay now.

He texted me a funny meme on Christmas Eve and followed it with several more, as well as a few pictures, on Christmas Day. He even sent me a photo of him wearing the footy pajamas his mom bought the whole family for Christmas.

So freaking adorable.

We texted quite a bit on Christmas Day. When I admitted that Jackson had canceled on me, Grant renewed the invitation to come to his parents' place but didn't push when I declined—which I appreciated. Instead, he told me he was off work the day after Christmas and asked if I'd be interested in playing racquetball with him at his gym.

I'd never played racquetball before, but . . . why not?

Initially, I worried that there might still be some tension between us, but those fears faded the moment he answered the door. Grant's sweet smile put me immediately at ease. But not even his patient tutelage could make me a passable raquetball player. My poor skills on the court made for some good laughs, however. After racquetball, we joined a drop-in yoga class—that man is full of surprises—and then grabbed some Chinese food to take back to his place.

Grant had to work the next day, so I didn't stay late.

The next evening, he showed up at my door with a bouquet of clear balloons filled with snowflake confetti and said, "Ready to have some fun?"

Who could refuse that?

After dinner at the pub, we tried—and mostly failed—to make snow angels. The snow that wasn't fluffy enough for angels, however, was perfect for packing and rolling. We built an impressive snowman and then had an impromptu snowball fight—that Grant instigated!—and ended our evening at Cocoa & Froth. It was our best date yet.

Grant is such a kind, considerate human. I shouldn't be surprised that he would ramp up his efforts now that we've almost reached the end of our wintertime dating arrangement. Still, every time my phone lights up, showing the date right beneath the time, it kind of knocks the wind out of me. We *are* nearing the end.

But we're good. It's all good. We have tonight plus two more evenings to spend together before the mysterious New Year's Eve date Grant has planned to, in his words, "*cap off our wintertime dating extravaganza and ring in a bright new year.*" It's gonna be a fantastic week.

January will probably suck, though.

Nope. I don't need to think about that right now. I need to get ready for tonight's date: the Iverson-Forsyth holiday party.

I want his bosses to see the fully realized human he's become—and know, without a doubt, that he is definite partnership material. When they see us together, I want them to notice the strides he's made toward getting that life his bosses require.

Luckily, I have the perfect outfit for the occasion.

Last summer, Adam flew me out for a visit, and I killed time exploring some of southern California's beachy areas while my brother was on set. One day, after walking down the Santa Monica Pier and riding the Ferris wheel a couple of times, I happened upon a high-end thrift shop. There, I found an amazing winter outfit they'd somehow missed when switching out their seasons. I tried it on.

Sold.

Now, as I'm slipping into the champagne sequin pencil skirt and its accompanying cream, off-one-shoulder cashmere sweater, I get another shot of the same feeling I got that day in Santa Monica; something Raquel and I refer to as "Thrifter's High."

The fit is perfection, and the materials? Straight-up luxury. Could I have afforded these designer duds when they were new? On a teacher's salary? Absolutely not. But could I force myself to eat forty-cent ramen packets for lunch for a week or two to buy them secondhand? Sure I could, if it justified spending eighty-five bucks on an amazing ensemble likely worn only once by someone who couldn't risk being seen in the same outfit twice.

And I did, even though I knew I might never get a chance to wear it. No regrets. But dang, am I glad to have it now. After meeting Grant's bosses and their wives at the fundraiser gala, this ensemble feels like exactly the right vibe for a party at the Iverson's lakeside home. I don't generally consider myself a vain person, but I might become so if I dressed like this every day.

A woman's face—and her ridiculously svelte figure—flashes across my mind, and I almost choke.

Shoot! I forgot about her. Will that Chelsea person from Grant's office be at the party tonight? Will she make bedroom eyes at him like she did at the gala and try to lay some groundwork to become Grant's next girlfriend?

She's ballsy enough to do it; I'll give her that. Even if she doesn't flirt with him tonight, I'd bet my shiny sequin pencil skirt that she'll be the first person to slide into his DMs when he wakes up single on New Year's Day.

Okay, maybe not this skirt, but I'd bet . . . my shoes. They're easier to replace.

Ha! As if Grant would go for someone like *Chelsea*. There's no way. Good luck, sister. You're not his type.

Or is she?

Nah.

In any case, he's mine for a few more days. Chelsea better keep her pointy manicured tips off my man tonight, or we're gonna have a prob—

Whoa there, Allie. Nope.

Nope, nope, nope. If Grant wants to date someone like Chelsea after we break up, that's his business. I don't think he would, and I hope he won't, but . . .

I look over at the clock. Deep breath. I should get going.

I arrive at Grant's condo at precisely 5:28 p.m. Grant's garage doors are open and exhaust fogs the cold air behind his running SUV. Before I can shift into park in the driveway, Grant waves me toward the space next to his in the two-car garage. I pull inside. By the time I've shut off my car, he's opening my door, offering his hand to help me out.

"There's a small chance for snow later." He kisses my cheek. "Since I have the space, there's no reason you shouldn't be using it."

"Thanks." He's such a good guy. I catch a whiff of a familiar citrus-and-spice scent through his snazzy wool dress coat. "You smell really good."

Grant smiles and ushers me to the passenger side of his SUV, which is already warmed up—including the heated seat.

"And you may be the most thoughtful person I know."

"You make it easy."

The drive to his boss's house takes about twenty minutes.

"I thought the head of an architectural firm would live in something less . . . traditional. Something made of cement, or a solar dome, or something super modern. Or post-modern. Is that a thing? Post-modern architecture? And if it is a thing, did saying that make me sound smart about architecture? Because I am definitely not."

Grant laughs. "Postmodern architecture is a real thing, yes. But picturing Howard and Elizabeth living in anything close to a postmodern style is, honestly, hilarious." He laughs again. "This house reflects their appreciation for the classics. Simple lines and unpretentious elegance."

"Huh." It's already dark, but from what I can see, this house is rather unpretentious, despite its high-dollar, enviable location. While it does somehow suit its wooded, lakeside lot, it would also totally fit within any traditional, upper-middle-class American neighborhood. With matching porch swings at opposite ends of the illumined front porch, it's postcard Americana.

"Have they loaned their house to the Christmas movie makers?" I ask. "Because if I were a jaded big-city executive, I would totally come home to visit my widowed mother in a house like this and then unexpectedly fall in love with the local Christmas tree farmer."

Grant's head tips back with the strength of his laugh. "In that case, I'm glad you're a kindergarten teacher instead of a jaded big-city executive with a widowed mother. But I'll have to keep all the local Christmas tree farmers away from you anyway, just in case."

"No worries, my guy. I think we're pretty safe from rogue Christmas tree farmers out here."

"A guy can't let his guard down."

He's quiet while parking the SUV, but every time I glance his way, he's smiling.

Dang, this guy looks good in a smile.

Inside, we're greeted by Howard and Elizabeth. Howard instructs us to hang our coats on a rolling rack that seems to have been placed in the foyer specifically for the occasion.

"So glad you could join us tonight, Allie." Elizabeth gives my forearm a grandma-like squeeze and then guides us to the rear of the house and a big family room where a few people have already gathered.

We're not the first to arrive and not the last. Which seems like a totally Grant thing to do. I'm big on punctuality, but this isn't the first time I've noticed that he's somehow learned to sense the perfect time to arrive.

The evening proceeds nicely. An informal cocktail hour is followed by dinner at the longest dining table I've ever seen in person. After dessert, we move back into the family room for after-dinner drinks. From what I can tell, only about seven or eight of the dinner guests work for Iverson-Forsyth. Everyone else is a plus-one of one sort or another. They're a nice bunch. Brenton—the company's IT guy—seems like he knows how to have a good time, in a 'bruh' kind of way that feels pretty dang familiar, thanks to having grown up with Adam and Jackson.

People have loosened up some now—good food and a little booze will do that. Every once in a while, a loud laugh breaks through the varied conversations, but the vibe here is definitely more muted than any gathering of teachers I've attended. This is a comfortable space, and everyone seems comfortable with each other.

Soon, I notice our hostess gathering dessert plates and wine glasses. Gathering a few myself, I follow her down the hall to the kitchen.

"Thank you, Allie. You didn't need to do that. You're a guest."

"Happy to help," I say. "Which ones go in the dishwasher, and which ones need to be hand washed?"

Elizabeth glances toward the hall we just passed through. "Don't tell anyone," she says with a wink, "but I put it all in the dishwasher."

"Even the crystal?" I feel the need to clarify. I adore my stepmom Michele, but I learned very early in our relationship that she is extremely particular about what does and does not go in the dishwasher. "No judgment," I add. "I just want to be sure my help is actually helping."

"All of it." She shrugs. "Haven't lost a glass yet."

"That's my kind of cleaning." I start rinsing and loading, careful not to splash anything on my cashmere sweater.

After one more round through the dining and family rooms to make sure we've collected all discarded dishes, the two of us linger in the kitchen a bit, chatting as she packs away some leftover desserts into the fridge—an appliance decorated with a collection of Christmas cards and photos.

"I like what I see when you and Grant are together," Elizabeth says. "You make a lovely couple."

Grant said he would be honest about our relationship with his bosses. Did he not do that? "You, uh, know we're only dating casually, and for a short time, right?"

"Oh, yes. Howard told me all about Grant's idea to ease himself into a social life. Quite the elaborate undertaking."

"You think?" What an odd way to put it. "It hasn't felt elaborate. It's just been . . . fun. Easy. Grant's a sweetheart."

"He is." Elizabeth smiles, and I feel the warmth of it all the way to my toes. "Grant has been a part of the Iverson-Forsyth family for years—and not just from a business standpoint. Howard and I—as well as Wallace and Claire—are all rather fond of him. He started as an intern, you see, and has been with the firm ever since."

"Yes, he told me that."

"Grant feels more like a nephew to me than one of my husband's employees. To be honest, I've even lost a bit of sleep worrying about that boy. He's been so single-minded about his career, so driven to succeed." She shakes her head, frowning. "That drive has served him well at Iverson-Forsyth, but by being so focused on his business life, I think he's missed out on the business of actually living. Until recently, that is." Her frown upends itself. "But I don't need to tell you what a wonderful man he is."

"He is that," I agree. "If I've learned anything about Grant Covington over the past couple of months, it's that he's much more dimensional than he appears."

"Indeed. Grant's entire outlook on life has undergone a change, and I think I'm looking at the reason for that change right now. You have been good for him, Allie. I'm glad to see it."

"He's been good for me too," I say, feeling a touch of heat in my cheeks. "I wish . . ." I trail off, not quite sure where I was going with that thought. "Anyway, it's been really fun dating Grant this winter. He's found his social groove." Not that I believe he ever lost it. "I don't think you need to worry about him so much anymore."

"You two do seem to get along quite well." Elizabeth smiles as she closes the dishwasher door. "Speaking of Grant, I suppose he's wondering where I've stolen you off to. Thanks for helping with the dishes, dear. Shall we rejoin the party?"

When we return to the family room, where the bulk of people are gathered, I find that Chelsea has taken the opening my absence provided to cozy up to Grant.

A sudden ache in my molars orders me to relax my jaw. But just because I'm smiling doesn't mean I'm going to overlook Chelsea's opportunistic rudeness. I'm a kindergarten teacher, after all. If she thinks I'm going to stand back and let her cut in line, she's got another thing coming.

Chapter 39

GRANT

I'm trying to figure out a polite way to extricate myself from Chelsea's conversational clutches when, finally, Allie reappears.

Allie says a quick word to Elizabeth Iverson and then crosses the room toward me. There's a determined grace to the way she glides through the gathering, bestowing nods and smiles as she squeezes through the tight spaces on her way back to me. Chelsea is still talking, but her words fade to a dull buzz, drowned out by the phrase repeating in my head:

I am in love with Allie Hayes.

When Rae asked that question at Mom and Dad's the other night, I wasn't sure I was ready to make a declaration that big quite yet. I knew I liked Allie. So much. I knew I craved her company over anyone else's. But did I love her? I wasn't sure then.

I am now.

Sometime between when Allie shoved a handful of snow down the back of my coat last night and when she pulled into my driveway this evening, that "Do I?" question cemented as a solid "Yes" in my brain.

I love her. I *love* her.

But I don't want to spook her.

It's been insanely difficult to hold myself back tonight when I just want to spill my guts and tell Allie how I feel. But if Rae's first gut reaction was correct, I can't make any sudden moves that might engage Allie's flight response.

I spent most of my free time over the past four days devising a plan that would hopefully help me convince her we should keep dating into the new year. I know it isn't a perfect plan, and definitely not a foolproof plan. I feel very much the fool, thanks to Rae's astute analysis of my actions—or, rather, my verbal lack thereof. But it is a plan I can hang some hope on.

Now that I know how deep my feelings run, however, I'm not sure it's enough. Especially given the ticking clock Allie references much too often for my comfort.

I'm going to cram as much wintertime romance as I can into the next three days. When I take her home after ringing in the new year, I will bare my soul. I will formally ask her to drop the "winter" from my boyfriend title . . . and maybe even let those big, golden words "I love you" loose on her—hoping against hope that I don't totally freak her out.

I love Allie Hayes. I want to tell her. So badly.

And I will. At the appropriate time.

I have a plan.

Chapter 40

ALLIE

I don't like to think of myself as a petty person, but it's more than a little gratifying when Grant simply walks away from his conversation with Chelsea to intercept my path. Her jaw drops, staying open long enough to catch a fly. Too bad it's winter.

Wow. That was mean. *Bad Allie.*

As Grant bends down to kiss my cheek, Elizabeth Iverson's voice rises above the hum of conversation.

"How about some music?" she asks. "It was such a treat watching you younger folks dance at Claire's gala earlier this month. What do you say we recreate that, if on a much smaller scale, hmm?" Her smile is wide. "Any musical requests?"

Silence falls. Heavily. Dancing is clearly not something this particular crowd expected or is comfortable with. At least not in this setting.

I glance toward Elizabeth. Her smile falters.

Nope. Not on my watch. We're friends now.

"That sounds fun!" I grab Grant's hand and drag him with me toward her, because no way am I giving Chelsea another opportunity to pounce. "If your sound system is set up for Bluetooth, I bet I could come up with a playlist on my phone pretty fast."

"I have one that will work," Grant says, surprising me.

A few minutes later, Grant's phone is connected to the Iversons' stereo, and the intro to a familiar song by BØRNS fills the air. It's an older song, but not old enough that I would have expected Grant to pick it as the first song at a party thrown by his soon-to-retire boss.

"Well, aren't you full of surprises." I laugh. "I love this song."

He grins at me over his shoulder. "I know."

Huh. I don't remember talking about it with him before, but I talk a lot, so I guess it's possible.

Grant adjusts the volume and then stows his phone in the back pocket of his dress pants before extending his hand. "Wanna dance?"

"Always." I slide my hand back into his. This is neither a slow song nor a fast, dance-ready beat. "Are you sure 'Electric Love' is the right vibe?"

"I'm kind of partial to its vibe." He shrugs, still grinning. "This song feels like . . . you."

"Yeah?" I laugh. "I'm flattered."

"Everything you do is electric, Allie." Grant squeezes my hand and then tugs me so close that not even the little gasp that motion surprised out of me could fit in the space between us.

Holy hot sauce. That was a certifiable *move*.

"And," he whispers into my ear, sending a rush of tingles through my veins, "I wouldn't want it any other way."

My breath stutters. I blink up at him. "Uh . . ."

"I said what I said."

My mind spins, and I'm a beat slow to follow Grant into a gently twisting sway. This isn't the sort of song I would put on a dancefloor playlist, but it absolutely demands motion. I can't deny the pull of its rhythm for long.

That spicy move Grant used to pull me close is still sending a twinkly rush of babymaker hormones directly to the melty parts of my knees, but soon I'm dipping my shoulders and relaxing my neck, letting my head bob to the beat. A wavy flow takes over my hips, and I lift my hands above my head.

Grant's rolling sway isn't quite as loose as mine, but his smile is everything. I'm not sure anyone would call what we're doing 'dancing,' but it's not *not*-dancing either. Whatever it is, I love it.

Grinning up at him, I turn a little circle.

Why isn't anyone else dancing?

All eyes are on us, and while a few heads are bobbing to the beat, several people are outright staring.

Ohhhh. Uh-oh.

My arms fall to my sides. Am I embarrassing him again? Like I did at the gala?

Oh, no. I didn't want— I didn't mean to—

"Hey." Grant reaches for my hands. "Relax. Their loss."

"It's okay, we can—"

"Keep dancing?" He tilts his head. "My thoughts exactly."

I don't know what has gotten into him tonight, but I like it.

Grant lifts our joined hands, pressing rhythmic little pushes and pulls into my palms to keep the motion going.

If he's okay, I'm okay. Far be it from me to stop my guy from acting on impulse.

The song starts to build toward the end, and I look up and meet Grant's magnetic gaze. When his lips form the lyrics of the final refrain, it's like he's pouring those sweet words all over me.

Talk about a move.

The song ends, and the next begins; it's a slower love song that has me wrapping my arms around his neck and laying my head against his shoulder. By the song's midpoint, several other couples have joined us, finding spots to sway between pieces of furniture.

As the evening goes on, almost everyone dances at one point or another—even Howard and Elizabeth. It's a sweet time.

It's nearing midnight when people start heading for the door. I make a pitstop at the bathroom, and when I come out, Chelsea is waiting, leaning against the wall opposite the bathroom door and looking like she is the recent recipient of some particularly spicy tea she's dying to spill.

Her lips tilt up to one side as she straightens and takes a step forward. "Just for the winter, huh?" Her low laugh is dry but doesn't carry a mocking tone. "Good luck with that."

And then she walks past me into the bathroom and shuts the door.

Uh . . . okay. Whatever.

When I get back to the family room, Grant is in the middle of a conversation with his two bosses, so I take a seat by the partners' wives as, couple by couple, the rest of the guests depart. Eventually, only the Iversons, the Forsyths, and the two of us remain, and then it's time for us to leave, as well. We're almost out the door when Claire Forsyth rushes into the foyer.

"Oh, good. You're still here. I can't believe I almost forgot, but I have something for you out in the car. Wallace!" she hollers toward the family room. "Are your keys in your coat pocket?"

"Left side," he hollers back.

Two coats remain on the coat rack, hers and Wallace's, I assume. She pulls a set of keys out and hands them to Grant.

"I got the publicity photos back from the gala photographer," Claire says. "There was an absolutely precious picture of you two, so I ordered a couple of prints. They came in today, thank goodness, because we wanted to make sure you got them before, uh . . ." She glances at me, and her smile wobbles the tiniest bit before strengthening again. "Well, we wanted to be sure you got them. One for each of you."

"Thanks," Grant says, and I echo him.

"You can just pop back in and drop the keys in Wallace's coat pocket after you get the pictures. Have a safe drive home."

Grant escorts me to his SUV and then goes back to collect the package and return the keys. Once he's in the car, he passes the bag to me.

I reach up to tap on an overhead light and then pull the two framed pictures from the bag, handing one to Grant.

It's a great picture, a candid shot of Grant and me on the dance floor at the gala. I'm smiling up at him, and he's smiling down at me with a tenderness and affection that makes my heart trip over itself.

"Wow." His tone is almost reverent.

"Yeah," I whisper. Whether it was dumb luck or highly-trained skill, the gala photographer captured that moment in a way that makes me wish I could crawl inside of it and live there forever. This picture makes me feel . . . like I felt with Grant tonight.

Grant and I look good together. *So* good.

If I didn't know better, I'd say we look like a couple in love.

And that scares the absolute crap out of me.

Chapter 41

GRANT

I've pulled out all the stops this week, trying to show Allie that I can be spontaneous and silly as well as conscientious and dependable. I want her to see me as the boyfriend she wants and the man—the partner—she could love.

I would give anything to be able to go back just two or three weeks in time, give myself a good shake, and say, "Wake up, idiot! Allie Hayes is the only woman for you. Stop fighting it." But I can't. Instead, I've spent every available waking hour trying to give her a reason to fall as hard for me as I've fallen for her. And . . . I think it's working.

I think.

But I'm not entirely sure.

We spent the evening after the Iverson-Forsyth party skating at an indoor rink I designed as part of a shopping mall renovation a few years ago. Allie is much better at ice skating than racquetball, and I have decent skating skills, too, thanks to several years on a youth hockey team. We were some of the oldest people skating, and I loved the way she cheered the little ones on.

Yesterday, I took the day off. We drove to a town known for its antique market and specialized candy shops and overindulged in both free samples and purchases. I don't think I've ever experienced such an epic sugar crash, and I'm pretty sure it hit Allie almost as hard.

Now, it's New Year's Eve—what was originally supposed to be our final date.

With everything in me, I hope it's not.

I pull into Allie's driveway, gripping the steering wheel like it's about to fly off the column. Excitement and hope zing off my skin; doubt, fear, and dread war for dominance in my chest.

My knees feel a little tingly. I don't have a backup plan. Loving Allie has become the only plan that matters. I am determined—and by determined, I mean terrified—to verbalize my feelings. Whether she accepts them or not.

Tonight, when I bring Allie home after our date, it will be the wee hours of January first. I will bring it to her attention that she has already stepped into the new year with me, and then I will tell her I love her and want to keep moving forward, together.

But first, we'll have some fun.

I've just shifted into park when a knock on the passenger window startles me.

The door swings open, and Allie practically vaults into the seat. "Happy New Year!" she shouts before adding, "A few hours early." Then she grabs my coat and pulls me over to kiss me right on the mouth.

It takes me off-guard, but in a good way.

"Happy New Year," I say back. "Ready to go?"

"Totally. I don't know what I'm ready for, Mr. Mysterious, but I am sooo ready."

"Are you disappointed it's not a fancy, get-dressed-up party? Be honest."

"Not a bit," she says, and I believe her. "I've had plenty of fancy winter dates with you. I'm entirely happy to be surprised by whatever this casual-attire date requires."

"Give me a sec to program our destination." I retrieve my earbuds from my pocket and put them in my ears. I shoot off a quick group text, making sure the phone faces away from Allie, and then press the "start route" button. I slide my phone into my coat pocket.

"Ooh," she says. "Are you secretly a spy and haven't told me?"

"If I were, you'd never know."

"Ha!"

Our destination sits only a few miles outside the Sterling Grove city limits, but I don't want to take a direct route and ruin the surprise. I head out of town, going in the opposite direction a sane person would go, and then make a well-planned series of twists and turns. My circuitous route was programmed into my GPS program ahead of time, thanks to a little help from Brenton, whose aid I sought after fighting against the app on my own for a while.

Finally, I head vaguely back in the direction we came from, making a wide circle around the town of Sterling Grove and using a bunch of backroads in the hopes of throwing her off.

"Um, Grant? Are you sure you know where you're going?" she asks. "Because I am totally lost."

"Mm-hmm." I smile. It worked.

We're on a gravel road in what feels like the literal middle of nowhere. As instructed by the voice in my ear, I stay on that road. Eventually, I'm informed that my destination is a quarter-mile ahead on the right.

At the crest of a hill, I look down and see lights. Lots of them. Right as we reach the driveway leading to the event venue parking lot, the GPS tells me we've arrived.

"I know where we are," Allie says. "Oof. I could have told you a much easier way to get here from my house. It takes, like, seven minutes, tops."

"Ah, but that would have spoiled the surprise."

Inside, we're greeted at the door by an attendant dressed in a fluorescent yellow jumpsuit, holding a clipboard. She has swirly designs painted on her face in that same yellow shade, with dots of other fluorescent colors scattered over any exposed skin.

"Welcome to Oakhaven Event Center and Adventure Park." She asks for our tickets. I hand them over.

"The bar and dining hall are through the doorway on my left. Just as a reminder, your meal, dessert, and unlimited bottled water are included with your ticket price. Soda, adult beverages, and a limited snack menu are available at the bar for an additional cost. At 11:45 p.m.," the attendant continues, "champagne—or sparkling grape juice, if you prefer—will be served to toast the new year. Only water will be allowed in the glow areas."

"The *glow* areas?" Allie asks.

The attendant shoots me a look.

"Surprise?" I say, hoping she likes this date. "This is a glow-in-the-dark event."

"Shut. Up." Allie gives me a little shove. "That is so cool."

The attendant looks at our tickets and then checks her clipboard. "Looks like you two are on the orange team. From here, you'll head down the hall to collect your protective jumpsuits, like mine, but yours will be orange. From there, you'll be directed to the paint station, where you can paint your exposed skin with blacklight-reactive body paint. Then, you can choose to hang out in the dining hall and bar, or you can engage in any or all of the glow activities available."

Allie lets out a cute little squeal.

"We have something for everyone," the attendant continues, "and you can go from building to building through heated, enclosed breezeways that connect all the spaces. We have a drum splatter area, blacklight mini golf, an art splatter room where you can create your own canvas using paint-filled water balloons, and, of course, dancing. Just through those doors"—she points off to the left—"you'll also find the dining hall and bar. Feel free to move from one activity space to another until your team—the orange team—is called to the indoor snowball fight arena."

"The *what*?" Allie beams up at me. "Oh my gosh. This sounds amazing!"

As the door opens again, admitting another couple, the attendant points us toward signs leading to the next step in our glow-party journey.

"This is going to be so much fun." Allie grips my hand and squeezes it. "I don't think they've done a New Year's Eve event here before, but wow! I love it. I heard about it a while back, but it slipped my mind until after you said you'd already made New Year's Eve reservations. And here we are." She laughs. "Grant Covington, you sly fox. This is freaking awesome. Hey! I wonder if we'll run into anyone we know?"

"Hmm. Could be." I grin as we round the corner and come upon several of Allie's friends.

Allie squeals again. "You guys! You're here!" She grins up at me. "Did you plan this? Oh, wait. What am I saying? You're Grant Covington. Of course you planned it." She laughs.

"I did."

I put the invitation out to the entire cocoa club one night when Allie ordered a cocoa refill. Paula declined due to another commitment, but Dylan, Lexi, Raquel, and her husband, Rob—who I'm meeting for the first time—are here, all suited up in fluorescent orange jumpsuits.

From the look on Allie's face, I think I did an okay job planning this date.

I bought our tickets in early December, back when I still thought New Year's Eve would be our final date. I wanted to make it the most Allie-centric night I could, to end our relationship on a high note. Now, I'm hoping it proves how well I've come to know and love the neon brightness of who Allie is. And how much she means to me.

So far, so good.

Chapter 42

ALLIE

By the time the orange team is called to the indoor snowball fight arena, we've eaten dinner and visited every activity on the roster. Our whole team is covered in festive, multicolored splatters of neon paint. I can't remember the last time I had this much fun or laughed this hard.

As I wait in line to receive my snowballs, I can hardly believe the cute guy covered in lime green and hot pink paint is the same Grant Covington who asked me out via multimedia presentation. I couldn't be happier with how his plan worked out.

But . . .

I'm having a hard time separating myself from the knowledge that this is our final date. Watching Grant sparkle with so much happiness and light tonight has really driven home how much I'm going to miss him. I know that's what I signed up for, but regardless of how amicably we will part ways later tonight, it hurts.

But I have to let him go.

Don't I?

That gala photo Claire Forsyth gave me must have been laced with some sort of gateway daydreaming drug or something, because it opened up all sorts of possibilities in my glitter-bomb brain. Even now, there's a shiny little question squirming around in there; a question loaded with too many 'what ifs' to count. I'm too scared to voice it. I'm almost too scared to acknowledge it.

Have I caught serious feelings for Grant Covington?

This whole winter boyfriend experience has been simply outstanding. Grant is courteous and kind. He's been more than willing to try to match my energy. The fact that I haven't short-circuited him yet is practically a miracle.

Does he understand that date-time Allie and regular-time Allie run on the same voltage? Doubtful. It's a pretty sure thing that if we kept dating those reserves he's been tapping into for my benefit would eventually deplete, forcing him out of the relationship for his own health and well-being.

Wouldn't they?

Or is Grant the exception to the rule?

I like him *so* much. I want—

"Your snowballs, ma'am." An attendant shoves a five-gallon bucket toward me.

I reach in and pull out what looks like the giant-sized version of the puffballs my kindergartners sometimes glue onto their animal pictures to represent fur. But size isn't the only difference. As I toss it back and forth between my hands, I realize these giant white puffballs are weighted the tiniest bit.

I look over at Grant. "I bet your racquetball muscles will get you some distance with these bad boys."

He picks one up. "Maybe."

Soon, a group in neon purple jumpsuits arrives. Like our group, the purple team is made up of six people. Once they've been given their buckets of faux snowballs, the attendant lays out the rules.

"Think of this like dodgeball, but with a glow-in-the-dark, wintertime twist. And without the rubber ball sting some of us remember from our younger days," he adds. "You must stay on your team's side of this line." He points to a thick, fluorescent yellow line going down the middle of the floor. "If you cross the boundary, the whistle blows, and you're out. If a member of the opposing team hits you with a snowball, you're out. If you catch a snowball thrown by the opposing team, the thrower of that snowball is out. The team with the last man—or woman—standing wins. Got it?"

People nod and murmur their assent.

"You are the final teams to battle tonight. Of all the winning teams of the night, the team with the overall fastest win time will be awarded free tickets to next year's New Year's Eve Glow Party here at Oakhaven Event Center & Adventure Park. The winners will be announced shortly before the countdown to midnight. Ready?"

Our teams separate to our appointed sides, and when the whistle blows, the overhead lights go off and the blacklights come on.

It's a crazy neon free-for-all as bright white snowballs start flying through the air, but their size and strange weight, combined with the blacklight effect, make them seem like they're moving in slow-motion. It's a hilarious contrast to the amount of effort and grunting we're doing to heft them the distance they need to go to reach our opponents. Nobody's hitting a darn thing, but everyone is giggling like a bunch of five-year-olds on a Pixie Stick and Pop Rocks high.

"I—I can't—" A woman on the purple team gasps through her laughter. "Somebody get me out before I pee my pants!"

Six orange-team snowballs immediately fly her way, and two actually make contact.

She bolts out the doors—toward the bathroom, presumably—and I catch a snowball I almost didn't see coming my way. "Gotcha!"

Her teammate heads for the sidelines while two of the guys on his team start rapid-firing at us.

"Nuts!" Dylan shouts a moment later. "I'm out."

Raquel dives to catch a ball, but it rolls out of her grasp. She's out. Rob nails a purple player in the gut, but when that guy pantomimes a dramatic death, it distracts Rob enough that he takes a snowball right to the face. Lexi is the next out. Now it's down to Grant and me against four purple jumpsuits.

"Score!" Grant's fist pumps the air as another purple jumpsuit leaves the court.

I sashay out of the way of two snowballs coming at once and then wing one at a woman whose eyes are on Grant. "Gotcha!"

The two guys left on the purple team make some kind of signal back and forth, nod, and then split, each to a separate corner of their side of the court.

Grant and I are side by side. And with them spread out like that, we can't watch them both.

"If you go low and aim for the guy on my side," Grant, always the strategist, says in a low voice, "I'll go high and take out the guy on your side."

"Why can't I go high?" I whisper and then duck as a ball sails directly over my head. "Kidding. I know I'm the one with the shortest path to the ground."

"On three." Grant holds a ball in each hand. "One, two . . ."

I don't just go low; I dive straight to the floor, only to have to drop my own snowball in order to catch the one coming at me.

But I do catch it. Right as Grant throws both of his snowballs toward the other player.

As the remaining purple player stretches up to catch one, the other one nails his arm.

He's out! Our orange-suited teammates break out in cheers.

Grant runs over, grabs me, and swings me up in the air. I'm breathless and laughing when he plants a hard, fast kiss on my lips.

Our teammates surround us, slapping our backs and whooping up a storm.

The attendant turns the overhead lights back on. When Dylan asks what our time was, the attendant informs us that our win was the slowest of the night, so we aren't in the running for the prize. We all have a good laugh over that.

On our way to the main event space to dance in the new year, Raquel, Lexi, and I stop off at the ladies' room.

"That didn't look like a first kiss back there," Lexi says coyly.

"Yeah," Raquel adds, crossing her arms. "Spill."

"I don't kiss and tell."

"*Riiiiiight.* My memories from *numerous* past conversations would argue that." Raquel snorts. "In fact, I bet I could recite your ratings of every guy you've kissed over the past eight years."

Yeah, she probably could. "Okay, fine. Our first kiss was a little over a week ago, the night that big storm came through. And there may have been a few more since."

"Yeah?" Lexi waggles her eyebrows.

Raquel tilts her chin down. "Dish."

"I just did."

"Rating system."

I take a deep breath and can't help but smile. "I'd rank Grant . . . at the very tippy top."

Her eyes go wide. "Better than Brody?"

"Ooh. That's tight race, but . . . yeah. Grant's got moves."

"I *knew* it." Lexi does a little dance. "So I guess you guys are done with the whole expiration date thing then?"

"Uh . . . nope." I swallow, hard. "We're both free agents again as of tomorrow."

"No way." Raquel wrinkles her nose. "I don't buy it."

"Me neither."

"That was our agreement."

"But you really like him." Concern filters through Raquel's tone. "Are you sure that's what you want?"

"It's for the best."

"It wouldn't hurt to bring up the idea of staying together," Lexi urges. "He's into you. I can tell."

"I agree with Lex." Raquel nods. "What's the worst that could happen? You're embarrassed for a minute? Fine. Let yourself feel a little embarrassed for a minute and then shake it off and do exactly what you planned to do all along. But at least you'd know."

"Yeah . . . so, I came into the bathroom for a reason, and it wasn't this. I'm just gonna . . ." I trail off on my way into a stall and close the door.

A series of hissed syllables chase me in.

"Oh, come on. I can hear you guys whispering."

At least two sinks get turned on.

These women are straight-up devious. *Gah,* I love them so much.

A few moments later, I emerge and turn the extra sink off with my elbow before I wash my hands. "Wasteful." I shake my head while giving them my strongest *I'm-so-disappointed-in-your-choices* teacher stare.

They just smirk at me.

Figures. You can't out-teacher a teacher.

After I dry my hands, they're both still standing there, staring at me. I plant my feet and cross my arms. After roughly three-point-seven seconds of this, I can't take the silence anymore.

"Pfft." I throw my hands upward. "It's been a fun time dating Grant. I like him. A lot," I admit. "But Grant's intention for the coming year—and he's been very clear about this, I might add—is to find someone he can settle down with in a sweet, comfy, thoroughly planned-out life. I'm not that girl."

"But what if—"

"No." I cut Lexi off. "Grant needs a planner, a thinker. Someone calm and steady who appreciates a well-ordered life, with budgets and schedules and spreadsheets and stuff. That's not who I am or what I want." I shake my head. "I don't fit into a rows-and-columns kind of life."

Raquel frowns. "He doesn't come off that way."

"Can we agree that maybe I know him a little better than you two do at this point?"

She nods, but the way her lips press together . . . it doesn't feel like an agreement.

"I really do like Grant, and I wish . . ." I trail off on a wavering breath.

What if I did bring it up? What if those daydreams Claire's gala photo drugged me into entertaining as possibilities actually. . . are?

No. They're not.

I give my head a shake to regain control from that momentary lapse. "I'm not going to try to force a relationship to work when it's abundantly clear that it shouldn't. We need to break up, as planned. It's the best thing. For both of us."

It feels good to have said it aloud. I needed to hear it. It's kind of a stark reality, knowing the magic of this particular wintertime season is ending, but isn't January always kind of a bummer that way?

Now that the truth of our situation is settled in my mind, I can relax, go back out there, and enjoy the snot out of my final date with this amazing man.

Will our breakup still feel a little bit like a gut punch? Sure. But that's Tomorrow-Allie's problem. Tonight-Allie needs to dance.

"Come on, guys," I say, giving Raquel and Lexi my biggest grin. "Hurry up and do what you came in here to do. It's New Year's Eve, baby. Time to party."

Chapter 43

GRANT

Allie expended a lot of energy dancing. She's fairly quiet on the much shorter, direct route back to her house. I wouldn't be surprised if the motion of the car sends her to sleep before we make it back to her house. I hope it doesn't. I need her to stay awake . . . just a little bit longer.

I turn down her street. This is it. This is the moment I've been waiting for all week. But since I'm still quite conscious of the very real possibility of spooking her, I want to ease her into it.

"So, hey . . ." I turn down the radio, hoping she can't hear my raging pulse with it at a lower volume. "I got an email that the winery is doing another paint and sip class a couple of weekends from now. I think it's beach themed. Want to go?"

"That was an excellent first date." Allie goes quiet again. When I look over at her, she's biting her lower lip.

"It's okay, Allie. It won't hurt my feelings if you don't want to do it again."

"No, it's not that. It's just . . . doesn't it seem like a waste of an opportunity?"

I pull into her driveway. "I don't follow."

"A dating opportunity."

Huh?

I shift into park and turn in my seat to face her. "I did think of it as a dating opportunity. I guess I was going for the nostalgia value, but it's not going to hurt my feelings if you don't want to do another class like that."

"No, that's not what I meant." She unbuckles her seatbelt and turns, tucking her left foot under her right leg. "That paint and sip class was a stellar, no-pressure first date. You knocked it out of the park with that one. You should absolutely use it again. But not on me, silly." She smiles. "You know what, though? The timing couldn't be better. Since it's not for two weeks, that gives you plenty of time to get your dating profiles up and going."

"My . . . what?"

"Your online dating profiles. Why waste that class on your ex-winter girlfriend when you could use it as a first date with someone new?"

Someone new? My next breath freezes in my throat. *Ex*-winter girlfriend?

"You know my neighbor Dennis? The writer?"

I nod, because my brain is a spin of chaos, incapable of forming speech. Of course I know Dennis. We ate lunch at his house. He made chili.

"I was thinking about how you're going to be diving into the dating pool this week. Why waste time with Phase II on the line? Hey, that rhymed! And so did that." She laughs. "You know as well as I do that you are more than ready to get out there and find your Phase II dream girl."

But . . . I already have.

My throat aches, feeling thick and swollen. My heartbeat echoes in my ears, and I have to make a conscious effort to hear the words still coming through her lips.

"You haven't put yourself out there on the dating sites or anything for a few years," she says. "If you want some help, I could show you how to sign up, and help you pick out photos for your profile and all that. Whaddya think?"

"I, uh—"

"And then, once we have the basics of your profile constructed, maybe Dennis could look it over from a writer's perspective and, you know, suggest ways to make sure it attracts the exact sort of woman you're looking for."

I am stunned. Gutted. Simultaneously overheated and freezing cold. I look down at my hands to make sure I still have fingers because the sensation of their existence is gone.

I thought the foundation I laid this week would naturally lead to a sure and solid "us." I dared to believe that, once I put my heart out there, her feelings would match mine. Or, if they weren't quite as far down the road as mine yet, she would indicate a willingness to see where our relationship might lead without an end date in mind. I had a plan. A good plan. Or so I thought.

I was wrong.

So, so wrong.

"Grant? Hey." She pats my knee. "You still with me?"

"I love you."

A tiny gasp pulls her backward as her eyes grow wide.

I reach for her hand. "I don't need to go out looking for something I've already found. I'm in love with you, Allie. You're the only one I want."

She shakes her head, scooting her back against the passenger door. "You can't— I—" Her shoulders contract, and I hear a shake as she inhales.

My pulse is still racing, but now it's feeding my words instead of stealing them. "It's been so hard to hold back, but I've always believed that old saying, 'actions speak louder than words.' I wanted to provide you with a definitive collection of criteria—consistent behaviors and actions—to support the truth of my feelings before I said the words to you, aloud. I had a plan to verbalize my feelings tonight, once I took you home. And I guess I did. But not at all like I planned."

She says nothing.

Perhaps it bears repeating. "Allie, I love you."

Allie closes her eyes and takes another trembling breath. Even in the dim glow of streetlights reflecting off snow, I note how hard she swallows before she speaks.

"I know your motivation behind all that is sweet and pure. But almost every phrase of that speech was evidence of why we would never work." She looks down at her lap. "You are an amazing man, and I'm incredibly honored that you would say, uh, *that*, to me. I won't deny that dating you has been awesome. We were good together, short-term. I think the world of you, Grant. But I can't see prolonging something that I know will end." She lifts her gaze, meeting mine. "We want different things out of life. Our real, after-wintertime lives. The futures we envision for ourselves would not blend well."

"I disagree. I think our differences complement one another."

She shakes her head. "I appreciate everything you've done to be my ideal winter boyfriend. And I hope we can stay in touch as friends. But I don't see any way around us being any more than that."

"We can make this work."

"It's January first, Grant. This is what we agreed to." She pulls her hand from mine. "Please don't make this any harder than it already is." She offers a tremulous smile and reaches for the door handle. "Being your winter girlfriend has been a privilege, and I wouldn't take a single moment of it back. But it's time to move on. Trust the process. You have so much to give the right woman. She's out there. I know it."

She opens the door.

"Wait. I—"

She holds up one hand, palm out. "Don't."

Defeated, I nod. "I'll walk you to the door."

At the door, she fumbles in her coat pocket for her keys. "I hate that you have an hour's drive home. It's so late." She bites the corner of her lower lip and looks up at me. "You could, um, stay over in my guest room if you're too tired to drive. Or if that's, uh, too uncomfortable . . . all things considered,"—she winces slightly—"I could give Dylan a call. He lives a couple of blocks over, and I'm sure he'd let you crash on his couch."

"No, that's not necessary."

"You're sure you can make the drive home safely?"

The thought of waking up steps away from an Allie Hayes who isn't my girlfriend anymore is all the impetus I need to stay alert on that drive.

"I'm sure."

Chapter 44

ALLIE

I've spent the first two days of the new year in the same pair of pajamas I put on the minute Grant backed out of my driveway for the last time. My activities since have alternated between eating handfuls of Lucky Charms straight from the box, gulping down guilt, and experiencing vivid mental reenactments of all those "what-ifs" Claire's gala photo—and let's face it, Grant himself—inspired.

The winter boyfriend plan was a good, solid plan. There was no "I love you" in that plan.

What happened to the plan, Grant?

I'm questioning everything.

Dragging myself off the couch, I give in to the magnetic pull of the fireplace mantel, where that framed photo lies, face down. I stare at the little cardboard kickstand on its back for a while and then walk back to the couch and curl up under a blanket.

I feel like I've just closed my eyes when the alarm goes off, announcing the first day back to school. With a groan, I roll off the couch and to my feet. On my way to the shower, I glance in the bathroom mirror. Is that a rainbow-shaped marshmallow stuck in my hair?

I lean closer. Yep. Sure is.

I guess dry shampoo isn't going to cut it today.

Thirty minutes later, my clean damp hair is twisted up and smashed into a claw clip. The kettle is plugged in; a couple of slices of bread are in the toaster, and I'm wearing a gray sweater dress, belted at my waist. A thin coat of mascara and a pair of riding boots later, the kettle screams that it's ready to be poured over some sliced lemons.

I let out a little scream of my own because I just remembered: I have no lemons, sliced or otherwise. I used the last one Friday morning and was so deep in my funk through the long weekend that I never went to the store to replenish my supply.

I have no lemons.

A hard, heavy weight fills my chest.

I have no Grant.

I miss Grant.

It's not the first time that truth has sucker-punched me over the last couple of days, but I can own it now. I miss him.

I *hurt* him.

That one still stings to admit.

I pull the crisped bread from the toaster, but even toast seems like too big of an ask for my gut full of guilt. I toss it in the garbage and head to work.

Chapter 45

GRANT

Work might be the best distraction from heartache, but as tempting as it is to fall back into my workaholic habits, I'm resisting the urge.

It's been two weeks since Allie and I broke up. The first few days without her were excruciating. Her absence is no less marked now, but the devastating hopelessness of those first few days has gone through a metamorphosis. I know I may be setting myself up to fail again. But what is that saying about never making the shots you don't take? Well, I love this woman, and I've got another shot left in me. I'm going to take it.

The when, where, and how is still undetermined.

Both Howard and Wallace have expressed their sympathy, and they both support my desire to win Allie's heart, as well as my partnership goals. To that end, I'm making an effort to keep the work/life balance my relationship with Allie created.

It's been years since I went to the early evening show at a movie theater, but I've done that twice now. Wallace even went with me once. I've taken long lunches in order to attend noon yoga classes at my gym several times this week, and I went to a hockey game with my brother-in-law last weekend. I even joined Brenton and the guys for drinks a couple of times after work.

All this extra activity has a two-fold benefit: it helps me remember the value of being a human in the world, and it distracts me from the constant bombardment of Allie-thoughts beating against my brain.

I'm days away from pitching the finalized school design to the Sterling Grove School Board. Unless Allie skips out on the meeting—which I can't imagine her doing—it will be the first time we've seen each other since New Year's Eve.

I wish there was some way to know if I was still on her mind, at least a little bit.

I don't need her to run up to me at the meeting and profess her undying love. I mean, it would be nice. And I'd be lying if I said I hadn't fantasized about that scenario a time or two. But I'd be just as happy with one of those signature Allie Hayes smiles and a warm hello.

Okay, not *just* as happy, but . . .

I miss her.

At night, Allie fills my thoughts. Each morning, I ache to hold her instead of the pillow my arms pulled close while I slept. I wasn't aware of anything missing in my life before Allie, but there's an Allie-shaped chasm in my life now. Regardless of the number of distractions I throw at it, it doubles in size every day.

I hope I get a chance to speak with her after the school board meeting. I need to gauge how she feels now that we've had some time apart.

I'm in love with a woman who doesn't believe we're compatible, but I'm a patient man, willing to put in the work to convince her otherwise.

I *will* win Allie's heart.

Somehow, I'm going to prove that we are exactly what a good match looks like, only more colorful than the norm. I can—and do and will—love her in a way that honors her unique Allie-ness. And I know she has the capacity to do the same for me. We're better together.

Do I have a plan for exactly how I'm going to accomplish all that?

Not even a little one.

I guess . . . I'll have to wing it.

Chapter 46

ALLIE

Somehow, I've made it through my first two weeks back at school. It probably helps that the first one started on a Tuesday. Now, it's Friday again, and I'm exhausted to my core.

When Dennis shoots me a text, asking if I want to test out the results of his new tomato bisque recipe for dinner tonight, I don't refuse the no-thought-required meal offer. Besides, I haven't seen Dennis in a while, other than an occasional wave if he happens to be outside shoveling his sidewalk when I'm coming or going from school. And I'm always up for some soup.

"I don't mean to be insensitive," he says as I slump down at his kitchen table, "but you look a little rough. Bad day?"

"Bad couple of weeks."

"Ah." Dennis is quiet for a bit. "I don't think I've seen that fancy SUV in your driveway for a while. The breakup happened as planned, I take it?"

"Yep." A wince tightens my stomach. "Well, maybe not entirely as planned. But yeah. It's over."

"I'm sorry it didn't work out."

"It wasn't designed to work out. That was never the plan. It's for the best." The line I used on Lexi and Raquel on New Year's Eve sounds as hollow as it feels.

"When you and Grant came over for lunch after that bad snowstorm, it was fairly obvious you were wrestling with some rather intense emotions. You barely spoke two words the entire meal. That's not like you."

He's not wrong. "Sorry."

"You couldn't take your eyes off him. By the time you two left, I had a feeling you were either going to end up with a happy ever after or a broken heart. I'm sorry it's the second."

"Grant told me he loved me." My throat tightens around the words.

"Did you say it back?"

"No. I don't want him to change who he is to keep up with me, and I refuse to tone myself down to fit into anyone else's idea of a perfect life. No one should have to change their personality to make a relationship work."

"What makes you think Grant would ask that of you?"

"Grant has a three-phase life plan all mapped out. He's a linear thinker. His brain craves structure and predictability. For me, even hearing those words feels kind of suffocating." It *does*. "I don't even plan a grocery list, let alone thirds of my life at a time. I live moment-to-moment, chasing whimsy and delight. I'm the furthest thing from a planner, Dennis."

"That's not true." Dennis narrows his eyes. "How long did you shop and plan for that blanket fort for your family's Christmas weekend?"

"About a year, but that's diff—"

"And what about your classroom? From all accounts, you're an excellent teacher. I can't imagine you just show up and decide on the spot what you'll be teaching that day."

"Obviously not, but—"

"And what about that thing you did with the dancing? On Black Friday. You can't tell me there wasn't a good deal of planning involved in that."

I open my mouth to argue but close it right back up because Dennis is on a roll. He recites a litany of zany shenanigans I've planned—and successfully executed—over the past few years.

"You see?" Dennis angles his chin downward, looking at me over the frames of his glasses. "You are quite the little planner, Allie Hayes."

"Lexi helped with the flash mob, so it wasn't just me. But outside of teaching, all of that other stuff was just for fun. In the larger scheme of things, it doesn't matter."

"Doesn't it? I think your nieces and nephews might disagree. Not to mention all those people who benefited from your organized Christmas cheer. Accept the evidence, Allie. You are a planner—and quite an excellent one."

I don't know how to respond to that. He has a point. All of those things were planned, meticulously, over time. It just didn't feel like planning because it was fun. Every one of them was a resounding success too—even if that success was only measurable in smiles.

"Exactly," Dennis says as if he heard my whirring thoughts. "Why don't you sit with that a little bit."

He gives me approximately two seconds.

"Have we established that perhaps you and Grant have more in common than originally thought?"

I swallow hard. "Yes?"

"And we've already established that Grant is trustworthy, intelligent, and kind."

"Yes."

"Has he ever indicated that he found your free spirit intimidating or embarrassing?"

My mind immediately goes to the gala, and how I broke some sort of rule about dancing before dinner. "Yes."

"Oh?" Dennis clearly did not expect that answer.

But was that Grant being embarrassed by me? Or was that just me, being self-centered and not taking the time to read the room?

My memory swerves to that moment at the Iversons' home when I realized we were the only people dancing to "Electric Love." Grant didn't care one bit that all of his colleagues—and both of his bosses—were staring at us.

"Actually, I think . . . that didn't really count."

Dennis releases a slow smile. "Since he is not a reckless man, prone to flights of fancy—"

"But that's the thing." I sit straight up. "I am prone. To all that. I'm, like, the prone-est."

"We're not talking about you just yet. We'll get there. I promise."

"Fine." I slump back into my seat.

"So let me get this straight. You believe Grant won't be able to accept that the woman he's fallen in love with over the past couple of months is the woman he's fallen in love with over the past couple of months."

"Um, what?"

"Did you, at any time," Dennis speaks slowly, "or in any way, pretend to be anyone other than who you are . . . while you dated Grant?"

"Absolutely not."

"And there it is." He smiles. "Grant didn't base his declaration of love on what he *doesn't* know about you, Allie. He fell in love with exactly who you are."

My breath catches on something in my chest.

"And if you search your heart," Dennis continues, "and replay all the things you've said and thought about him, I think you'll realize that you are in love with exactly who he is."

There's a strange pressure at my temples. Something flutters in my belly.

"Come to terms with that, my dear, and all those things you consider deal-breaking differences will show themselves for what they truly are—complementary strengths."

My hand lifts to my throat. I take a short gasping breath.

"Now you're coming around to it."

Dennis slaps his hands down on the tabletop and then stands, completely ignoring how the movement made me startle. "How about I pack up some of this tomato bisque for you? I think you need to go home and sit with this revelation for a bit." He moves toward the stove. "But not too long, of course." He chuckles. "You need to put those unique Allie Hayes planning skills to work.

Figure out a way to show Grant you're willing to take a chance on that happy ever after, after all."

I cross my arms at my chest and scowl at Dennis's back. "I just *had* to move next door to a romance novelist, didn't I," I grumble, but I can't help but smile. "You're a sly old menace, Rosalie Dennis."

Dennis's laugh booms so loud I feel the vibration through the floor. But when he finally turns to face me, his face is as serious as those true crime novels he writes under his real name.

"Love is worth any risk," he states emphatically, and then . . . he winks. "Would you like some more bisque?"

He got me. Again.

But he's definitely got me thinking.

And perhaps planning a little bit, as well.

Chapter 47

GRANT

I arrive in Sterling Grove about half an hour before the board meeting is scheduled to start. Since the school board expects a large turnout for this particular meeting, they've moved it to the high school auditorium and made it open to the public. It's a big night. On so many levels.

Wallace and Howard are on their way—for moral support, they said. But I know, at least in part, it's a test to see if I truly have what it takes to level up and move into Howard's position when he retires in March.

Just before the meeting is called to order, I spot Allie near the doors at the back of the auditorium. She's wearing a bright blue coat with an orange knit scarf. Her hair is down in loose blonde waves that surround her beautiful face like a white-gold frame. My thirsty eyes drink her in as she walks about halfway down the right-side aisle, picks a row, and takes her seat. It's the first time I've seen her in almost three weeks, and she is . . . stunning.

I was still at work yesterday when my phone alerted me to her text, inviting me to join her for cocoa after the school board meeting. I nearly fell out of my chair.

I couldn't think of anything clever to say, so I simply typed, "Sure," hit send, and immediately threw up in my trashcan. I went home sick for the remainder of the afternoon, most of which I spent staring at that picture Claire Forsyth gave me.

I wonder if Allie kept her copy after we broke up?

Allie meets my gaze and gives me a thumbs-up, but her smile seems nervous. This reminds *me* to be nervous. Not about my presentation to the school board, because I feel fairly confident about that, but about what comes after.

I know it could be *just-two-friends-having-cocoa* for her, and I can respect that. I need to know where she stands so I can figure out how to sweep her off her feet.

But could it be that she's missed me? Might she be open to more?

To . . . me?

There's really no way to know. I guess I'll just have to improvise.

And that is . . . terrifying.

As the auditorium fills, the space hums with hushed conversations. I try to smile and nod at those in the crowd I recognize—especially the committee that helped inform my design. Dennis is here, as is Rainey, who owns the pub. There's a big, bearded guy in the back wearing a baseball cap and glasses who seems familiar, and when I glance at the guy sitting next to him—Allie's stepbrother, Jackson—I know why.

Ah. The school's mysterious benefactor is here.

Considering the lengths to which Allie goes to be able to spend time with Adam, I'm surprised she would ask me to join her for cocoa at the expense of spending time with her twin. And with Jackson here too . . .?

Oh, no. Please tell me she did not invite her brothers to get cocoa with us.

But even if she did . . . it'll be all right. I can wait.

She's worth it.

Wallace and Howard enter just as the board secretary hands me an agenda. The meeting is called to order a few minutes later.

Other than the usual parliamentary procedural things, my presentation and a Q&A session are the only items on it. While the minutes are read, I try to focus and mentally review my presentation. It's not easy.

The school board secretary leaves the podium, and the elementary principal steps forward.

"Thanks for coming, everyone," she says. "I know you are all excited to see the architectural renderings for the new school, so I will make this quick."

After reminding everyone of the unique funding source for the project, she gives a brief overview of Iverson-Forsyth Architectural Associates as well as my qualifications as the lead architect on the project.

Finally, she turns to me. "Mr. Covington, the stage is yours."

It takes about forty minutes to get through my presentation, but it goes off without a hitch. After twenty or thirty minutes of Q&A, the school board president calls for a vote.

It's unanimous. Sterling Grove is getting a new elementary school, including indoor recess rooms with constellation ceilings.

The auditorium breaks out in cheers.

This time, when I meet Allie's eyes, they're already on me. And she's smiling big. She mouths something, and I think it's somewhere in the vicinity of "I'm so proud of you."

It's a place to start.

Who am I kidding? It's all I can do to keep myself from jumping off the stage and running to her. I want to pick her up, spin her around, and then kiss her with everything I've got.

But I don't. It's not time for that. Yet.

A little voice in my head warns that, maybe, that time will never come.

But I don't want to hear it.

There's still hope.

No plan . . . but still hope.

Chapter 48

Allie

We celebrate Grant's victory at Cocoa & Froth. As we sit in one of the booths, sipping our whip-topped cocoas, I realize it's not as weird being here with him as I feared it might be. It feels . . . comfy, like coming home after a long time away. And there's a big part of me that doesn't want to wreck this vibe.

But I know what I have to do.

I know the risk I'm about to take, but I won't back down.

What's the worst that could happen? If, during our time apart, he's decided he's not into me as more than a friend, we can just keep on keeping on until our friendship gradually fades into the ether of "that one time I had a winter boyfriend." He'll become a partner in his firm and then find a nice girl to settle down with. Together, they'll raise a couple of kids, and their perfect little family will take fabulous adventure vacations because Grant now appreciates the value of spontaneity.

Meanwhile, I'll shrivel into a sad, dry husk of a human. All because I was too stupid and stubborn to admit I'd fallen in love with the best man in the world when I had the chance.

Sounds peachy.

I can't think like that. Grant isn't the type of guy to tell a girl he loves her and then simply change his mind because she didn't say it back. He would *never*. And the fact that I know this about him makes me feel safe and warm and as rich as the dark chocolate cocoa in my mug.

Our conversation has kept a steady, comfortable flow. But I know time is running out—and not only because Cocoa & Froth closes in forty-five minutes. If I'm going to do this, it needs to be now.

I take a deep breath. "Hey, so . . . I have something I'd like to show you. Do you have time?"

"Sure."

He didn't consult his phone, watch, or the clock on the wall above the menu board before answering. When Grant is with me, he's with me one hundred percent.

One more thing to love about him.

Oof. I sure hope I don't mess this up.

My hands shake a little as I pull my laptop out of my bag and fire it up. "I put this presentation together kind of last minute, so it's not as polished as it could be, but I'd appreciate any feedback you're willing to give."

"Sure. No problem."

He's so accommodating. It melts me.

I cue up the presentation. "I, uh, don't have a snazzy remote like yours. Mind if I sit beside you?"

He scoots closer to the wall, and I slide into the booth beside him, spinning my laptop around to face us. His arm moves around the back of the booth, and his hand rests on my shoulder for barely a breath before he pulls his arm back.

"Sorry. Old winter boyfriend habit."

"No, it's fine." *And more of that, please.*

I click to the first slide. "This is a color wheel. I'm sure you've seen one of these before."

He nods.

"Right." I click to the next slide. "First, we have our primary colors. Red, blue, and yellow. These colors are amazing on their own, but when we combine them in certain ways, we get some pretty magical results."

I click to the next slide, complete with a sparkle transition because I am who I am. "Yellow and blue make green." *Click. Sparkle.* "Likewise, both red and yellow are required to create orange." *Click. Sparkle.* "And blue combined with red makes purple. Are you with me so far?"

"It seems like a very appropriate lesson on colors for your kindergarten students," he says. "Good job."

"Thanks. Now back to the color wheel." I click through another sparkle transition to reveal a repeat of the first slide. "I've only mentioned six colors by name, but as you can see, each color contains numerous shades of itself, from light to dark."

I click to the next slide, a photo I took of a piece of white construction paper with two puddles of watercolor paint, one blue and one orange, with a little space between them. "Here we have two colors that look very nice together. But what happens when we combine them?" I pause to click to the next slide. "A murky, lifeless sort of brown." Another click leads to a photo of one of the older watercolor sets from my classroom. "And thus, many a watercolor paint set is ruined."

Click. Sparkle. "Back to the color wheel."

I've replaced the original color wheel with one that has text and graphics.

"Do you see these arrows?" I run my finger across the screen, following arrows connecting purple to yellow, blue to orange, and red to green.

Grant nods. He's so adorable.

"These arrows all show colors that, if mixed together, would create similar shades of that lifeless brown mess that ruins a watercolor set. You see, green was never meant to take on the properties of red. Purple would become ill if you tried to make it be yellow. And . . ." Another click-sparkle repeats the photo of my watercolor puddles mixed together. "Blue sucks the very life out of orange."

I glance at Grant, whose attention stays solidly on the screen. The arm that had momentarily been behind me now crosses his waist, almost protectively. It tugs at a deep ache in me.

"But there's something interesting about the colors these arrows connect," I continue. "Neither color's individuality can survive when it tries to become its opposite. But when each color is allowed to be fully itself, *next to* the other one, they work together to create a beautiful and vibrant harmony more powerful than either could be alone."

I try to ignore the way Grant suddenly sits up straighter, but my pulse speeds up a little bit. Is he getting it? I think he's getting it.

I point to a small caption in the bottom corner of the color wheel graphic and read it aloud: "'*Colors opposite each other on the color wheel are called complimentary colors.*' This means that each opposing color's individuality complements that of the other without ever having to try to be something it's not. Blue makes orange a truer, brighter orange. Orange makes blue a truer, brighter blue. You follow?"

"I think . . . I think maybe I do." Grant glances at me but quickly returns his gaze to the screen. But even in that quick glance, something in his eyes reached for my heart.

I'm trying not to bounce in my seat, but I'm not sure I'm succeeding. I take a deep breath. "As an educator, I need to meet the diverse learning style requirements of all my students. It can be difficult to nail down exactly what medium will best serve an individual student's needs, and it sometimes helps to approach the curriculum from a different perspective. So . . . I made a spreadsheet."

Grant visibly jolts. "You did what now?"

"I made a spreadsheet."

"Who *are* you?" Laughter dances in his eyes, but a look of mock horror covers the rest of his face. "What have you done with the real Allie Hayes?"

"I know, right?" I grin. "Okay, so . . . I'm kind of new to making spreadsheets, and I can't promise all of the rows and columns will make sense right away. If there's any part you find confusing, let me know. I'll do my best to clear it up for you."

"How about you walk me through it."

Chapter 49

GRANT

As I look back toward the screen, I lift my mug to take a sip of cocoa.

Allie takes a deep, deep breath . . . and one click and sparkle transition later, her spreadsheet is revealed.

Shock forces a breath in through my lips, and I immediately regret that sip of cocoa. Allie rubs my back until the coughing subsides.

She gives my back a little pat and then gestures to the screen. "Yeah, so . . . I printed off a blank spreadsheet and colored in some of those rectangular box thingies," she explains. "Then, I took a picture of the finished product to upload into my presentation. Whaddya think?"

"This says . . ." I jab my finger at the screen but then have to cover my mouth for another cough. "This says . . ." I swallow, take another sip of cocoa, and then meet her gaze. "'I love you.'"

"I love you too, Grant."

I tear my eyes from Allie's earnest face to stare at the most amazing spreadsheet I've ever seen. Within those rows and columns, she's colored in specific cells in alternating blue and orange to spell out 'I LOVE YOU.'

I'm not sure there is such a thing as a reverse gut punch, but I feel like fresh oxygen has injected life into my core.

"I love you, Grant." Her voice falls to a whisper. "I'm so sorry I hurt you."

"You made a spreadsheet for me, and you . . . just put it right out there."

She presses her lips together and nods.

"You love me. You *love* me."

"Yup." A smile stretches her cheeks, turning sideways with the playful tilt of her head. "Can we get to the part where you tell me you love me too? I mean, I made a spreadsheet and everything. I feel like it's the least—"

I smash my lips into hers, reaching up around the back of her neck to thread my fingers into her hair. Allie does not hesitate to kiss me back.

Our kiss is a desperate, fiery thing that could consume us both . . . if not for its underlying tenderness. Instead, it soothes the stark loneliness of these past few weeks and fills the deep longing that has haunted me—and clearly her, too—since our breakup. The kiss deepens, and I'm lost in it. In her.

When we finally come up for air, I grip her shoulders and look straight into her big, beautiful blue eyes.

"I love you, Allie."

Our next kiss is calmer, but it carries the richness of every warm, delicious moment we've shared alongside frothy hints of all the sweetness yet to come.

When the kiss ends, our foreheads rest against each other.

Allie exhales a contented sigh. "It was the spreadsheet that won you over, wasn't it?"

"That was unexpected. But no."

"Was it the sparkle transitions?" she asks. "Because I've always suspected you were a secret fan of the sparkle."

"I'm a fan of *your* sparkle. Of all the bright and shiny things, you're my favorite."

"This has been a rough few weeks," she admits. "I've had a lot of time to think about our relationship. And if I'm being honest, I think I started crushing on you on our very first date, when you got paint on your face and then tried to rip my clothes off."

"That was an accident, and you know it." I laugh. "But if that's the case, you sure hid that crush well."

"Yeah." She exhales a short puff of air. "Even from myself."

I kiss the tip of her nose and straighten.

Allie sighs. "I guess this means your perfect winter plan failed."

"I guess it did." I drape my arm around her shoulders and pull her tight against me. "And I am absolutely okay with that."

Chapter 50

ALLIE

Grant holds an umbrella over us as we walk to Cocoa & Froth. We had to park a lot farther away than usual. By the time we got back to Sterling Grove, after the ribbon-cutting ceremony that unveiled the new logo for Forsyth-Covington Architectural Associates, every parking spot near our favorite little cocoa shop was already full.

"I know this weather begs for a cup of hot cocoa," he says as we take one of the paved pathways through the boulevard's grassy, park-like median, "but I've never seen this place so packed. When we drove by, it looked like standing room only in there."

"Yeah, it did." I try to hold back my smile.

"We could get our cocoas to go," he offers. "Head back to your place, snuggle up on the couch, watch a movie . . . Unless you think Jackson will mind?"

My stepbrother has taken up temporary residence in my guest bedroom, which he's actually sharing with Adam and Tulip for the weekend. But Grant doesn't know Adam is in town. Yet.

"I bet there's room for us." It's a sure thing. "But if not, you know I'm always up for your snuggles."

Oh, there will be snuggling. For sure. Later.

Jackson and Adam can skedaddle on out of there if they can't handle it.

When we're safely under the entrance awning, out of the cold April rain, Grant collapses the umbrella. He extends and collapses it a few more times to shake off the water. With his attention diverted, I glance over my shoulder to find Lexi waiting just inside the door.

I give her a nod. She grins and races toward the back of the building.

After securing the snap to hold his umbrella closed, Grant pulls the door open. "After you."

I reach up on my tiptoes to kiss his cheek, hoping those extra few seconds give Lexi the time she needs. It does. Just as I walk through the door, the lights go out.

"Power outage?" His forehead furrows. "That's odd. I haven't seen any lightning or anyth—"

The lights surge back on, and shouts of "Congratulations!" and "Surprise!" fill the air.

Grant's face is a mask of shock that quickly transposes into a smile when he sees a big banner—printed with his company's new logo—suspended over the tables in the center of the cocoa shop.

He turns his smile on me. "You planned this?"

"Me?" I press a hand to my chest in melodramatic denial. "Are you accusing *me* of planning a surprise party to celebrate you finally reaching your Phase I goal?" I laugh. "Yep. That was me. Surprise!"

"I love you." He leans down and presses a kiss to my forehead.

"I love you too." I wrap my arm around his waist. "You did it, Grant! You made partner." I give him a squeeze. "I am so crazy proud of you."

He drapes his arm around my shoulders. "I couldn't have done it without you."

The crowd surges toward us. So many people we love, all in one place.

Grant's parents move in first, wrapping us both in a giant hug. The Iversons are here too, fresh off Howard's retirement party last night, as are the Forsyths and several of Grant's former coworkers—now his employees.

I give a little wave to Grant's sister Rae, who's here with her family. She lifts her mug to me and then returns to what looks like a lively conversation with Dennis.

Adam is here—in disguise, of course—as is Jackson, all of my parents, and a couple of my other stepsiblings. Of course, our entire Thursday-night cocoa club is in attendance. I wouldn't dare leave them out.

Finally, I break away from the crowd to order our cocoas. Josie, my favorite barista—not that there are any bad ones at Cocoa & Froth—informs me that they've just released their updated spring menu, so I decide to try something new, even though it sounds a little weird. She assures me it's delicious, and I know better than to doubt her.

By the time our cocoa is ready, almost everyone has found a place to sit, including Grant. I take my time getting over to him. There are a lot of people in here, and I don't want to accidentally tip these mugs off their saucers and into somebody's lap.

"What are we drinking tonight?" Grant asks as I place his mug on the table.

"Basil-infused dark chocolate cocoa with artisan lemon meringue marshmallows."

"Sounds adventurous." Grant's smile angles off to the side, highlighting that dimple I love. "Perhaps even a bit . . . whimsical?" He winks and scoots his chair over to make a little more room for me.

"You know me." I shrug, and then take my favorite seat: the one beside him. "I'm all about the whimsy. All the time."

He drapes his arm around the back of my chair, and his smile is as warm, rich, and cozy as any cocoa could ever hope to be. "I wouldn't want it any other way."

A Note from the Author

Dear Reader,

Thank you for taking a chance on this book. I hope it provided a sweet escape and a story you'll happily recommend to your friends. If you'd consider leaving a review online, it would be much appreciated.

For many of us, the past few years have been heavy ones, full of loss, anger, confusion, grief, disillusionment, and reckoning. The echoes of our collective and individual traumas remain active, and they can still deliver the occasional gut punch. I hate that for us. But I also know how the power of stories and art can help get us through hard times.

The idea for this book was born before the word "pandemic" became a part of our daily lives, but the bulk of it was written between 2021 and 2022. While writing, my desire was to put into the world what I most needed—and still need—*from* the world: warm, cozy comfort . . . and some good, frothy fun.

I want the Cocoa & Froth rom-com books to embody the rich, sweet, and flavorful layers of gourmet hot cocoa—with plenty of froth on top. In these pages, I hope you found a sweeter world in which to retreat from our sometimes inhospitable reality; an atmosphere in which:

- *blended families come together, experiencing peace, good times, and harmony as their norm,*

- *neighbors become like family,*

- *and friends always have your back.*

And a place where:

- *an anonymous force invests in a small rural community to help it survive, grow, and thrive,*

- *a company values its employees in a whole-person context instead of treating them like performance drones expected to work themselves into early graves,*

- *and a cozy cocoa shop crafts mugs full of both comfort and adventure.*

I endeavored to insert those ideals within Allie and Grant's story in order to create the kind of world I'd like to see. I hope you'll come back to Sterling Grove with me to discover more of those sweet and cozy vibes through the entire Cocoa & Froth series.

Until next we meet in Sterling Grove, please be kind to yourself, hold on to hope, love with all you've got, and take every opportunity to cozy up with a cup of hot cocoa and a really good book.

Here for it,
Vanni Shaw

About the Author

Vanni Shaw lives in a small midwestern town much like the fictional town of Sterling Grove—minus the famous secret benefactor throwing big dollars toward community improvements, of course. In her free time, she reads *allthebooks*, takes her elderly dog for short walks that take a long time, mindlessly scrolls the socials, intermittently obsesses about the Enneagram, and frequently loses track of time while lost in her latest hyperfixation.

Over the past fifteen years, this pseudonymous author has worked within several areas within the publishing industry, including professional book reviewing, book editing, and copywriting under both her real name and her original pseudonym, Serena Chase. A multi-published, award-winning author of epic fantasy and young adult romance under her original pseudonym, *The Perfect Winter Plan* is her debut writing as Vanni Shaw, and her first published rom-com.

For book updates, general tomfoolery, and recipes for the cocoas featured in this series, subscribe to her newsletter and follow @vannishawbooks on social media.

Connect with Vanni: vannishawbooks.com

Books by the Author

Flirty, frothy, & fun romantic comedy by Vanni Shaw

Cocoa & Froth

The Perfect Winter Plan

Epic fantasy and YA romance, written as Serena Chase

Find yourself in the fairy tale.

Eyes of E'veria (4-book epic fantasy series)

The Ryn

The Remedy

The Seahorse Legacy

The Sunken Realm

Standalone (YA romance)

Intermission

Acknowledgments

Thank you, readers! I appreciate you more than you will ever know. I hope you'll return to Sterling Grove with me soon for (drumroll, please!) Jackson's story. (Yes, THAT Jackson.) Please connect with me online. I'd love to hear from you.

Ellerie: This book would not exist had you not mused aloud your wish for a just-for-the-winter romance all those years ago. As the dedication reads, this one's for you.

Delaney: Thanks for being the first person to read the almost-final draft of this novel and for becoming so invested in the story that you walked outside expecting snow . . . in September.

Charity Tinnin: Thanks for your editorial insight. The story is so much better for the changes you led me toward. Our Marco brainstorming sessions are life-giving, as is your friendship.

Amanda G. Stevens: It's exciting to be chasing fresh genre adventures alongside such a talented author and good friend. Thanks for jumping in last minute with an extra pair of editorial eyes.

Crystal Ferry: I don't even know how to thank you for all you do to encourage, assist, and ground me. You know I respect the snot out of you as an author and entrepreneur, and I 100% adore you as my friend. Never doubt it. You freaking amaze me.

Lucy at Cover Ever After: Thanks so much for going over and above what I expected from a cover designer. I love your design for *The Perfect Winter Plan*, and I'm excited to be doing this series with you on my team!

To anyone who came to this book after first knowing me as Serena Chase: thanks for following me over here.

To anyone who knows the real me and just now found out I'm an author or is reading one of my books for the first time: welcome to the circus of my imagination. Thanks for your support!

To my Patreon subscribers: Amy S., Kathy McGee, Stella Bixby, Rebecca Miller, Melannie Johnson Savell, Liz G., Collective Perspective, Samantha Taylor, and Trisch Beezhold. This book was supposed to be a side project to help feed my creative brain toward reworking Patreon Project One and finishing Patreon Project Two. Instead, it became the whole thing—and I actually finished and published a book for the first time since 2016. Thanks for sticking with me through those first two yet-unpublished/unfinished projects. Your encouragement has meant so much through that rough season and as this book took shape. The final product is much different than the first and second drafts you read on Patreon. But I believe—and I hope you think so too!—that it's so much better for the changes made.

To all the readers, influencers, authors, librarians, bookstore folks, and the many friends who have recommended or will recommend my books to others: YOU ARE THE BEST! Thank you so much.

To Kali Suzanne of Kalioke Movement Lounge: I miss coming to Gentle Yoga since moving out of Burlington! Thank you for your inclusive and trauma-informed space, and for teaching me the practice. You inspired the glow party in this book, as well as a few moments of zen.

And lastly, to the Castle Kitchen Food Corp of Canada: BLESS YOU for making a dairy-free/gluten-free/vegan/plant-based cocoa mix I can actually drink without getting sick. And all the bonus points, because every variety I've tried tastes AH-MAZE-ING. Your cocoa mixes are my go-to for testing out all those Cocoa & Froth drinks I made up for this book. (Not an ad. I just really love the cocoas.)

Here for it,
Vanni

www.ingramcontent.com/pod-product-compliance
Lightning Source LLC
Chambersburg PA
CBHW021644110726
47902CB00007B/1820